DOOM WAS SPELLED WITH THREE LETTERS

DNA. The secret code of life that scientists seek to master, so that they can shape the future of the human race. But a "safe" DNA experiment that goes wrong creates a force that controls the scientists themselves—unleashing on the world a new virus that lowers the intelligence of all it attacks!

*   *   *

Like THE CHINA SYNDROME, this story is fiction. The *fact* is that today in laboratories all over America, despite the protests of concerned scientists, DNA research is being actively pursued. This research, officials assure us, is perfectly safe...

*   *   *

IQ83
ARTHUR HERZOG

"A THINKING READER'S
ABLE EVENT!"

D0818361

IQ 83

ARTHUR HERZOG

A BERKLEY BOOK
published by
BERKLEY PUBLISHING CORPORATION

IQ 83

A Berkley Book / published by arrangement with
Simon and Schuster

PRINTING HISTORY
Simon and Schuster edition published 1978
Berkley edition / March 1980

ISBN: 0-425-04433-5

A BERKLEY BOOK ® TM 757,375
Berkley Books are published by Berkley
Publishing Corporation,
200 Madison Avenue, New York, New York 10016.
PRINTED IN THE UNITED STATES OF AMERICA

ACKNOWLEDGMENTS

The author wishes to thank the following sources for permission to quote material in this book:

The American Psychological Association.

Michael J. Hindelang and Travis Hirschi, "Infelligence and Delinquency: A Revisionist Review," *American Sociological Review,* vol. 42, August, 1977.

Macmillan Publishing Company for eight lines from "Sailing to Byzantium," reprinted from *Collected Poems* by William Butler Yeats, copyright © 1928 by Macmillan Publishing Company, Inc.; copyright renewed 1956 by Georgie Yeats; M. B. Yeats, Miss Anne Yeats, and The Macmillan Company of London and Basingstoke.

Mensa, Dept. 60, 1701 West Third Street, Brooklyn, N.Y. 11223, for test material on pages 136 and 137.

The Psychological Corporation for remaining test material.

Random House, Inc., for seven lines from "If I Could Tell You," copyright © 1945 by W. H. Auden, reprinted from *Collected Poems* by W. H. Auden, edited by Edward Mendelson, copyright © 1976 by Random House, Inc.

The author wishes to express gratitude to the following individuals and organizations:

Center for Disease Control, HEW.

Children's Hospital of Philadelphia: Drs. Gertrude and Warner Henley, Joseph Bongiovanni; Shirley Bonhem.

Educational Testing Service: Robert Solomon.

Electronucleonics Laboratories, Inc., Bethesda, Md.: Drs. Ed Bond, Dan Zimmerman; Ron Southerland.

Memorial Sloan-Kettering Cancer Center: Pat Molino.

National Council on Alcoholism: Dr. Albert N. Browne-Mayer.

Psychological Corporation: Drs. Jerome E. Doppelt, Wimburn L. Wallace, Mildred E. Katzell.

Stevens Institute of Technology: Dr. Karl Springob.

Drs. James Wetmur, Marshall Goldberg, Bernard Wagner, Robert Brooks, Mira Rothenberg, Selma Snyderman, David Kahn, William A. Blank, George Jervis, Lawrence Cohn. And to Professors William J. Goode, Richard Wolf, Walter Weiss.

Also to my intrepid researcher, Hilary Bruns, and wonderful typist, Millie Becerra.

Some of the quiz questions are courtesy of Mensa, the high-IQ society. For further information on Mensa, write Mensa, Dept. H., 1701 W. Third Street, Brooklyn, New York 11223.

My special thanks to Don McKinney, Ross Wetzsteon, Jim Wetmur and Dick Wolf for reading the manuscript for factual and textual accuracy.

... so far as it makes sense to talk about a "standard" American population ... there is no particular reason to think that the intelligence of that standard population has been stable, in either genetic or environmental terms ... the standard American has no reason to feel confident that he is one of an unchanging, reliable mental type.

John Calhoun, The Intelligence of a People

The paranoia of stupidity is always the worst, since its fear of destruction by intelligence is reasonable.

Arthur Miller

PART ONE

MARCH

ON A SUNDAY EVENING in early March the Healey family was en route to New York City after a country weekend. A persistent drizzle fell on heavy traffic that finally gave up and ceased to move altogether. James Healey drummed the steering wheel with short straight finger-nails and thought about the time people wasted in cars.

"I told you we should have started earlier," said Ruth, inevitably. "You had to go on a hike."

"I saw a deer. I was tracking it," he said, as he had before.

"I'll never understand you. You don't even own a gun."

"Tracking was enough." He had followed the deer almost an hour, moving noiselessly in tennis shoes, keeping upwind, fascinated. The animal would not have spotted him at all if he hadn't deliberately made himself known. Watching it leap over a hill, flatten itself against the sky, vanish, he had felt a rush of pure pleasure at being able to outwit the beast without the slightest desire to harm it. "The radio said nothing about rain."

"Now you believe what they *don't* tell you?" Ruth said tartly.

As though the four-lane highway had a reason for being, the traffic lurched forward, but not for long. "I have to pee," Jennie said from the back seat.

"We'll be home soon, honey," Ruth said. "Let's play a game to distract ourselves. How about geography, Jen?"

"Okay. I'll start. 'Essex.'"

"That's no fun. Jennie knows all the places that end in 'x.' Anyway, we've played it a hundred times," Paul rumbled in the deep voice that still surprised his father. "How about only military geography? I just made it up. You use only the names of places where battles have been fought—plains, rivers, cities, blockades, naval engagements..."

"You'd win that one hands down." Jim Healey disapproved of his sixteen-year-old son's incessant war gaming. "Let's see who can name the capitals of the fifty states."

"That wouldn't be much of a contest, either," said Paul, his face appearing in the rearview mirror. He had his mother's oval face and brown hair. "You remember all of them."

"I might forget some," Healey teased. "Try me."

"South Dakota?"

"Pierre."

"See?"

Ruth said, "What about anagrams?"

"Funny how everybody picks the game he or she is best at," Healey observed. "Okay, what's the word?"

Ruth put her hand to her cheek and finally said, "'Charade.' What words can you make of 'charade,' Jen?"

Jennie, who was ten, thought a moment and said excitedly, "'Red' and 'race' and 'car.'"

4

"Good! Paul?"

"'Cad,' 'ade,' 'ad.'"

"Good again! Jim?"

"'Card,'" he said. "What about you, Ruth?"

"'Char' and 'aha.'"

"'Hard,'" said her husband.

"'Chard,'" Ruth added.

"That's three words for all of us except Daddy, who's only got two!" Jennie shouted.

"You're too smart for me. I'm *sure* there are more."

"I know one!" Jennie bubbled. "'Raid.'"

"There's no 'i' in 'charade,' honey," Ruth told her.

"I meant 'read'!"

"'Hear, hear,'" Ruth said.

"'Are,'" Paul said.

"Watch out, folks! I'm about to catch up," Healey announced. "'Dare' and 'dear.' That's four for each of us. It's a dead heat. What a bunch of brains this family has."

"'Ear,'" Jennie said at once.

"'Heard,'" said Ruth.

"'Head,'" Paul said casually.

"'Acre,'" Healey responded.

"'Ahead,'" Ruth said jubilantly. "I have six words now."

"Okay, 'arc,'" responded her husband after a pause.

"'Care,'" Paul put in.

"'Care*d*,'" Jennie squealed at last.

"Tied again!" Ruth cried. "That won't do. 'Ache.'"

"'Raced,'" Healey said.

"'Ached,'" said Paul.

"'Aced,'" said his mother.

"'Arched,'" said Paul.

"'Arced,'" said Healey.

The children were silent. Ruth took a while to answer. "'Carder,'" she said finally.

Healey pondered. "'Era.' Maybe it's a standoff for once."

"'Had,'" Ruth proclaimed. "Jim?"

When the car behind brushed theirs, Healey assumed it was a mistake, and said nothing, but the second and third taps, in quick succession, had to have been intentional.

"What's going on?" He shifted to "park" and undid his seat belt.

Ruth's face looked frightened in the half-light from the dashboard. "Jim! Be careful! That person must be crazy!"

"I'll come too," called Paul.

"I'd better handle it alone."

The station wagon appeared unscathed, but abrasions covered the old car in back. It stood motionless, its bumper a few feet from theirs. Healey approached warily, wondering what to expect—maybe a crowd of teenagers, hopped up on dope, dangerous—but the car contained only the driver. Staring straight ahead, he did not seem to notice Healey. As he bent to the open window, Healey could hear him rant, "Fucking cars, fucking cars..." A whiskey bottle lay on the seat beside him.

Healey said brusquely, "Hey! What is this? What are you trying to do?"

"Huh? What?" The head jerked, and Healey, with a practiced glance, took in the physiognomy. Triangular face with a broad forehead and narrow chin. Tight blond curls, blotched complexion, short nose, oddly hung upper lip that might be the result of a cleft palate operation but probably wasn't. The expression was remote except for the dull cunning that crept into the wide-set eyes. "Oh! Hah! You're the bastard just backed into me!"

Healey won a struggle for self-control. "I struck *you!* Lord, that's a laugh. Listen, I'll let it pass this time, but do it again and you're in for real trouble."

"Yeah, sure."

"I'm warning you."

Confident the episode had ended, Healey moved away, but the man jumped from the car, gesticulating and shouting. "You dent my bumper. You pay for that."

"Pay," Healey said with contempt. He pointed to the

vehicular ruin dripping with rain and said, "I suppose I put a hole in your grille, too?"

"Yeah."

The young man was taller than Healey by several inches but slender; from shoulders to hips he seemed almost columnar. Healey stared at him glumly. A fistfight would have been pointless, humiliating, risky. People watched from their cars; Ruth and Paul had their heads out of the side windows, while Jennie looked from the rear. Healey said carefully, "You don't have any business driving in the first place. You're drunk. Go sleep it off."

"Who says?"

"I do."

The two cars occupied the outside lane. When the man advanced, swaying slightly, Healey retreated to the shoulder. He'd hardly ever used his fists and wondered distractedly if he'd need them now, at forty-one. Should he summon Paul? That prospect displeased too. Paul had become vaguely truculent ever since he'd started war gaming; his son might end any chance of avoiding violence. "Listen . . . ," Healey said.

"You . . . ," the man with the odd mouth tried to articulate, ". . . pay . . . or . . ."

"I'll call the police!"

"Yeah, sure."

The man's eyes rolled, and Healey stepped farther away. The man turned to his car, reached through the window across from the steering wheel, groped and brought out the whiskey bottle, which he held waist high. His back was to the road. *Good God! Am I about to be bludgeoned by a crazy drunken fool in the middle of a traffic jam on a superhighway?* No one seemed aware of his plight. Keep talking, he told himself, eyes on the bottle the man held by the neck, concealing it from onlookers with his body. "Put that down. You don't know what you're doing. You've lost your senses."

The man was horrible angry. Veins bulged in his

throat. "You ran into me!" The bottle rose swiftly.

He really believes that. He's stupid, unbelievably stupid. What impresses stupid people? Credentials! Authority! Use yours. He made his voice as cold and hard as he could. "Do you know who I am? I'm a physician. A doctor. Look at my license plate if you don't believe me! Make trouble and they'll lock you up and throw away the key."

"They will, will they?" said the man, but the head turned and confidence drained from the triangular face. "Doctor, big-shot doctor smacks into my car, but who'll take *my* word for it? I got all the luck, don't I? *You* could get my car fixed if you wanted. You got the insurance. They'd listen to you. People like me don't got no chance. You can afford . . ."

Pressing his advantage, Healey commanded, "Pull off the road. Let me see your driver's license."

"I wanna see yours!" The bottle sank.

Horns brayed around them as though the altercation had caused the tie-up. The man muttered to himself, shuffled, scowled. He retreated to his automobile as Healey started for his, still on the shoulder. Suddenly the battered machine lurched and came toward him. Healey jumped, but his foot slipped on the wet pavement and his head lightly struck the edge of the metal luggage rack on top of the station wagon.

"I'll get you!" he heard a voice cry.

Healey stood still for a moment, breathing in gasps as he watched the old vehicle roar down the shoulder and disappear at a nearby exit. There hadn't been time to get the license number, but that was just as well—good riddance. *Are you okay?* he asked himself, deciding that he was despite a ringing in his ears, a little dizziness and some pain. He climbed into his car. The incident couldn't have lasted more than a minute or two.

"Are you all right?" Ruth asked.

"I guess so." He patted his face with a tissue from a packet on the dashboard.

8

"What happened exactly?"

Healey decided not to mention the blow on his head. Ruth would try to make him see a doctor. Like most doctors, Healey stayed away from doctors as much as he could. Anyway, the headache was already subsiding. He said, "Some idiot trying to work off his traffic frustration on us. There ought to be an IQ test for drivers."

"Any damage to our car?" Paul asked.

"I don't think so."

Ruth laughed, as though to ease the tension. "In heavy traffic, I have to admit, I've had the urge to bump into cars in front of me and knock them out of the way."

"Probably lots of people have, but they don't act on it," said Healey. "Anyway, the man was drunk." He gripped the steering wheel angrily. He could be lying dead on the asphalt now. He was terrified by senseless acts—there seemed so many of them, as though anarchy lurked everywhere. State of fools. Rough beast slouching toward Bethlehem to be born. He said, "I hate jerks, especially drunken jerks."

"Daddy!" remonstrated his daughter, who had blond hair and clear blue eyes. "It's not good English to say 'jerk.'"

"It'll do. Listen, no matter what they tell you about letting go, inhibitions are important. Take away self-restraint and what do you have? Stupid violence. Barbarism." He stared moodily at the monotonous windshield wipers. For Healey, it sometimes seemed miraculous that society ran at all.

"Want me to drive?" Ruth asked as the car before them began to move slowly.

"I can do it, thanks."

"Shall we talk about something else? Let's finish the game," Ruth said.

"Okay. Whose turn is it?"

"Yours."

Healey forced himself to concentrate and said finally, "'Rad.' That's a radiation unit."

"I'm not sure that's fair," Ruth muttered. Soon she smiled and said, "Why, it's so obvious. We all missed it. Meet the champion, darlings. 'Ace,' which is me!"

WEEK ONE

DAY ONE

On Monday, Healey rose early, leaving Ruth asleep. He dressed quietly and ate a stand-up breakfast in the kitchen. Around him morning noises began to sound in the roomy apartment, but Healey, mind on the day ahead, left without seeing his family.

In the back hallway stood a nondescript bicycle, and Healey brought it down in the service elevator. It was 7:15, and Phillip, wearing a visored cap, a bow tie and a neat blue uniform, had just come on duty. Other doormen—dozens, it seemed—had come and gone, but Phillip, an Indian from Bombay with dark skin and prematurely white hair, had served the old co-op on the East Side even before the Healeys bought an apartment there five years before. The morning dialogue between Jim and Phillip often sounded the same.

"What's it like out?"

"Bad."

"Oh?"

"Mmmmmm. Not a nice day, no. It might rain."

"Well, I've got a raincoat, and I need the exercise." Healey aware that he worried unreasonably about gaining weight, patted a nonexistent roll on his stomach.

"You are a man of action, and men of action change the world," the doorman said, gravely regarding him. Phillip claimed clairvoyancy and tried to collar those who passed his way to predict their destinies. He touched Healey's arm with a clean white glove, murmuring, "This will be an important day for you. Very significant. Mmmmmm."

"Maybe so," Healey said pleasantly as he pushed the bike past the door Phillip held for him. "Family okay?"

Healey suspected that Phillip's family was too large to keep track of, but the doorman nodded and said, "Mmmmmm." Phillip always said, "Mmmmmm."

Phillip was right for once. Today would be important one way or another.

For almost a year Healey—a doctor and research scientist who specialized in inherited disease and whose only patients were children—had been pursuing the National Institutes of Health in Washington for permission and a grant to conduct an important experiment. The government body had been slow, and not simply because it was a bureaucracy; Healey's landmark research required the combination—recombination, scientists called it, for obscure reasons—of various types of DNA, including human.

The DNA (deoxyribonucleic acid) molecule, a virtually weightless film fully a yard long coiled in every normal cell, was the stuff of genes. DNA determined both the inheritance and the functioning of plants and animals. In the early 1970s researchers learned how to cut, splice and rearrange DNA in a laboratory. For the first time science had the ability to piece together genetic material from separate and different living organisms.

Controversy had raged ever since, with scientists, philosophers, so-called bioethicists (students of biological ethics), legislators and journalists joining the fray. Critics of gene splicing worried what such experiments as these might create—Armageddon virus, for instance, a Doomsday organism for which humanity lacked resistance or cure. Some feared that genetic transplants would lead to the terrifying day when humans would be cloned in test tubes and males would become superfluous. Some argued that man had no right to meddle with evolutionary processes nature had taken billions of years to establish.

Healey was sympathetic to such concerns but believed that the guidelines established by scientists from within and without the government to regulate DNA research were sufficient. The long list centered on the use of high-containment facilities designated P-4, the highest, down to P-1 ("P" for physical). It was true that the facility at the Kellogg–Bryant Institute, where Healey worked, was classified only P-3, but that was because the P-4 designation involved certain (and in Healey's view unnecessary) constructional niceties. Even so, it should have been good enough, especially since no pathogenic organisms were to be employed there. Still, NIH had stalled because of the *human* DNA questions, as if human DNA was too complex, mysterious and therefore too worrisome to be tampered with.

How many times had Healey opened another brown envelope with government franking, only to say to Coral Blanchard, his secretary, "Lord, they want *more* information now. We'll need a truck to get all this to Washington." He continued to argue that the human DNA was no more dangerous than any other, that safety checks would be made at every step of the way.

If Healey tried to be patient, his colleague, Ad Wallon, wasn't. "Jesus, they're hysterical ninnies at NIH!" he exclaimed. "*Everything* involves risks, from crossing the street to getting married—I should know! But to claim something could happen is another world from saying that it *will*. They're letting them clone bacteria to produce insulin, give wheat and corn the power to nitrogenize themselves, eat garbage or clean oil spills, but when it comes to our work, the most important of all, they drag their feet. Sometimes I think to myself . . ."

"Guess what? We got the green light," Healey said to Wallon a couple of days later. "And what did it? My impassioned arguments? New proof that the work was safe? Nope, it's the Russians. The Russians plan a similar experiment. Now NIH wants to know why we've been slow in starting! Can you beat it?"

"What are we waiting for?" cried Wallon excitedly. "We ought to hurry before they change their minds again."

The team, long since selected, had been assembled at once. Virologist Adelein Wallon, who had changed fields from surgery, and electronmicroscopist Walter Benson were both old-timers on the Kellogg–Bryant staff. Bacteriologist Linda Summer, from Cornell, had just joined it. Robin Frazer, M.D., biochemist and enzymologist, took a short leave from Johns Hopkins for the experiment. Healey himself wore a number of hats— medical doctor, Ph.D. immunologist, human geneticist, university professor.

How much had been done in a week! Healey reflected as he pedaled along. Work had begun the Monday before. Cultures had been prepared of *Escherichia coli*, a bacterium that inhabits the human gut, though this K-12 *E. coli* was not able to live outside a laboratory. In it had been grown an organism called the lambda virus, also attenuated, or weakened, for safety's sake. DNA from the lambda virus and from a normal human placenta had been extracted, with detergent and a high-speed centrifuge, and placed together with a so-called restriction enzyme that cut the DNAs at specific sequences, leaving "sticky ends" that attached to each other in random order. (This was the "shotgun" technique dreaded by critics of such experiments because the nature of the new DNA combinations was unknown.)

So far, so good. The reason for combining viral and human DNA was to provide the latter with a home. On Wednesday evening the lambda virus, with the human DNA inside it, was grown in ten thousand petri dishes, with still another substance added to the mixture, an assay, or test reagent, brilliantly devised by Robin Frazer. The problem was to identify which, if any, of the DNA pieces contained the enzyme they sought. With a special dye, Frazer tricked the enzyme into announcing itself by turning the culture blue.

By Thursday morning the petri dishes were covered with plaques, pinholes on the culture showing the locations of the lambda virus. Visible to the naked eye, about five hundred plaques dotted the surface of each dish, or five million plaques in all. The five team members spent the day eye scanning the dishes. Finally, in the late afternoon, Wallon cried, "I've got one!" Linda Summer soon found a second, and Healey the third.

"Three blue plaques!" Frazer said proudly. "That ought to do it."

Excitement mounted. The critical pieces had been trapped in the viral net. The three plaques, in turn, were propagated and placed in test tubes to be cleaned in a centrifuge. On Friday morning Walter Benson, who had been monitoring the experiment with the electronmicroscope, examined DNA samples from each test tube at high magnification. What he saw was a microorganism sandwich—a lambda piece on each side of the needed human piece. But the human section had to be as short as possible to rule out extra, unwanted DNA beyond the desired enzyme. Benson emerged from his lair, the EM room, and in a sharp, high voice objected, "Two of them are completely unsatisfactory. The DNA's too long." He showed them the results, and even Wallon, a skeptic about safeguards, agreed. Benson went on, "The third's no good either, in my view."

"Come on!" Wallon shouted. "Are you trying to shoot us down, Benson? You work for the Russians or something?"

Benson said coldly, "I am merely presenting my professional opinion. Whether it's respected is another matter."

Wallon insisted that the minuscule additional portion of DNA in the third sample represented no problem whatever. He wanted to press on and finish that evening. The dispute went to Healey, the Responsible Investigator, who said, "Run more checks, Walter. Then we'll see." When the fussy little electronmicroscopist failed to prove his point, Healey concluded, "Let's go on."

"The Nobels are ringing," Wallon laughed, but Healey, always cautious, refused to cheer until Monday.

This was where matters stood as the front wheel of Healey's bicycle grazed a pothole, almost making him fall. He found himself contrasting the brilliant achievements in biology, which had progressed further in the past ten years than in the previous two hundred, with the dismal performance of society. Why, the streets of New York looked as if they'd contracted smallpox. Surely the wear and tear on cars must be more expensive than the cost of filling the holes. Any fool could see that.

A medium-sized man with sandy hair, gray eyes, light, slightly freckled skin and small dimples in his cheeks that seemed at odds with his keen face, Healey locked his bike to the rack near the ambulance entrance. As he turned toward the hospital he squared his shoulders unconsciously.

Named for its industrial founders, Kellogg–Bryant was both a two-hundred-year-old hospital and a research facility, hence the word Institute in the title. It occupied a newly renovated eight-story building on Manhattan's East River. Highly automated, with an auditorium, a heliport and the latest in scientific hardware, the

eighty-five-million-dollar establishment was foremost in
work in inherited disease.

Squares of recessed concrete, the building front offered
little in architectural warmth, but, inside, the reception
area opened abruptly into a large atrium courtyard,
where small trees—*Ficus berjumentis*, or figless figs—
grew in boxes around a fountain. High above, the
courtyard was topped by an elaborate skylight. Between,
the stories presented a complex design: windows of
various shapes—square, oblong, circular, diamond;
sections of floors that protruded; railed walkways; aerial
gardens. Drawings could be seen in the ward windows—
flowers, hearts, faces, moons, suns, scrawled words like
"hello" and "love"—drawn by the patients, principally
children.

Healey rose in a white elevator to the eighth floor,
emerging in an immaculate hallway with no-smoking
signs, smoke sensors in the ceiling and protruding shower
heads to wash off acid in case of a spill. Air conditioning
hummed softly in the background. He passed a maze of
labs bristling with equipment and reached a door marked
JAMES E. HEALEY—CHIEF OF PEDIATRIC RESEARCH. The
long, narrow office had an enclosed place for his
secretary, not yet in. Beyond lay a sort of reception room
with a blackboard, chairs, leather couch and coffee table,
on which were journals like *Cell*, *Nature* and *Gene*, along
with a brochure for Scandinavia, which the Healeys
hoped to visit next summer. A case housed medical books
and pieces of Mayan statuary. There was a photo of
Healey and his family, all smiles, taken at the country
house in Connecticut. Plants crowded the windowsills.
Healey's secretary insisted that she be the only one to
water them.

Behind a glass door at the rear was Healey's private
office—steel desk, chairs, filing cabinets with drawers for
cards which recorded information on patients seen at the
hospital during the seventy-odd years of its existence. The

cards bore inscriptions like "Down's syndrome—mongolism," "galactosemia," "Tay-Sachs disease," "Friedreich's ataxia." Some cards were yellow with age, others freshly white, like that for isovaleric acidemia, a strange condition that caused the skin to smell as though it were rotten, or for the bizarre Lesch-Nyhan syndrome, whose youthful victims would, if unrestrained, literally eat their own flesh, nibbling and swallowing fingers, arms, shoulders, lips, with no indication of pain. New inborn errors of metabolism were being identified all the time; the writer of a textbook on the subject had complained that at the present rate of discovery, future editions of his already expensive tome would be so large as to price it out of the market.

Healey hung up his raincoat, scanned the weekend hospital report and saw nothing new. The routine blood tests for himself and his team of four showed nothing unusual either—had they, he would have heard immediately. He turned his daily calendar to Monday, March 3, and, in an old sports jacket with patches on the elbows, went back into the hall. It was just past 8 A.M.

Healey's destination was a metabolic ward and a little girl who suffered from a rare disease.

Occurring in one out of ten thousand births, phenylketonuria (PKU) had formerly accounted for 1 percent of mental defectives, but no longer. The condition arose from a superabundance of the amino acid phenylalanine in body tissues, leading to brain starvation. The disease could be identified at birth with a blood test, required in most states, and a special diet free of phenylalanine, which existed in most foods, kept the content of the substance normal and prevented damage, so that PKU retardation was increasingly rare. But the diet—a gray liquid served from bottles—was troublesome. Nobody was sure at what age, if ever, it could be safely discontinued, and it was hard to enforce, since it meant little or no ordinary food. If parents were lax and let a PKU child eat normally, the child might begin a

20

dreadful descent down the IQ percentiles. Cathy, who was six, had been such a case.

As Healey had learned the story, Cathy's mother, twice divorced, had two normal children from her first marriage. (Cathy's father must have carried the PKU strain, since the disease was inherited.) A new man entered her life, and the mother began to neglect the child, failing to enforce the diet and omitting clinical visits for metabolic maintenance. In kindergarten in upstate New York, where they lived, Cathy started to change from a willful, spirited child into a withdrawn one. Several times in the previous months she'd run a high temperature and refused to eat, so that her body fed off its own phenylalanine-filled tissues, literally poisoning itself. Cathy had been identified as slow in the first grade. Fortunately, the damage hadn't been permanent. The school authorities had been responsible for bringing Cathy to the hospital, where dietary treatment and mental stimulation had wrought wonders. Mel Orenstein, the psychiatrist, calculated that the girl's IQ had risen fifteen to twenty points since admission, and it was still going up. Even with the diet, PKU children where seldom smart, but Cathy showed exceptional promise, and though the girl was a charity case and expensive for the hospital, Healey wanted her in a controlled environment as long as possible.

Healey had another reason for keeping Cathy on hand. PKU had been selected as the first inherited disease on which to try genetic surgery because the abnormality was so well understood. The problem was a failure to convert phenylalanine into substances vital to brain operations because the genetic instructions to do so were lacking. If human DNA containing those instructions could be introduced into the chromosomes of a PKU victim, the condition would be cured. Many other inherited diseases could be treated in the same fashion, hence the importance of what Healey hoped to accomplish in the subbasement lab.

Quite by accident, Cathy had been at K–B when the work got under way, and among the cultures employed was one from her white blood cells. If the experiment succeeded, PKU victims like her would be safe from the terrible symptoms even without a special diet; if for some reason, the team failed today, Healey would need more of Cathy's leukocytes and fibroplast to try once more.

People made a pet of Cathy Gobrin. The little girl could have paid for her stay at the hospital by selling kisses. Nobody could resist her, not even Herman Herrmann, the austere director of the Institute.

Healey, proud of her progress, looked in on her whenever he could. Arriving on the fifth floor, he stopped dutifully for a red light that meant a procession of tots was about to charge down the hall to the playroom. The light changed, and Healey stepped into the convergence of various halls. The morning shift had just come on duty, and the floor seethed with activity—orderlies bearing medicines, nursing assistants moving young patients, nurses in different-colored uniforms scurrying everywhere, doctors and interns in loose white coats conversing in animated clusters. Healey smiled around and stepped behind a semicircular enclosure.

Olga the head nurse, stood there, white uniform beaded with gold insignia. To Healey, she always looked like a general, and he jokingly referred to her as such. Almost as tall as he, with a square jaw and gray hair under a cap pointed like a weapon, Olga ran the floor with furious efficiency. A nurse or orderly who got instructions wrong, mixed up people's X rays or forgot to take a temperature soon learned of the head nurse's intolerance of error. If the hospital had an *esprit de corps*, a powerful desire to avoid sloppy standards, as could all too easily be found in medical institutions, those with a strong sense of discipline, like Olga, were responsible.

"Good morning, general," Healey said as he reached

for Cathy's folder. "How's my patient?"

"Couldn't be better, doctor. The little cold she had on Friday is completely gone." She listened intently as a cylinder plopped from a pneumatic tube and opened it while she talked. "Dr. Wallon's already been to see her. He just left."

"So early?" Healey said in surprise. Wallon usually came in later. He scanned Cathy's file as Olga watched, seemingly casual but really reading the doctor's face for possible complaints, of which he had none. Weekend care seemed perfect, with Cathy's behavior faithfully recorded. There was no sign of the symptom Healey watched for most carefully, a return of the shy, withdrawn behavior the girl had displayed a month before, when she entered Kellogg-Bryant. "Okay," he said.

"Doctor..." Olga hesitated. "Don't you think Cathy could have a little real food? She's driving us crazy."

"Has she had any?" he asked quickly.

"What kind of floor do you think I run? No. But since she's coming along so well... The synthetic diet doesn't have everything. Sooner or later..."

"Not quite yet. Let's see what happens."

A motorized cart bore down on him as he started across the hall. It stopped, tiny antenna waving. A recent innovation at the hospital, the carts were equipped with a simple device that took them unerringly to any in-house destination ordered; they halted abruptly if an obstacle appeared. Healey was skeptical as to how much time and money the vehicles saved, but the kids adored them.

The room Cathy shared with three other children was painted in bold colors. Puzzles, books, art supplies, games and music boxes covered the tables. A wall poster showed a cat on a chinning bar with the legend "Hang in there, baby!" Tropical fish swam in a bubbly tank. Recorded sounds played discreetly in the background—dogs barking, pans rattling, grown-ups talking indistinctly. Hospital life was meant to seem as normal as possible, to ease the transition home; and with classes, the playroom and the sunroof, most children spent little daytime in bed.

In a pinafore, Cathy, azure-eyed, rosy-cheeked, sat on the edge of the bed, legs dangling. "Hi, doctor! Kiss!"

He kissed her. "How's my little friend today?"

"Fine." She frowned suddenly. "Can I go home soon? I miss my brother and sifter."

"Sister," he corrected lightly. "Not your mother?"

"Oh, her too. But she comes to see me sometimes, and they can't. Why can't they?"

Her mother visited damn seldom, he thought, and wished there were some other place for Cathy when she quit the hospital. He said, "Too young. Kids under twelve can't visit. It's a crazy rule if you ask me. Anyway, you'll be leaving here soon. What are you reading, dear?"

Cathy glanced at the picture book in her lap. "It's about King Arthur. He had a table with knights. One was called Lanfalot."

"Lancelot."

"Lan*sse*lot. He was in love with King Arthur's wife, whose name I can't speak."

"Guinevere," said Healey.

"Do you think Lancelot slept over?"

"Slept over?" he asked.

"With King Arthur's wife," she said slyly.

"Sure he did," another kid said.

You could certainly pick up things at hospitals, Healey thought. "Well, I don't know," he said. He hoisted Cathy and patted her behind. "Gaining weight, aren't you?"

The girl pouted. "I wish I could have i-scream."

"Ice cream?"

"Ice cream. I want some. I want some now."

"Will you settle for anything else but ice cream?" Milk products were loaded with phenylalanine.

"Meat," said she.

"Okay. Be patient, dear. You can have a little meat soon."

"Promise?"

"Yes."

Mel Orenstein hurried into the room. In his early sixties, gray-haired, flat-faced, intense, the psychiatrist was always in a rush.

"Hello, Mel. What's on the agenda today?" Healey put Cathy down.

"WISC. The Wechsler Intelligence Scale for Children. Let's see how smart our girl is this morning," Orenstein said rapidly. He had a stentorian voice that sounded almost mechanical.

"*Real* smart," Healey said.

"I don't like tefts. They're too hard," Cathy protested.

"Tests. Come on, Cathy, cooperate. You gave me a tough time last week." To Healey, Orenstein muttered, "She's hell on wheels, this one. Willful as all get out. Got the makings of a first-class bitch. Sexy one at that."

"I don't want to be dumb, do I, doctor?" Cathy asked, a little anxiously.

"No. And you're not, either," Healey said. He watched with surprise as Orenstein opened his attaché case. "You're testing her here?"

"Why not? It won't take ten minutes. Kids don't need absolute privacy for accurate testing, the newest literature shows." He took out a form and a pencil, glanced around the room and ordered, "You children be quiet, okay?" He pressed a button on his stop-watch and began, "Tell me, Cathy..."

"Kiss first," Cathy bribed him. Orenstein pecked her on the forehead, seeming embarrassed. "Evening is to dinner as morning is to... what?"

"Breakfast!" Cathy shouted. "I want some!"

"Of all the questions," Healey said, laughing.

Out in the hall again he saw the director advancing with a small retinue, among them Tish Wyler, a tiny, excitable young woman with a face upturned like a buttercup, who ran the Institute's publicity staff. Herman Herrmann towered over her. A bacteriologist turned administrator, the director was a powerhouse in the medical world and famous because of his (to Healey) rather farfetched book, *Genes and the Year 2000*, which argued that human evolution would soon be controlled by man himself, marking his final mastery over nature and the beginning of his freedom from natural forces. Herrmann, tall, bald, gaunt, beak-nosed and wrinkled beyond his forty-eight years, was intensely busy but took the time to make personal inspection tours. No detail of the Institute's life escaped him.

Healey watched the cortege—two assistants with notebooks and pencils who recorded the director's every utterance as he strode along, bending, peering, poking, examining everything, while little Tish Wyler scampered to keep up. In a bass voice Herrmann was saying to her as he came within earshot, "Hospital food shouldn't be bad, but it shouldn't be good, either. Eating is an ego issue, maybe a superego issue. Ego must be discouraged in patients. It interferes with care. Eating is *sui generis*, but the menu is not..."

Herrmann's eyes, protruding like searchlights, had found Healey and stayed on him. "Ah, Dr. James Healey."

"Good morning, Dr. Herman Herrmann," said Healey, who was amused by the director's name.

"This is *der Tag* downstairs, isn't it?"

"Yes, I guess we'll know something today, Herman," Healey said casually.

"We're all terribly excited," exclaimed Tish Wyler. "The press release is written, and it'll make headlines!"

"I believe Dr. Healey's work will make headlines, not the press release," Herrmann rebuked Tish Wyler, who glanced at her note pad uncertainly.

"Better keep the release in the drawer for a while, Tish. You never know about these things until the returns are in," Healey said.

Cathy appeared in her doorway, saying to Herrmann, "Hi, doctor. Kiss!"

Herrmann muttered, as he bent to her, "The little tart."

• • •

While Healey was above, Dr. Adelein Wallon entered the subbasement holding a plastic coffee cup he was forbidden to bring into the containment facility. Upstairs, Wallon had tried to be his ordinarily ebullient self, but he did not feel well and stared morosely at the flaming-orange symbol by the door. Words beneath it said:

BIOHAZARD

ADMITTANCE TO AUTHORIZED PERSONNEL ONLY
HAZARD IDENTITY: RECOMBINANT DNA RESEARCH
RESPONSIBLE INVESTIGATOR: JAMES E. HEALEY, M.D.
IN CASE OF EMERGENCY CALL:
  DAYTIME PHONE 555-1042 HOME PHONE 555-7966
AUTHORIZATION FOR ENTRANCE MUST BE OBTAINED
FROM THE RESPONSIBLE INVESTIGATOR NAMED ABOVE.

They overdid the biohazard stuff, Wallon thought, lighting a cigarette. *They*, to him, meant the Americans, even though the virologist had been in the United States twenty-five years, was a naturalized citizen and spoke perfect English, so that he was more American than Belgian now. The DNA experiments seemed to arouse an unconscious, almost tribal fear of biological intermixing. Was that in some fashion related to how *they* still felt about the race question, to their deep fright that assimilation of the black gene pool by the white would destroy Caucasian capability? What nonsense! So was their constant concern about health. Never had there been a people so health conscious as *they*, a nation of hypochondriacs. Look at the safety features required for the subbasement, like mechanical pipettes and glove boxes. The microorganisms used in the experiment were not even remotely pathogenic—even if they could escape their double-walled laboratory prison, which they could not. The precautions were far too elaborate; with less stringent ones the work could have been completed last week, as he had urged. That damn Healey!

Wallon fumbled for his lab key. Where was it? Had he left it home? He couldn't remember. He *had* to stop drinking, he warned himself stormily, scouring his pockets. Look what booze had cost him already: three wives, then a succession of girlfriends, not that any could carry on a decent conversation.

Wallon's problem, he knew, was a tendency to become morose despite his outward bonhomie, and so he drank, which didn't help his sinuses any more than did cigarettes. Recently, because of headaches, Wallon had prescribed cortisone for himself to reduce inflammation. A fool of a patient had himself for a physician, Wallon thought; he wasn't at all sure how well steroids and whiskey mixed. Badly, to judge by last night's performance. He had been in a poker game with fellow doctors and was so far ahead—You cheat a little with your quick fingers, don't you, Ad? he asked himself, ashamed, and nodded—that he'd permitted himself a drink and then another and another. Toward the end he played stupidly, and in the last hand, *knowing* (oh God!) that he should have folded, he tried to bluff and lost everything. At home, as solace, he drank more, slept, woke before dawn and took a pill against nausea which kept him awake for the rest of the night. And now the missing key, minor in itself but worrisome, like a signal.

He found it at last, cuddled in his watch pocket, opened the door and entered the facility through the air lock. The quarters were cramped even though the lab had been built to accommodate only a small team—how the Americans loved to save money! As he'd hoped, five clean uniforms lay folded on the bench in the changing room, for Wallon—childishly, he knew—felt that being first to work might somehow restore his fallen virtue.

Undressing, Wallon wondered how he would comport himself if Linda Summer burst in. The girl . . . woman— he could never decide what to call her; she was a first-rate

28

woman bacteriologist, but she was also young, mid-twenties, he supposed, so "girl" seemed right—was extremely pretty, and perhaps displaying his lust would affect her. But he doubted it. None of his other blandishments had received the slightest encouragement. In any case, shy Summer always knocked. How ironic, Wallon's mind went on, that for all its expensive safeguards, the facility had only one changing room. Nobody seemed to have considered that female scientists might work there too. When Linda put on or took off her uniform, she hid behind the shower curtain.

Wallon pulled white trousers over thick legs and thrust heavy arms into a jacket that buttoned in back. *They* even worried about the contamination of buttons! Covers went over his sizable shoes and a white cap on his large head. He was about to leave when he remembered that he still wore contact lenses, forbidden in the containment area because microorganisms might lodge behind them. Crap! Wallon retrieved eyeglasses from his locker and left the contacts there.

The atmospheric pressure in the changing room, and in the animal chamber next door, read -0.1" W.G., -0.2" in the corridor past the second air lock, and -0.3" in the central lab area, so that all air flowed inwardly until it was exhausted through a series of extremely fine filters and an incineration system. When Wallon entered the third air lock the slightest breath of air went with him. The forty-four-foot square lab was a world of its own. Walls coated with layers of plastic presented a completely smooth white surface, as did the ceramic-tile floor covered with invisible plastic. Equipment crowded the oppressively low-ceilinged chamber—stainless-steel cabinets and worktables loaded with paraphernalia, glove boxes, sinks (liquids leaving the lab were boiled), centrifuges. Surrounding rooms could be seen through windows: one contained the Phillips electronmicroscope, others racks where cultures were grown. A steel door opened to a conveyor belt on which glass and metal containers were sent to the outside "kitchen" to be cleaned, having passed through an autoclave, or sterilizer.

Over the weekend Wallon had propagated a quantity of Simian Virus 40, still another DNA combination. The lambda virus had provided shelter for the normal DNA, from the placenta, but to deliver it to human tissues a stronger, bolder virus was needed, meaning a cancer virus, as Simian Virus 40 was. Years before, through a gross error, the early Salk polio vaccine, which had been prepared in monkey cells, was found to contain SV 40, one of almost fifty monkey viruses. SV 40 could cause cancer in monkeys, and there was fear of what it could do in people. The vaccine was recalled, but 30 percent of the population had already gotten polio shots and had SV 40 antibodies in their systems. Although they harbored the virus, none had contracted cancer as a result, according to extensive follow-ups. Alarmed scientists had also given SV 40 in massive doses to convict volunteers, who developed nothing more serious than benign tumors at the injection sites. Even so, Wallon's SV 40 had been purposely attenuated as a further safeguard. In itself, the monkey virus could cause no harm.

Wallon had spliced the lambda-human DNA from the blue-plaque test tube to the SV 40, producing a new virus, and wanted to see how well it had grown. Wearing elbow-length rubber gloves, he removed sealed petri dishes from the incubator. As he carried the dishes, Wallon experienced a shudder of nausea and stood still for a moment until the spasm passed. He placed the dishes inside a laminar-flow hood and pressed a switch. The hum meant that an air screen had been created; it would prevent organisms from escaping the cabinet through the long, narrow aperture intended for human hands.

The virologist's next step was a clear infraction of the regulations for a top-level physical-containment facility, which decreed that manipulation of certain classes of microorganisms, within which the new virus clearly fell, had to be conducted in a glove box, a sealed container with rubber gloves attacked inside. Instead, Wallon removed the lids from the petri dishes in the laminar-flow hood, where he added a dye, careful, however, not to touch the culture with his gloved hands. He replaced the lids and brought the dishes across the room to a Zeiss high-resolution light microscope.

Again, he was breaking the rules. Wallon should have sealed the dishes with clear plastic before using the microscope. But the plastic slips made microscopy less effective, because the objective, or lower end of the instrument, would be farther away from the culture. A meticulous scientist in his own fashion, Wallon put an uncovered petri dish beneath the objective.

He could not see the virus—the far more powerful Phillips EM would be required for that—but he could extrapolate its presence from the condition of the monkey cells it grew in. Most cells looked healthy, but some had died, meaning the virus lived. As he turned delicate dials of the scope for still better resolution, the image blurred; he had permitted the objective to touch the culture.

Even then he was in no danger of contamination; the lense would be wiped with a tissue, as Wallon did, the tissue disposed of in a bag for autoclaving. But nausea chose that moment to attack again. His stomach contracted, and his clammy brow extruded sweat. Unthinkingly, he patted his forehead with the tissue, a corner of which passed before his nose.

Though Wallon was oblivious to the contact, his psyche must have pressed a button like the one on the wall for signaling an accident. This time, in a glove box, he carefully covered the next batch of dishes with clear plastic covers before bringing them to the microscope.

Walter Benson was first to arrive after Ad Wallon. Short and spare, a lifelong bachelor of fifty-one, with a perpetually startled expression, Benson had quit medicine, having correctly decided that his grumpy disposition antagonized patients. Benson took a Ph.D. in cell biology, branching into histology, the study of organismic organization, and then into electronmicroscopy, where his seeming arrogance protected him from eager researchers who always panted for pictures of the microorganisms they worked with. Benson was one of the best EM men in the business.

Grumbling "Good morning," Benson approached Wallon's table. A self-appointed sergeant-at-arms in the lab, Benson peeked into the disposal bag, saw the tissue and, with a reproachful look that Wallon, preoccupied, failed to notice, dropped the bag into a sterilizer, using tweezers, which he autoclaved as well. He continued to his domain, the EM room. Benson's job today was the same as it had been throughout the experiment—to run controls. He would make grids of the new virus cultured over the weekend. The EM's capacity was mag 160,000. If necessary, pictures could be blown up much larger.

Robin Frazer came next. A muscular thirty-four-year-old black man with a clipped mustache, a radiant smile and carefully articulated speech, Frazer had demonstrated his talent for innovation with the elegant blue assay. He had left his family in Baltimore, expecting to stay a week or two at most. A superb athlete, he had a national rating in squash, which he played whenever he could.

Linda Summer followed. The job of the Ph.D. bacteriologist had been to make most of the cultures, and that done, she would work today with Frazer to test the new virus for protein production. Summer was twenty-nine, though her seamless skin made her look younger. Red-haired, blue-eyed, tall, slim, exquisitely constructed, Summer was a little awkward, withdrawn, even stiff, perhaps because of her beauty. Now and then her gaze drifted surreptitiously to the air lock through which only Healey had yet to pass.

Healey changed into a uniform but did not enter the lab immediately. He walked instead to the animal chamber down the corridor. He felt oddly apprehensive. He had no reason to distrust the experiment, so that couldn't be it. The suspense that had been building the whole week must be responsible. He sought momentary diversion. The end cage contained an African green monkey named Lucky with which Healey had developed a routine. He stood before the cage, his gray eyes peering deeply into Lucky's brown ones. Playfully, the monkey rattled the bars, whirled, grabbed wooden blocks from the back of its cage and constructed shapes with them—a square, a triangle, a crude star. Healey patted Lucky through the bars and handed the animal an apple from a crate.

Healey had already made a culture from Cathy Gobrin's cells: the ultimate test was at hand. He added the new virus prepared by Wallon. If it took, growing rapidly and revealing its presence by the blue assay, the genetic splice had worked; DNA from the normal placenta, carrying information which caused the proper conversion of phenylalanine into other needed substances, had combined with Cathy's substance. A cure for PKU had been developed. Unless Benson and Frazer turned up something new, the experiment could safely be called a success.

As noon approached, with no alarum having been sounded, Healey suggested that they skip the lunch break, which would mean a shower and a change and rechange of clothes, and finish. He felt he was close. At 12:32 Healey looked up from the Zeiss and said, "Okay, I guess that's it."

Linda Summer ran over, bent as though to kiss him but extended her hand instead. Frazer's smile lifted his mustache. Wallon shouted, "Ever cautious Healey! We had it last week, Jim, and you know it!"

Healey murmured, "I like to be sure." But he smiled too.

"Well, we've done it," Wallon said, beaming. "We might as well start testing the animals with it. Have to, sooner or later."

"What's the hurry?"

"I want to get some sleep."

"Any objections, Robin?"

"Not from here. Nothing's shown up, and I don't see why it should," Robin said easily.

"Okay."

Wallon went to inoculate monkeys and mice with the new virus, and then he went home. A lack of symptomatology in the animals would be further confirmation that the virus was safe, not that anyone thought otherwise. More elaborate testing would follow, then the publication of papers and finally the new virus would be tested on a PKU victim, perhaps Cathy herself. There were dreams to dream now that they had proved that an inborn error of metabolism could be genetically corrected. Someday, Healey thought as he bent over the microscope, babies or embryos would be analyzed with a computer for their propensity to disease. If trouble lay in their genes, genetic surgery could be used to correct it. A new field of defect medicine might be at hand.

Benson strode from the EM room, looking grim. Still disliking the DNA section, he had been making ever greater enlargements of it. From what he could tell, he reported, the new virus might have mutated over the weekend, which probably meant nothing, but still . . . Healey, expressionless, turned to Frazer. With Summer's help, the biochemist had been synthesizing and testing the viral protein products with low voltage applied across the gel to separate small molecules from large ones. The results appeared as bands on a photo plate. Frazer had found only a single band, indicating only one foreign protein, the enzyme which, in a human body, would counteract the overproduction of phenylalanine. That was exactly as expected.

Upon Benson's caveat, however, Frazer performed the test again, on the chance, unlikely as it seemed, that another, slower-appearing protein might emerge, given the extra time. Examining the plate, the biochemist saw two bands instead of one, meaning that the virus made two proteins. "Oh boy," he said.

The new protein was either the result of mutation or the extra snip of DNA Benson had complained about on Friday, but nothing more could be explained at that point. It was one of tens of thousands of unknown substances in the mazelike, largely uncharted subworld. Frazer said, "Well?"

Healey's long silence had to do with disappointment, not indecision. Uncertainty had appeared, and his job as Responsible Investigator was to avoid risks, no matter how small, with recombinant DNA. "Let's scrub it," he said in a low voice. "We'll have to start over. Herrmann won't like it, but it can't be helped."

The others nodded reluctantly. A sample of the new virus would be frozen, the rest autoclaved as a further safety measure. The animals would be closely watched for symptoms. That the scientists might not know what to look for, not recognize symptoms if they appeared, was simply not considered. There was no reason why it should have been.

DAY THREE

On Wednesday Healey came home to find Phillip
standing door, looking glum. The man's moods wandered
like a pilgrim. He could be open and friendly or austerely
remote, as now.

Healey thought back quickly; it seemed to him Phillip
had been on duty every day for at least a week. "Don't you
ever take time off?"

"This was supposed to be. Other man got sick."

"Well, take my advice and don't overdo it." Healey
gazed at the gloomy countenance, the color of cocoa,
draped in long white hair. 'All work and no play
makes—"

"Phillip a dull doorman. I know." He seemed to
brighten at the prospect of a conversation. "But I like my
work. It gives me a chance to observe people closely,

understand their inner concerns, see what drives them on. People are miraculous, all people, no matter how humble. Don't you agree, doctor?"

Healey had limited tolerance for generalizations such as Phillip often offered. He pushed his bike across the lobby and said, "Sure."

Phillip followed implacably. "People believe man's greatest gift is intelligence, but compassion is far greater. It separates man from animals in a way that intelligence does not, because animals have intelligence too. Modern man is too smart for his own good. Look at the weapons he has invented. Consider the dangerous experiments he undertakes. Mmmmmm. And his intelligence interferes with his compassion, prevents him from achieving his full potential for happiness. Man cannot live by brains alone."

"By brains alone. That's not bad," Healey complimented from inside the elevator, wishing Phillip would unhand the door.

"In terms of evolution..."

Healey had heard Phillip on this subject before. When the doorman paused for breath he put in, "How's the family?"

"Fine."

"How many kids do you have, Phillip? I forget."

"Eight. Some say that's too many but..."

From the shaft above knocking sounded. "Somebody wants the elevator," Healey said gratefully.

The morning mail lay on a chest by the front door, and Healey riffled it. Postcards from friends. Announcement of a summer music festival, which the Healeys wouldn't be able to attend because they'd be abroad this year. Solicitation from the public broadcasting channel. Bulletin from Common Cause. A small check from the government for a few days' consultation in Washington: "Please Do Not Bend, Fold, Spindle or Mutilate." A bill from the utility. For months the bills had been wrong in the utility's favor, even after countless phone calls and letters from Healey. At last it seemed to be right.

A rattle of pans reminded him of Flo. Flo Robbins, a rotund widow in her forties, really ran the capacious old apartment. She had been with the Healeys for a decade. Five days a week she arrived in the early afternoon to clean, shop and cook dinner before going back to Harlem, where she went to church most evenings. Healey held Flo in high regard: she was competent, pleasant, perceptive, quick.

"What's for dinner?" he asked her.

"Roast beef," Flo said in her fluty voice. "Pink as you like it. Hash browns. Not much in the way of vegetables around. You'll have to settle for squash, Jim."

"Okay," he said with a small sigh. The ribs stood in a roasting pan, and he prodded the meat with his finger. "That's a lot of beef," he observed.

"You folks have company, remember?"

"Company?"

"That nice big doctor and a girl. Is she his girlfriend?"

Yes, it was Wednesday, when the Healeys often entertained, because on that day he taught at the university and could be depended on to get home on time. He'd forgotten all about Wallon, who was bringing Linda Summer. He said a little too insistently, "She's not his girlfriend. At least, I don't think she is."

Flo's eyes widened. "You like that girl yourself?" she asked cagily.

"Now, Flo, don't get the wrong idea." *Too* perceptive. "What about the kids?"

"I'll feed Jennie first. Paul's eating at his friend's."

"Again! More war games?"

"Guess so. Dinner won't be late, will it? I got church."

"You'll be out on time, Flo. We don't want to keep God waiting."

"You'll get well-done roast beef if you do."

"The Lord's revenge."

Healey backed out of the kitchen thinking of Ruth's revenge if she knew about his peckish urge for Linda

Summer. Nothing had happened except in the sternest sense of the commandment on lust. He had not so much as stared at the young woman, at least when she had been looking. He had observed the proprieties to the point of formality. Linda must think him a cold fish! On the other hand, she would probably have been shocked were she aware that the Responsible Investigator would like to investigate her. She was so timid, he so married. Yes, better that nothing showed.

Healey went to the bedroom, putting the exquisite redhead with the unlined face out of his mind. Ruth sprawled on the chaise in a dressing gown working on the crossword puzzle to classical music on the FM radio. "Hello, dear," she said, without moving her dark eyes. "What does something *organoleptic* affect?"

"Spell it." She did. "I should know? You're the wordsmith in the family."

"At least you're the better speller," Ruth said with a touch of condescension. "How many 'l's in acrylic?"

"One," said he. He crossed the room, bent past the folded newspaper to kiss her. Their lips met perfunctorily. Sex, thought Healey. Good Lord, it's been *two weeks!* Soon I'll forget how!

"I have it! Something organoleptic affects the *senses*. I'm too smart for the *Times*," Ruth exulted.

In his walk-in closet he took off his clothes. Ruth was smart all right. A tax lawyer, she was employed by a firm that permitted her to work part time at almost full pay. Equipped with a dazzling memory, she could recall legal precedents and locate relevant decisions with ease. Ruth could have earned big money if she chose, but preferred to paint her detailed miniatures and be available for the kids. His own income as a researcher and teacher was hardly princely. The family got by, barely, the only contention being over the small stipend he gave his mother, to which Ruth objected, sometimes strenuously.

Ruth lowered the paper as he emerged, wearing his

undershorts, and said, "Speaking of female smarts, I was right."

"Right about what?" She had an arrogant way of expecting him to understand her references.

"Jennie's IQ. I told you she was going to take a test. I called the school today. She scored one fifty-four."

He whistled. "Well, I'm not surprised—look at her parents. But we oughtn't to go overboard. People make too much of IQ. It's got predictive value for school, but that's about all. It's really a middle-class measurement."

"So we're middle class! The whole country is, mostly, so IQ does mean something, no matter what they say. I bet you Jennie goes ahead and becomes a mathematician."

"Come on, she's only ten. She'll change her mind a dozen times."

"I wonder. She's very determined, and she's very smart. Admit you're proud of her."

"I am! But smarts aren't everything. You're forgetting Jen's maturity. Look at Paul. I bet he's got the highest IQ in the house, and what's he doing with it? Playing games."

Ruth's eyes rolled up. "It's all he ever does anymore. Other kids his age have interests, but Paul has only one. He's obsessed. He's been in his room talking ever since he got home from school. I'm almost sorry we got him his own phone."

"We couldn't use ours if we didn't. Ask him about his homework?"

"I tried. He says he does it, and maybe it's true—the kid's so fast! But how much can he accomplish when all he does is study war?"

"Sometimes I hardly feel I know him," Healey said.

"I don't, either. This morning he told me he may not go to college. You can't pay the rent playing war games, I said, but he never listens to me anymore. You'd better talk to him." He nodded. She peeked at him. "Maybe you ought to get dressed, Jim. You want to be ready for that girl, don't you? The one with the gorgeous bod?"

Ruth's smile was more than vaguely taunting. How did women know what went on in a man's dream loins? Somehow they did. Sensuous sentinels, always on the alert. "When they passed out bodies, you didn't get a bad shake, either," he teased.

"Is that supposed to be a compliment?" said Ruth, running a finger down her cheek. "Some men appreciate me."

"Now, Ruth..."

"Like Wallon," she went on saucily. "He finds me attractive, I know he does."

"Why shouldn't he? You are. But don't take it too seriously. Ad wants to be liked. He always comes on strong, especially with women."

"Please! Don't spoil my fun. I like to be flirted with. It makes me feel young."

"Good Lord, Ruth! You're hardly an old lady. I only meant that Wallon tries a little *too* hard, it seems to me."

"Oh? You'd do better, I suppose?"

"When it comes to women I'm a little out of practice—eighteen years' worth," Healey replied, slightly exasperated.

"I'm not a woman now?"

"You know what I mean." As he started for the bathroom his wife called, "Isn't that too long?"

"Isn't *what* too long?"

"To be faithful."

"Not for me. What about you?" he demanded.

"Not for me, either," Ruth said, he thought a bit sadly. "I was just talking. Anyway, I feel sorry for Ad. He's just a kid under the surface—he brings out the mother in me. As for that china doll, you wouldn't kick her out of bed, because—"

"Ruth..."

"She'd break."

• • •

42

The Healeys ate at seven to accommodate Flo, and guests who wanted cocktails were urged to come well before, especially Ad Wallon, a frequent visitor. It was almost seven when Phillip called on the house phone to announce him. Jim grumbled, "Here we go again. Ad's late, and he'll want a drink."

"You could refuse," Ruth said. The Healeys rarely took more than a glass or two of wine.

"Try holding back the sea." At the front door he wondered what took so long. Phillip of course. He could visualize the scene: rarely silent Ad Wallon standing openmouthed as Phillip harangued him on his destiny.

Ruth came to the door as the guests entered. Wallon bowed in a courtly manner and kissed her on the lips. "You remember Linda?"

"Of course! We met at the hospital. Hello, dear. How stunning you look."

"Thank you. Hi, Jim."

Healey had never encountered Linda Summer socially before. In a sleek black-velvet pants suit, blouseless and cut surprisingly low in front, with her long red hair and pretty pink mouth that needed no lipstick, she looked sensational. Almost despite himself he began to compare the two women. Linda: youthful, tall, big-breasted, hesitant, graceful. Ruth: short, thin, vivacious, maturely lovely under a bell of brown hair, yet a little pinch-faced right now, feeling uneasy, maybe, because she had a decade or so on the other. Yes. Ruth *would* react that way. Wallon was saying expansively, "That's some character, your doorman. He told me I'd figure in history, but not for anything I accomplished, like I might be remembered for something terrible. How do you like that?"

"Phillip calls them as he sees them." Healey laughed. Wallon had a habit, European, Jim supposed, of speaking with his face close to his listener's. There was liquor on his breath. Healey took a step back and examined him—

43

Wallon's broad, usually ruddy face seemed pale. "You don't look so hot."

"Me? I'm fine. All I need is a drink. Time for a quick one?"

"Flo's the boss. Ask her," Ruth said.

"I will! Linda?"

"Not for me, thanks."

Wallon went to the kitchen, seized Flo in his burly arms, hugged her and begged, "Miz Flo, I'm dying for an itty-bitty drink. Do I have your generous permission?"

"Drink's bad for you," Flo reproved. "But we don't want you to die. You have ten minutes before dinner—not a second longer, hear, doctor?"

"Yes ma'am," Wallon said.

Wallon emerged with a tumbler of amber liquid garnished by a single ice cube. He plopped himself between the two women on the low-slung couch. "I don't mean to be unfriendly, but you I see all the time, Jim. Ruth's a different matter. She's my best girl, or would be if you weren't in the picture."

Healey disliked foolish banter of this sort, especially from a forty-five-year-old man he liked and respected, but with Ruth grinning idiotically he had to go along. "She likes you too, I hear," he observed.

"Is it true?" Wallon said to her.

"I refuse to answer on the grounds of possible self-incrimination," Ruth replied.

"Ah, the bitches," said Wallon, lighting a cigarette. "You never know where you stand with them. You have to guess, because they won't tell you. And if you're wrong, watch out. They never change their minds. The bitches have been a problem for me my whole life, and I'm afraid they always will be." He picked his glass from a coaster, set it down again hastily and coughed.

"Catching cold?" Ruth asked.

"Doctors catch things like plague or Lassa fever, but not colds. I have a little sinus trouble, that's all. I'm trying to clear it up by the weekend. I'm taking medicine," Wallon grumbled.

"What are you taking?" said Healey.

"Cortisone."

"What's happening this weekend?" Ruth wondered.

"I'm going to Boston to visit my kids." He glanced at Linda. "They live there with their mother. The kids and I always have a great time."

"Is Linda coming with you?" Ruth said.

"I hadn't asked her, but it's a terrific idea," Wallon said with hearty sincerity. "Want to, Linda?"

"Sorry, I can't."

"She can't." Wallon nodded, apparently to himself. He drank and placed his arms on the couch back, framing the two women, turned his round visage to each and said, as if determined to be charming. "If only I could be positioned between you two forever. We'd be as stars in a constellation."

"Sounds cold," Ruth said archly. "What would you call us?"

"Well, let's see. My kids tell me I look like a bear." Healey was sorry Wallon had said that. It was one of those things you never forgot. Wallon *did* resemble a bear, with his big head, shaggy hair, large nose, wide mouth, heavy body. "Ursus. Ursus and his nurses. Want to be part of a new constellation, Linda?"

"Not me, thanks."

Neither woman appeared to notice, but anger slashed Wallon's face. Linda must have said no to him a lot, Healey thought; he feels rejected. Even so, the reaction seemed extreme, especially for Ad, usually so jocular. Healey stared in surprise and, puzzling Healey further, Wallon stared back, as if asking Healey to forget what he'd seen. Then Wallon replied lightly, "Is that all you ever answer, Linda?"

"No."

"How are things at the hospital?" Healey put in to

break the silence.

"Okay, I guess," Wallon said. "I gave a big kiss for you to . . . the little girl."

"Cathy," said Healey.

At dinner in the dark-paneled dining room with an old chandelier, Wallon, between bites of beef and gulps of wine, began an elaborate discourse concerning science and art. Refuting an English writer whose name he couldn't remember, nor the title of his book ("C.P. Snow, *The Two Cultures*," Ruth supplied), Wallon declared that the two were not fundamentally different.

"Flo," Ruth broke in when dessert and coffee had been served, "why don't you go ahead? We'll clear up."

Already in hat and coat, Flo emerged. "Good night, then."

"Great dinner, Flo! The Yorkshire pudding was wonderful," Wallon exclaimed. "Where was I?"

"Something about art and science," said Ruth patiently.

"I see science and art as both essentially creative, scientific insights being no less—"

Jennie, in her bathrobe, ran in. "I came to say good night!"

"Hey, here's my real girlfriend," Wallon bellowed. He scooped up Jennie and kissed her. "Where's Paul?"

"At the neighbor's," Ruth said. "This is Jen, Linda."

Jennie curtsied and continued around the table.

"Time for a card trick after we eat?" Wallon asked.

"No, it's almost bedtime. Don't forget to brush your teeth," her mother told her as she scampered off. "You were saying, Ad?"

"Where was I? All these interruptions . . ."

"Science and art . . ."

"Are fundamentally alike. Scientific insights are like writing poetry, composing music, painting a picture. Science is really an art form," said Wallon. He opened his mouth again, closed it and said to Healey. "Do you agree, Jim?"

Healey said, "Not exactly."

"Why?" demanded Wallon.

"A couple of reasons. Science involves math, while art doesn't."

"A minor matter," Wallon assured him.

"And a lot of science is plain old dull technical benchwork that has little to do with insights, artistic or otherwise," Healey went on.

"That's you all over, Jim," mocked Wallon. "Logical, tidy, precise, linear. You stick too much to clear-cut causality. You don't like to make big leaps. I told you about that English fellow, C.T...." Wallon floundered.

"C.P.," Ruth said.

"Stow."

"Snow."

"He was right about two cultures, only he had the wrong two. Did I tell you I'm going to give a lecture at the Aspen Institute this summer? No? Well, I am, expenses paid. That'll be my thesis. The real two cultures are *science*, which includes art, and *politics*, which subsumes business, law, communications, legislation..."

Wallon's point might have been interesting if he hadn't mixed up so many words and gone on at such great length, with Ruth encouraging him. Wallon seemed at the point of ending his diatribe, when he stopped speaking in midsentence and stared at them with hollow eyes.

"Yes?" Ruth asked.

"...is...is...is..."

"Are you all right?"

"I feel...sort of confused. I've been a little under the weather all day. It must be the medication," Wallon said limply.

Ruth put a palm to his forehead. "You don't have a fever."

"I'll be okay." Wallon smiled bravely under her hand.

"Where was I? Funny, I don't remember. I guess I haven't yet thought through my ideas."

"Funny, all right," said Healey later in the bedroom. "Funny peculiar, not funny ha-ha. I hardly understood a word he was saying. Did you?"

"Sort of," Ruth said.

"You certainly *acted* like you did. Well, it must be me. But he kept forgetting things."

"Too much wine."

"He didn't really *seem* drunk. Also, before dinner, he had a temper tantrum, though he got control of himself. But I suppose you're right—booze. Unless he's coming down with a bug. If he is, I hope none of us catches it."

"The only bug I worry about you catching is that Summer girl. What a creep. She said practically nothing except 'no.'"

"Maybe she was a little intimidated by you. You have that effect on people before they get to know you."

"Nuts. She needs to get laid, if you ask me. And you're a candidate. Did you see how she blushed when you looked at her? The woman adores you."

"You exaggerate. Shall we go to bed?"

"Do I get my good-night backgammon? It's only ten-thirty."

"One game is all I'm good for."

Almost always she beat him. They kept a running score, and every Christmas he bought her an extra present. This time, having covered the key points, he thought he might win, but toward the end Ruth got lucky with the dice, played smart, took well-calculated chances and wiped him out.

"You did it again. Ready for bed now?"

"Yes, dear. I'm ready." Ruth giggled girlishly. "Maybe it's perverted, but winning makes me aroused."

Speedily, she aroused him, her familiar hands touching familiar places, and his hers. They had techniques that always worked—a kiss at the base of a shoulder blade, a slight scrape with fingernails, gentle tugs at coarse lower hair. The two of them, male and female, stiff, wet ...Linda Summer, unannounced, flowed into his mind and hovered there, summoning. No! No! Just in time, Healey triumphed over fantasy and finished precisely when Ruth did.

DAY SIX

Healey woke with a start, almost uncertain of where he was until he patted Ruth's rear for reassurance. The luminous numbers on the digital clock radio said 3:12. Normally a sound sleeper, he wondered what had roused him so early and then remembered pieces of a dream, chunks as though from a fallen mosaic: driving... the station wagon to... a massive hospital high on a hill... something very important to do... man stepped on the road... Healey swerved, but the man darted to the other side... again and again Healey swerved, but the man continued to jump up before him screaming "Fucking cars!" until the station wagon struck and Healey saw the face disintegrate—the vacant triangular face of the man on the expressway.

The dream had more pieces than that, and while trying

to remember them, Healey heard retreating footsteps and a few soft words. He went quickly to the hall and knocked sharply on Paul's door, underneath which light shone.

"What is it?" Paul said.

Paul's tone annoyed him. Breaking a house rule, he entered without being asked. His son was dressed. "Paul! It's after three and Buddy just left!"

"Today's Saturday."

"I don't care what day it is! I won't have you playing games all night."

"All night," Paul mocked.

Healey pulled on the belt of his robe. "Most of the night, then! You're still sixteen and don't forget it. Let's talk in the morning."

In bed again, as if to hypnotize himself to sleep, he watched the numbers turn on the clockface, seconds becoming minutes that dropped into place, one by one, with a tiny whir and a click, audible in the silence. *Whir, click, whir, click, whir.*

It commenced with a little *pop!*, which was followed by a gentle hum, as if from light electrical machinery. He believed at first that the clock radio was acting up, until he realized that the buzzing came from deep inside his head. What was the trouble? He blamed sleeplessness, or his anger with Paul, for causing the mind sound, which eventually stopped, to Healey's intense relief. But into the void came distinctly

> *Round and round it goes.*

What? Whose childish voice was that? His! He had recited the lines when he was a little boy.

> *Round and round it goes.*
> *Where it stops nobody knows.*

This time the voice was bolder, as though it had proved it could speak. Healey tried to find a means to quell it, but sounds exploded—screams, yells, high-pitched laughter. Then:

> *Beans, beans, the musical fruit—*
> *The more you eat, the more you toot.*
> *The more you toot, the better you feel,*
> *So let's have beans at every meal!*

Good Lord! How old was the memory store that doggerel came from? He couldn't have been more than eight or nine when he'd learned those lines and hadn't thought of them since. *Go away!* he pleaded with the voices.

> *The more you toot, the better you feel.*
> *Where it stops nobody knows.*

Please! he shrieked to himself, opening an eye: 3:47. *Beans, beans*: 3:48. Healey staggered from bed and swallowed one of the tranquilizers Ruth sometimes used for insomnia. The last time he looked, the clock announced 4:12. *Round and round*, a voice still said, as though from afar.

The clock announced 11:00 when Healey woke, sluggish and heavy limbed. He hadn't slept enough. What, he wondered, had his body been telling him last night? That he'd been pushing it too hard? He attributed the hallucinatory voices, now mercifully quiet, to minor fatigue; after all, he'd been working long hours for almost two weeks, ever since the experiment started, as it would again on Monday. Yes, he ought to rest this weekend.

He reviewed the plans. Take Jennie to a museum for a special exhibition of dolls, as he'd promised. Talk to Paul about his future. Prepare next week's lecture for his class at the university. There were papers to read. Attend a concert with Ruth that evening. See his mother...the schedule, undemanding as it was, seemed too heavy.

The bathroom mirror told him what he'd already suspected—lines troubled his eyes, and his sharp face was pale beneath its dusting of freckles. Could he be sick? He took his temperature. Thermometer in mouth, he washed his hands and combed his sandy hair, which had begun to recede, making his forehead look more domed and professional than he liked, though Healey wasn't vain.

No fever: in fact, the mercury stood at slightly below normal. The malaise that afflicted him this morning could account for that, though why the malaise in the first place? Tiredness and/or a bug that he could have caught from Wallon on Wednesday perhaps. If so, it couldn't be very serious. Yesterday Wallon had said he was okay.

In his closet Healey had the sudden sense that the voices hadn't left him at all but surrounded him like his clothes. The voices were silent because Healey refused to let them speak; he was suppressing them with conscious effort. No wonder he was tired! Deliberately, he opened a window in his brain to investigate and heard, at once:

> *Beans, beans, good for your heart—*
> *The more you eat, the more you fart.*
> *The more you fart, the better you feel,*
> *So let's have beans at every meal!*

Stop! Good Lord, he thought, is this you? *What* is happening? He backed out of the closet in haste.

In a T-shirt, old trousers and slippers Healey padded to the kitchen to find Ruth at the table with coffee and the crossword puzzle. "Good morning."

Ruth looked up, startled. "I didn't hear you come in. Are you all right?"

"Guess so. Why?"

"You were thrashing and talking in your sleep."

"Oh? What did I say?"

"'No, no!' was all I could understand. It must have been a bad dream."

"Sort of. I ran over a man on the road. Do I talk in my

sleep often?" He poured himself coffee from the pot.

"I can't think of a last time. How I envy the way you sleep."

"I'm sorry I woke you."

"I wouldn't have minded except I lay with my eyes open until after three."

Healey was perplexed. He had woken from the dream after three. Might he have been wrong about the time? He didn't believe so; he'd said "after three" to Paul. Could it have been later than that? Everything had become confused. "Are you sure it was after three?"

"I think it was. I almost woke you. I wanted to talk, but it didn't seem fair. I felt strange. I had a lot of crazy ideas. I was depressed." Her dark eyes clouded.

"You could have woken me," he said carefully, almost sure he had been awake and she hadn't. "What a silly thing you are."

Ruth smiled wetly. "You're right. I am a silly thing. I'm about to get my period, is the truth of it."

"You're sure that's why you're depressed?"

"Sure I'm sure. It always effects me that way, though I forget every time. I bet I go on forgetting, month after month, until I have my change of life."

"That's a long way off," Healey remonstrated.

"Not so long," she muttered, wiping her eyes with a napkin as she pretended to study the puzzle.

"How can I cheer you up?" he said, though needing cheer himself. "Would you like to come to the museum with Jennie and me?"

"I don't think so. I doubt Jennie will go either."

"She's been looking forward to it all week!"

"She has a headache, she says."

"What is this place, an infirmary? Is Paul up?"

"Haven't seen hide nor hair."

"I'll talk to Jennie after I eat something," he said. Opening a cabinet for a box of cereal, he spotted, printed on a Campbell's Soup label, "M'm! M'm! GOOD IDEA." Instantly, not a single voice but a chorus began to chant,

M'm! M'm! GOOD IDEA. M'm M'm! GOOD IDEA. M'm! M'm! GOOD IDEA, louder and louder, until Healey wanted to put his hands over his ears. *M'm! M'm! GOOD IDEA.*

The children had selected the colors for their rooms. Jennie's was a pinkish pastel, with white trim and flimsy white curtains on the two windows. Neat little miniatures, outdoor scenes painted by Ruth, lined the walls. Against the upholstered headboard of Jennie's neatly made bed leaned a collection of dolls and stuffed animals. Wearing pajamas, Jennie sat at a small white desk. "I thought you were sick."

"Not really."

As he kissed her braids he saw a math book and the electronic calculator he'd given her for her tenth birthday. "Hey! Are you allowed to use that for homework?"

"Teacher says so. I can do the numbers without it. It's faster with the calculator, that's all."

"Do you think Einstein could have doped out the mathematics of the universe if he'd practiced with a calculator when he was a kid?"

"Maybe he'd have done it sooner."

"Quick on the uptake, aren't you? Something of Einstein's I've always liked. Want to hear? He said, 'My gift for fantasy meant more to me than my talent to absorb actual knowledge.' No, it must have been 'positive knowledge.'" *M'm! M'm! GOOD IDEA.*

"What does that mean?" she asked.

"Just that he daydreamed, used his imagination, which to him was more important than facts."

"Do you feel the same way?"

"I do, now that you ask. I thought you had a headache."

"It went away. Only, my eyes hurt a little." Jennie coughed.

"Maybe you ought to stay in today, just in case." Jennie, who took her health seriously, nodded gravely.

Healey studied her. "Have you been reading a lot lately?"

"Quite a bit, Daddy."

"Let's get those eyes of yours checked, okay?"

"Okay."

He stood in the hallway, pondering the voices. They came and went, without warning or, apparently, reason. What was behind them? Healey didn't have the slightest idea. The brain did peculiar things. He had to hope the voices would simply vanish.

Hearing Paul on the telephone, Healey knocked on his door as he had on Jennie's. His son called, "Who is it?"

"Me."

"Oh, all right, come in, Pop. Call you later, Buddy. I checked with Fenwick, and he thinks Napoleon could have done it if he'd thrown in his cavalry earlier. Right. Okay."

Listening to his son, Healey had to confess a certain admiration. Paul was sharp, decisive, analytic, poised, confident—a leader. If only he used his abilities for more serious purposes. Healey surveyed the room.

The walls, painted by Paul in martial olive green, were covered with maps marked with crayon and pins. A small cannon lurked in the corner. A tall wood chest with glass doors housed all manner of military memorabilia—medals on felt, old sword, Prussian officer's cap, bayonet, naval pennants.... Paul did little else these days but refight wars of the past on large boards with pieces and cards, which strewed the floor. Paul put down the phone and said, "Well?"

Healey nodded at the debris. "What's this—the officer's *mess?*"

"Ha, ha." Paul stood up. He was taller than Healey, with spidery arms, big hands, long stringy dark hair and a masculine face that would captivate women when the acne cleared—*if* Paul ever stopped war gaming long enough to notice girls. "You want to talk to me."

"Obviously. Paul, I'm worried about you. All you do is play games."

"They're not just games. They're *history*."

"Just the same, I wish you'd do other things, like study."

"Something wrong with my grades?" Paul asked peevishly.

"I haven't seen a report. I don't look. You're too old. Your grades are your business now."

"If you haven't seen a report, how do you know something's wrong with my grades?"

"I didn't say anything was wrong with your grades," Healey replied in exasperation. "I only meant that you couldn't have much time for schoolwork with all this." He nodded toward the board on which Waterloo had been resurrected. "Remember the lab I set up for you at the country house?"

"Why wouldn't I remember it?"

"You don't go near it."

"Too busy," Paul snapped.

"But busy doing what? Maybe war games are fun, but what will you get out of them in the long run? You wanted to be a biologist once."

"Not anymore."

"Look, you know as well as I do that you get by at school because you're smart, not because you're studying. You've got intellectual capital, but sooner or later you'll use it up."

"A sort of mental savings account?" Paul asked mockingly. "What about interest? Don't I collect that?"

"Listen to me, Paul! Intelligence is fine, but there's such a thing as maturity too. I wish *that* was measured by IQ tests. A lot of people's scores would go down, yours included, I'm afraid." *Round and round.*

"I'm as grown-up as anybody else," Paul yelled.

"Wasting so much time isn't very grown-up."

"Wasting! Do you understand who plays war games? Scientists, lawyers, professors..."

"But they're *already* scientists, lawyers and professors! That's what they went to college for. What about you? Have you given up on it?"

Paul looked away. "I'm...not sure."

"Think about it, will you? And will you promise to get to bed earlier and study some?" *M'm! M'm! GOOD IDEA.*

"Okay, okay," said Paul bleakly, "though I really wonder about becoming a professional person. I've told you that."

After lunch, Healey settled down in the small room that Ruth called a den to prepare for his Wednesday lecture. He began perusing scientific articles he had brought from the hospital. "...whereas the reconstruction in vitro of replication by DNA polymerase action alone had remained inadequate. The basis for this discrepancy in progress is rooted in a biochemical fortuity. By means of enzyme fractionation procedures, RNA polymerase was isolated from cell extracts as a large multisubunit transcriptase. Isolated DNA polymerase, on the other hand, is only one component of a multienzyme DNA replicase. The purpose of..."

It was no use. Healey understood the point of the article, but he couldn't concentrate because of the din in his head. Deciding to put the lecture notes aside for the moment, he dug in his desk and emerged with a thick loose-leaf binder in a heavy canvas cover. Many times, Healey had attempted to keep a diary but invariably failed because there was either too little or too much to write about. He had settled instead on what he called, wryly, "Healey's Book." In it he recorded his random ideas as they had occurred to him, on any subject, with no set order, sequence or effort at literary style. He tried, not always successfully, to make entries in the notebook once a week, as a mental exercise. They were always brief and unpretentious.

On Professionals

Paul isn't the only one who doubts the value of professionals. A lot of people do. To them, professionalism is a trick—a means of pretending that the professional has more knowledge than he really has, a way of covering up mistakes, a device for keeping others out of one's field. There is truth to these accusations.

Just the same, once we admit that human knowledge is limited, precarious and subject to error, the value of the professional becomes clear: he possesses *skills*. I worry that skills aren't sufficiently respected, despite the time it takes to acquire them. Because if knowledge is limited, *skills are what we are best at*.

I see things as constantly wanting to run down—all things. Skills represent order in the world whose fundamental urge (demiurge?) is disorder. Those who make light of skills are asking for chaos.

But at the same time the professional should not exaggerate, make false claims about, the extent of his expertise. Modesty behooves...

Which led him to

On Arrogance

When I see intellectual arrogance, in myself or others, I think of Walt Whitman's brain, which I believe was abnormally large and was kept in formaldehyde for study. But a lab worker dropped it, swept it up and threw the brain away.

Must tell Herrmann that story.

On Suicide

Read in the paper—*must* try to keep up with the *Times*, but Lord what a chore!—that a famous writer died after a brief illness whose nature wasn't specified. Suicide, I bet. But why conceal the fact? In a word, shame.

While feeling ashamed about suicide may be silly, in another sense I think it reflects a profound and correct human attitude. Except in cases of extreme incapacitation or terminal (how I hate that word!) illness, I believe suicide to be a biologically stupid act. I am aware, of course, that depressed people aren't fully in possession of themselves, but if we consider intelligence precisely as the possession of self, then suicide becomes stupidity in those terms. Broadly considered, life *is* intelligence.

Beans, *beans*. How strange to have voices flap about in his head like bats in a cave! Could they, in some way, be related to *his* intelligence? Was his mind flying apart? Healey began to become alarmed. He wrote hastily

On Functioning Intelligence

Intelligence—I don't mean IQ; people confuse the two terms, but IQ is only a numerical index of intelligence, not intelligence itself—is to me the ability to manipulate abstractions, to examine and choose between large numbers of alternative possibilities—combinatorial play, I think Einstein called it. But with intelligence, flashes of insight must be associated. Nor can intelligence be separated from the rest of the personality, for it is also the sum total of all our experience up to the present moment. Clearly, intelligence has many dimensions...

He gave up. His ideas wouldn't stick together; his cerebral glue wouldn't hold. For distraction, he decided to balance the checkbook, which was usually easy to him. This time he had to borrow Jennie's calculator.

The concert that evening was spoiled for Healey by the voices that rang in his head, drowning the music.

On the way home they bought the Sunday paper. In the bedroom Ruth started the crossword puzzle, soon asking, "What does 'salubrious' mean?"

"It seems like I ought to know, but I don't."

"Same here."

After minutes of intense concentration he said, "'Salubrious' means 'healthful.'" Shouldn't such a word have been at the tip of a doctor's tongue?

In bed he silently recited the names of the state capitals in alphabetical order and was delighted to remember all fifty.

DAY SEVEN

On Sunday, not quite up to facing his mother alone, he asked Ruth to come with him, but she declined. "I have too much to do."

"Like what? We don't have to stay long."

"What difference how long we stay? She doesn't remember we've been there."

"She remembers. Mother is mostly lucid. Mother has bad days, that's all," Healey said defensively.

"When was the last good day! Like I've said, Henrietta ought to be in a nursing home, a cheap one at that. Don't tell me she'd hate it—that's pure projection on your part. You're worried about what might happen to *you* when you get old."

"Really!" he objected.

"Don't 'really' me," she said crankily. "I'm not the one

who keeps us broke supporting *my* mother in the style she thinks she deserves. It's disgusting how well she lives when she's done nothing her whole life."

"Your mother's dead! As to mine, you exaggerate and you know it. I'm not supporting her. I help her a little, that's all."

"She could invade that goddam capital of hers."

"She doesn't want to. Old people are strange about security."

"She's strange, all right. She's senile."

"Did you get your period?"

"No. Why?" Ruth asked in surprise.

"I wish you would," he snapped. "Maybe your mood would improve."

So he went by himself, on foot, pondering Ruth's accusation. Though she had spoken in anger—he did not know why—there was a kernel of truth. Old age didn't frighten him, but senility did. Be reasonable, he told himself. Henrietta undoubtedly had some arteriosclerosis, and the tendency to senility could be inherited— granted. But as far back as he could remember, Henrietta had been vague and forgetful, used wrong words, made factual errors, confused tenses, given instructions that she quickly countermanded. These probably had been precursory symptoms, and he, far older now than she had been when she began to display them, showed no such signs of eventual impairment. Besides, his mother, bright as she was, had always pampered herself, giving her brain an easy life, while his had had plenty of use. Healey sometimes compared the human mind to a watch. His had a fair share of jewels (though nothing like his idol Einstein's), and he kept it clean, well oiled, in good shape. Healey did not believe he would be sandbagged by senility.

So why the anxiety? He supposed it was bound up deeply with the response he had developed as a child to his mother's ineptitude and imprecision. Even then he had liked things to be exact, thorough, complete. For Healey, senility stood at the antipode of that which he so highly valued—capability, and if senility terrified him it must have been because his self-system was a little bit *too* organized, as a defense. *M'm! M'm! GOOD IDEA*, a voice seemed to congratulate. He tried to ignore it.

Also, he decided, everything else in his background and bent conspired to make him a creature of the cranium, who would be in double jeopardy if his powers faded. The expensive private schools he'd attended justified themselves as providing a better shot at a first-rate university; his training initiated him into a cabal whose specialized corner of knowledge could not be entered by those without it; the professional cadre, of which he was a part, regarded mental acuity as the *sine qua non*. Healey had respect for assembly-line workers, miners, firemen, veterinarians and farmers, but he had never had a desire to be one. His gift was conceptualization. His universe had been built on his brains.

On occupation, Healey had been clear. He would be a doctor like his father, James Healey, Sr., who had a rich practice as a heart specialist on New York's East Side. Midway through Harvard medical school, though, James Jr. began to wonder. At the back of his mind he had the notion that the summit of human accomplishment was helping others, and while medicine was such a road, there might be another, more exciting one in scientific research. Healey supposed he shared a common human desire for heroism, which he might best fulfill through the discovery of what wasn't known and therefore didn't yet exist.

By this time Healey was dating Ruth, a slim, serious senior at Radcliffe with a compact figure and limpid dark eyes. Ruth admired his dedication while confessing not to share it. Ruth wanted nothing less conventional than children, a house and a career that gave her time to enjoy them; she had chosen law, specializing in corporate taxes, because, she reasoned shrewdly, after a few grueling years of study, easier ones would follow. Jim warned her that a research physician couldn't expect to earn anywhere near what a specialist like his father did. That was all right with Ruth, though she had rather hoped for a house with a tennis court.

He'd chosen her, he imagined, partly because she was as organized and foible-free as he. (But why had she chosen him? he sometimes wondered.) After his M.D. and internship they were married. Ruth was in law school, and he pursued his Ph.D. It had gone almost exactly as he'd hoped. He was fortunate in every way—content, well respected, secure, free to research as he liked. Things couldn't have been in better control, before yesterday at least, when the voices had started to transmit.

In his usual neat but old sports jacket, a blue shirt with a button-down collar and no tie, gray flannels and brown suede shoes a little worn at the heels, Healey neared his mother's residence. Henrietta had always patronized her only child for his simple style. In fact, his parents had been surprisingly improvident, so that after James Sr., died some years before, Henrietta came to Healey for help from time to time.

Henrietta lived in a fairly expensive apartment-hotel on Madison Avenue. The Park Hudson, with its plush lobby and restaurant, catered mostly to permanent guests—well-to-do people, as Henrietta purported to be. Rather than dispel it, she deliberately fostered the aura of wealth. Using her props like an actress—her cane, her anachronistic lorgnette, her blue-gray hair, her jewels, her antiques. The jewels were mostly real, the antiques weren't. After her husband's death, Henrietta had been forced to sell the good pieces. Only junk remained, which didn't prevent Henrietta from displaying it with pride to gullible neighbors, older people like herself.

When Healey arrived, Henrietta was exhibiting her possessions to an elderly gentleman to whom he had been introduced several times before. "This is my son, Judge Crum. Ah, you two have met? The old forgettery's at it again. Anyway," she went on hastily, as though embarrassed, holding out a glass egg that lay in her hand, "I acquired this *objet* in Venice, where, as you know, some of the best glass is made. By hand, of course. The glass is quite old, which you can tell from the rough places on the surface. There is some sort of design inside—I can't make out just what it represents. I believe it was used by a doge—a Venetian prince—as a paperweight. Do come back, Judge!"

"Mother, Mother," Healey sighed as he stooped to kiss her. "*What* are you telling the man? You bought that glass egg in Woolworth's! It got the rough places when I played catch with it. I know what the so-called design inside is too. It's the Empire State Building."

"Well, it's hard to see, and Judge Crum's eyes aren't what they might be," Henrietta replied firmly. "He's hooked, and that's what's important."

"Why, for Lord's sake?"

"Why? Use that famous head of yours. Judge Crum—he sat on the circuit court or something—is impressed with my, ah, possessions. He's a total stick, of course, though I don't tell him *that*. But he's company. And when I die you'll be grateful."

"Grateful?" he asked in surprise.

"You'll do land-office business at the auction, mark my words."

"Auction? What are you talking about, Mother?"

"When I die, and how I crave the day when I shuffle off this mortal..."

"Coil?" he offered.

"You'll shuffle off my things. It's in my will. You have the auction here. The whole building thinks I'm stuffed with valuable antiques. They'll come running. You'll make money, son."

"You expect me to hold an auction?" he asked in surprise.

"I do. And if you sell anything cheap my ghost will rap with the cane." She had her cane in her other hand and banged it on the floor, smiling prettily.

"Nobody's stupid enough to *buy* this stuff, Mother," he said.

"They are, though. Greed makes people dumb. You'll

see. Now come along. I ordered tea from downstairs, and it'll get cold."

Walking briskly with the cane, Henrietta went into the living room, and Healey followed. The place had the dusty, cryptlike smell he associated with old age, probably because elderly people didn't open windows. Not that Henrietta was so terribly old, nor did she look it. At seventy-one, she had clear gray eyes like his and the same keen, angular face. Her thin body appeared youthful. She looked attractive in her jewels and dress of black silk.

They seated themselves at a small table, and as Henrietta regally poured tea into cups initialed for the Park Hudson she asked, "Milk or lemon?"

"Lemon, Mother. You know that."

"How are the children? And ... your wife?"

"Ruth isn't feeling well," he lied. "The children are okay. They'll come to see you soon."

"I hope so! It's been months."

"Now, now. They all visited a few weeks ago."

"Did they?" Henrietta changed the subject. "James, you look tired. Does ... take good care of you?"

"Mother, we've been married eighteen years. You ought to know Ruth's name by now."

"I do! I remember the day you first brought her home." She put a lump of sugar in her tea and sipped it. "I thought Ruth looked a good bit like me. Is he, ah, marrying his mother? I asked your father. I remember exactly what he said. Word for word. 'Good thing if he does.' Such a devoted man. Except ..."

"Yes?"

"Except he played around," she said.

"Mother, why upset yourself? You don't know that for sure." She'd said this before, without offering proof.

Now, though, Henrietta laughed harshly and cried, "Oh, but I do! Come, I'll show you." She went to a wall covered with photographs and pointed to a group photo taken at their old summer house. In it was Jim as a small boy—his expression halfway between quizzical and serious—and a young woman named Jody, a college girl hired to take care of him, he recalled. "I caught them, her and your father..."

"Don't get excited. Calm yourself."

"And her!" Henrietta pointed to a different photo. "She was a neighbor, called Roberta. I remember... Oh, what does it matter. And her! There were quite a few of them."

"Mother, you'll give yourself a heart attack." He turned to guide her back to her chair, but Henrietta shook free, staring silently at her gallery. How strange that Henrietta had waited all these years to detail his father's transgressions, as if only just remembering. Did senility release the past? *Beans, beans, round and round*—was something like that happening to him? Why? What was wrong with him? Was he, in fact, showing signs of senility? He felt almost dizzy. Could he have hurt himself? When? Last Sunday he had hit his head on the luggage rack. Good Lord! He touched his cranium gently. No pain. No swelling. He hadn't thought of the incident the whole week. It couldn't be, could it? Or could it? *M'm! M'm! GOOD IDEA.*

Henrietta's voice lurched him out of reverie. "Jim," she was saying, "you oughtn't to do that."

"Do what?"

"You know very well!"

"Mother...," he said.

"Bastard! I bring this little girl into our house and what happens?" Her wrinkles glared at him.

"I didn't..."

"You thought I didn't know! You put sleeping pills in my coffee. How bitter that coffee was! I drank it. I became woozy, you put me to bed. You kissed me. Turned out the light. You left. After a while I got up. I retched in the toilet. I needed you but couldn't find you. I walked to the other end of the hall and heard moans and cries. I saw you, Jim, in Jody's room! I peeked through the keyhole. I couldn't sleep, so I went to Jim Jr.'s room. That was when I found him in a fever, and I screamed! You came, finally, in your clothes. You pretended you'd been outside. It was raining, remember? Your shoes were absolutely clean! I've never told you before. I waited a whole week to fire that young bitch so you wouldn't be suspicious. Do you remember now?"

"Henrietta," he asked abruptly, "who's President?"

"Why, Roosevelt, of course. The idiot."

"Mother, let's have our tea."

WEEK TWO

DAY EIGHT

On Monday, Healey woke restored, voices silent. He decided to forget about his head until he had further cause to think about it.

Downstairs, he attempted and failed to waive the usual augury from Phillip. He biked to the hospital. Nearing it, he saw intersection after intersection jammed with cars. Good sense dictated, as did the law, that drivers refrain from entering crossings until a place existed on the street across, but good sense didn't always prevail. Compelled by an instinct that seemed to possess them when competition for space occurred, the motorists crowded into crossings, blocking traffic in every direction and honking horns as though others were to blame.

Healey was of two minds about human nature. Sometimes he was unpleasantly convinced that people were nothing more or less than hosts for genes whose only goal was to reproduce and survive. Genes were totally, ruthlessly selfish and made people that way too. But selfishness could be self-defeating and therefore stupid. Since nature obviously didn't favor stupidity in the battle for survival, Healey mused, there had to be genes that made for cooperation... Healey watched appreciatively as an ambulance approaching the hospital's emergency entrance stopped quickly to let a pedestrian pass.

Healey's schedule that morning called for several inescapable hours in the outpatient clinic, but first, stethoscope dangling from the pocket of his white coat, he visited the fifth floor. As he opened Cathy's chart, Olga, the head nurse, materialized. They conducted a rapid exchange.

"General, how's my—"

"Frankly, doctor, Cathy seems a little listless. Blah." He raised his head. "Why?"

"Search me. It happens sometimes. After a while they miss family life. Emotional deprivation. You know."

"She doesn't have much of a family life to miss."

"She thinks she has."

He pondered that. When he got right down to it, Olga was the real expert on children in the wards, and he accepted her judgment. "Maybe it'll be different at home this time. She'll be leaving us soon."

"I'll be sorry to see her go. You get attached to the little things, much as you try not to," the general said, the hard lines of her face softening. "Any new instructions on her diet? Cathy seems completely stabilized."

"You're a regular Jewish mother when it comes to food, nurse." he bantered. "I'll need a little blood this morning. After that she can have normal food in small amounts as a supplement. Let's see how she handles it. If there's any change, I want to know about it right away."

He found Cathy dressed but lying on her bed, eyes on the ceiling. She stirred at the sight of him. "Hi, doctor! Kiss!" she said faintly.

"What's the matter, dear? Are you sick?" he asked, sitting beside her and providing the required osculation.

"Oh noooo."

"Sleep good?"

"Oh yes. I dreamed about Sir...Lansselot. He was bringing i-scream to that queen of King Arthur's."

"Guinevere. Did she like it?"

"Oh yes. So would I."

"I don't know about ice cream, Cathy, but you can have some real food from now on. But not too much of it. Remember that when you get home."

Cathy jumped up and bounced on her bed. "Goody! Can I leave soon?"

"Yes, dear. Soon. Okay?"

"Okay!"

Healey spent the next few hours seeing children in the clinic. Most were doing well under various regimens designed to combat metabolic disorders, such as the boy who had displayed steadily increasing levels of cholesterol. His father had died of a heart attack while under thirty years of age, and so in all probability would he, were it not for special plastic beads, prescribed by Healey, which grabbed cholesterol and carried it out of the body in the excreta. The successes made him proud, the failures bitter—and there were failures, kids who showed symptoms of rare, fatal diseases, maybe inherited, maybe viral, because the exact cause, much less cure, was unknown. So much was unknown; anybody who chose to look could see that greater knowledge revealed only greater uncertainty. It seemed to him sometimes that he stood on a mountainside in a new land. The higher he climbed, the bigger the land appeared.

Late morning, Healey returned to his office to find his secretary watering the plants. Coral Blanchard loved greenery; on her own time, as a volunteer, she filled the visiting rooms with verdure. Potted plants and flowers frequently came as gifts to the hospital or for children about to be discharged. Through a staff network she maintained, Coral was apprised of the harvest; she kept the excess in a cold room on the eighth floor—cold rooms were ordinarily used for storing drugs, but Coral had expropriated this one—distributing her bounty when the supply was meager. Healey had told her that she should have been a florist, meaning, though he didn't say so, instead of a secretary. Coral was sweet but inefficient.

Taking off his hospital coat, he said, "How are you today, Coral?" and waited. Do I always ask that? he thought. Yes. It's what doctors say. And the reply is mostly the same, from children and adults alike. They say "fine." With Coral it'll be "fine but."

"Fine," said Coral, "but..."

A long-faced woman in her fifties, Coral Blanchard was something of a hypochondriac.

"But what?"

"Oh, nothing, really. I have a lump."

"A lump? Where?"

"Behind my right ear."

"Did you hurt yourself?" Coral was what lay people called accident-prone. She always barged into things.

"Not that I know of."

"Okay, let's have a look," he grumbled.

Coral set down her watering can and came to him eagerly. He pushed back her thick white hair and inspected. "It's only a pimple. Coral, at your age! You should be ashamed of yourself."

"For having a pimple?"

"For worrying."

Healey had just sat down at his desk when he heard, inside his head, a hollow *pop!* A voice muttered, *Fine but, fine but, but, but, but...*

> *She has pimples on her but I love her.*
> *She has pimples on her butt/I love her.*

Faster and faster repeated the voice, becoming a chorus that sang tonelessly. *She has pimples on her but I love her.*

76

Shehaspimplesonherbutt/I love her. Shehaspimpleson-herbutIloveher. ShehaspimplesonherbuttIlove her. She has... He shrieked silently, *Stop! Stop!*

Healey was much shaken by the new outburst—or inburst, as he thought of it. That "but-butt" business had been a joke when he was in the third or fourth grade. Why had it returned? *What* was wrong with his noggin? Had he broken some vital vessel when he fell against the luggage rack? Perhaps blood was dripping into his brainpan. Fatalities resulted from such invisible injuries. That stupid son-of-a-bitch with the triangular face had caused all this.... *Cease*, he commanded. He sounded like Coral.

Badly needing distraction, Healey glanced at *The New York Times* on the corner of his desk but instead plucked from his out box the hospital newsletter titled *People in White*, published on weekdays by Tish Wyler's publicity people. The four-page bulletin reported on events at Kellogg–Bryant—marriages, divorces, transfers, leavings, retirements, awards, donations, social functions, and so on—and had the usual editorial tidbits, including a self-quiz which always had a "Tillie Green" section for the young patients. "Tillie Green hates red, but she loves ———." The right answer had to contain repeated letters, as in Tillie Green. "Yellow," Healey supplied. "Tillie Green hates horses, but she loves ————." "What? Why can't I... Mmmmm. Fillies."

Next came a harder question.

Helen's daughter is my daughter's mother. What is my relationship to Helen?
(a) Her grandmother
(b) Her mother
(c) Her daughter
(d) Her granddaughter
(e) I am Helen

That's easy, Healey thought. Why, it's... His mind began to rock. It's... Now, let's see, Helen's daughter is...He *knew* the answer and yet failed to grasp it. *Helen's daughter is my daughter's mother*. Meaning...He took a yellow pad and wrote on it, needlessly, since the words were all in the question: "Helen's daughter is my daughter's mother." Obviously, that made Helen...who, for Christ's sake? he asked himself urgently. *Helen's daughter is my daughter's mother*. Lord! He couldn't spend all day on this. If only the voices in the back of his mind would shut up and let him think. He wrote: "If Helen's daughter is my daughter's mother, then..."

Helen...

Her daughter...

I am...

I am Helen! Sure! He turned hungrily to the answer on the last page.

(c) Her daughter

I see it, he thought. The daughter of Helen has got to be me because I am my daughter's mother. How simple, and yet he'd failed, outfoxed by a ridiculous riddle. What's the matter with you, Healey?

He was pondering a visit to Mel Orenstein, the psychiatrist, for an examination of his head, when he realized that Coral Blanchard stood over him. "Dr. Healey?"

"Yes?"

"I've been calling you. Didn't you hear?"

"I was thinking about something."

"I admire your powers of concentration." Coral hesitated looking contrite. "I forgot to tell you. Dr. Herrmann called."

Healey pulled himself together and asked, "When?"

"A couple of hours ago."

"Thanks," Healey said heavily. Coral put concern about a pimple ahead of the director. *She has pimples on her*...Stop!

78

His secretary answered the phone, and Herrmann came on the line at once. "Jim? Herman." How absurd, Healey thought. He knows it's me and I know it's him, yet he recites our names. "Jim? Are you there?"

"Yes, Herman."

"You sound distracted. Are you all right?"

"I'm fine." Fine but. *She has . . .*

"Seen the paper today?"

"I haven't had time," he lied.

"The antirecombinant DNA bunch is still around, apparently. I told you about them, didn't I? They're called the Coalition for a New Public Health, whatever that means. I stylize myself as believing in the 'new,' but public health is hardly new. Anyway, they think the work is dangerous. They plan to protest DNA experiments in this area. They know about yours."

"Why wouldn't they?" The plans for the experiment had been routinely published by NIH in the Federal Register and even in the hospital newsletter. "Who's in the group?"

"The usual Nervous Nellie scientists and impressionable kids. I doubt if there could be many of them, but even so we don't want a demonstration. Our benefactors wouldn't like that. Tish Wyler's quite concerned. What state is your experiment in?"

"My bunch is in the lab now making cultures."

"When do you plan to finish?"

"I want to move a little slower this time to avoid another mistake. We're scheduled to finish next week."

Herrmann moaned, "That's not what I had in mind. I'll have to make a statement before long—public anxiety about recombination still exists. I'd like to be able to say that the work is done. If you've got a success—how can you miss?—it'll be too important to bitch about. Could you possibly wrap up this week?"

"We can try," Healey said reluctantly. *M'm! M'm! BAD IDEA.*

"Keep me posted. I'll be flying in and out for the next

few days." Herrmann was so busy that he used a helicopter that landed on the roof.

Healey started for the subbasement lab but, changing his plan, emerged from the elevator on the second floor, where the cafeteria was, and spotted the group at a side table. They'd broken for an early lunch, as he'd suspected. Healey bought a sandwich and coffee and joined them. "The boss himself!" said Robin Frazer, exhibiting square teeth. "How's it going, Jim?"

"Fair," Healey said as he sat down. Linda Summer, across from him, smiled prettily but said nothing. Neither did Walter Benson, who nodded. Benson didn't mean to be rude, Healey thought; gruffness was his natural manner. His attention went to Ad Wallon. The pallor of the previous Wednesday had returned. Did his eyes convey a peculiar intensity? "How are things downstairs?" Healey asked.

"Smooth. Linda has the lambda virus so well trained it's practically culturing itself," Frazer told him.

"Don't joke. That's what people are afraid of," said Healey with a comic grimace. "Herrmann wants us to wind down as soon as we can. He means this week. Can we?"

"What's the hurry?" Frazer asked.

Healey explained the situation. "He wants to make an announcement."

Wallon said loudly, "He could make one now."

"That's what you claimed before," Benson said.

"We'll do it this time, I'm sure. To success!" said Wallon. On the table before him stood three glasses close together, each half full. Wallon's hand moved quickly as he picked up a glass, raised a toast and drank.

"That was my glass," Benson complained.

"In fact," said Wallon, "you don't know which glass it was. My hand is too quick. Didn't you know I'm a magician? I was a surgeon too, before I decided I didn't like the color red. Just couldn't stand it. I don't know why." As he spoke he rapidly rearranged the glasses. "Now, tell me—whose glass is whose?"

"Much too easy. The glass on the left is the one you drank from," Frazer said from the end of the table. "The one in the middle is Benson's. On the right is mine. You're not much of a magician, Ad."

"You're mistaken, Robin," said Wallon. "Even when my hand is shaky it's quicker than the eye."

"*You're* wrong, and I'll prove it," Frazer said playfully. He sipped from a glass. "See! It's mine!"

"How can you tell?" Benson asked.

"Why, from the taste!"

"The taste?" Benson sipped from the tumbler. "It tastes like water. I don't see any difference."

Frazer's black mustache tilted up. Wallon laughed, and Linda said softly, "They're teasing you, Walter. All three of you drank from the same glass." Benson scowled.

Healey said, "I still want your opinion on whether we can finish this week."

"I see no reason why not," Wallon replied. "We've got the routines down pat. It only means doing more things at the same time. It ought to be easy—if Walter doesn't get in the way."

Benson's high voice protested, "My job is to perform the necessary checks, remember?"

"Obstacle course is more like it."

"Look, the requirements call for—"

"You don't have to be such a goddam perfectionist!"

"Hey," Healey said, a little surprised at Wallon's overheated response. "I'm sure Walter will do the best he can. He has a responsibility, after all."

Benson nodded. Frazer said merrily, "You won't work us too hard, will you, Jim? Did I tell you about the squash tournament at the Yale Club. I have all this excess energy, with my old lady in Baltimore."

Still shifting water glasses, Wallon upset one. "Jesus, I'm sorry."

"Did I embarrass you, Ad?" Frazer asked.

Wallon muttered, "You don't embarrass me. I do."
Just for a second, Ad looked oddly apprehensive.

The scientists trooped down to the elevator. In the
subbasement the men stood outside talking while Linda
changed, then followed her.

Before entering the lab, Healey paid another call to the
animal room and stood before Lucky's cage. The African
green monkey stared back, rattling the bars with hairy
fingers, and turned to grab the wooden blocks. But this
time the monkey failed to make shapes; it merely looked
from one block to another and cast them down.

He said to himself, What's the matter, Lucky? And the
monkey seemed to reply, *If I could tell you I would let you
know.*

"If I could tell you I would let you know." Whose line
was that? Whose? He could see the name but couldn't read
it. What did it mean? "If I could tell you . . ." Endlessly
circular, circularly endless. But circles *were* endless. No
answer: only riddles, nonsense. Whose? Auden, yes. Go.
Away. So. Know. Then he had the last stanza.

> *Suppose the lions all get up and go,*
> *And all the books and soldiers run away;*
> *Will Time say nothing but I told you so?*
> *If I could tell you I would let you know.*

"Here, Lucky." The monkey snatched the apple he
handed it.

DAYS NINE TO TWELVE

For the rest of that week Healey listened closely to the unwanted voices in his head as they recited slogans, doggerel, snatches of poetry he hardly knew he remembered. There was no pattern to them, no set time, nothing to indicate how his tangled brain chose among *Round and round, Beans, beans, M'm! M'm! GOOD IDEA, She has pimples, If I could tell you* or whatever other incantation it decided to produce.

Had he gone quietly crazy? He didn't think so, though it certainly couldn't be ruled out. Nor could obsession-compulsion, anxiety, masochism or other kinds of neurosis, including hypochondria. He *could* be imagining the voices in order to convince himself he was sick. Again, he couldn't quite believe it. Deep psychological troubles of that sort would have shown up earlier in some form, if they existed, or so it seemed to him. Unless, of course, he was in fact displaying onset symptoms of premature senility. But that idea he couldn't accept. Healey preferred to think that whatever was the matter with him had an outside source, of which he could think of only one, the fall against the luggage rack.

He relived the incident on the highway endlessly, rolling it back and forth in his mind like a piece of film. The bump, the triangular blotched face of the driver, the flourished bottle, the old car's lurch, Healey's leap to safety, his feet slipping on wet pavement, his head striking the luggage rack—had the blow been harder than he remembered? It must have been.

Healey knew he should consult Orenstein but found convincing reasons not to. Head injuries were notoriously hard to diagnose, and the psychiatrist might err. If, on the other hand, he *was* seriously ill, Healey, like anyone else, preferred to put off knowing about it as long as possible. Also, the voices might vanish of themselves in a few days, and Orenstein would laugh at him.

If it were possible to record the voices and play them back he might get an insight of some kind, but loud as they sounded to him they existed only in the sound tracks of his mind. Searching for other means to establish his brain's condition he thought of the quizzes in *People in White*. Perhaps testing his capacity would tell him something. He dispatched his secretary for all the back issues she could lay hands on. Coral looked at him as though to speak but departed.

An hour later he spotted her in the corridor. "*Where* have you been?" he demanded.

"Putting greenery in the cold room. Didn't I tell you?"

"No." At least he didn't think so. Suddenly he wasn't sure. Was his memory failing now? "Did you pick up the back issues?"

"I forgot."

She retrieved them, and he turned to the tests.

"Tillie Green hates fun, but she loves to be _____."

"Silly," Healey provided without difficulty.

"Tillie Green hates herbs, but she loves_____." What? Oregano, basil, sesame, rosemary, marjoram, bay leaves, thyme. Good Lord! Arrowroot? Not an herb. Sure! He wrote "fennel," adding, with a kind of glee, "tarragon."

"Tillie Green hates houses, but she loves_____." He was hung up for minutes before he found "dwellings."

That questions designed for kids sometimes seemed hard discouraged Healey no little. With trepidation he tried ones for grown-ups.

Complete each analogy by writing one word in the spaces, ending with the letters printed.

Example: high is to low as sky is to /E/A/R/T/H/.

thermometer is to temperature as clock is to / / / /E/.

"TIME," he wrote.

brave is to fearless as daring is to / / / / / / /I/D/.

No use! he sighed to himself, and stared at the answer: "intrepid." Healey, are you dumb! You don't know your head from your ass.

In each line below, underline the two words that are most nearly opposite in meaning.

short, length, shorten, extend, extent

"Shorten, extend," Healey selected, pleased to find himself right. Then

punish, vex, pinch, ignore, pacify

He stared at the words in apprehension, as though they were enemies, at last choosing "pinch, pacify." The answer was "vex, pacify." But one's about as good as the other, Healey thought.

In each group of words below, underline the two words whose meanings do not belong with the others.

shark, sea lion, cod, whale, flounder

Easy! "Sea lion, whale." Mammals. He was getting sharper.

stench, fear, sound, warmth, love

Stench-fear-sound-warmth-love! None seemed out of place because they *all* seemed out of place! Many answers equaled no answer. His head was a jungle. Dejectedly, he learned that he should have selected "fear" and "love."

Healey began to feel guilty. Hotshot scientist, university professor and chief of pediatric research at a famous hospital, he was immersed in silly self-tests. Nonetheless, he had to continue.

Barbara's brother Matthew has one more brother than he has sisters. How many more brothers than sisters does Barbara have?

Healey's mind-motor coughed and gave out. He read the answer: "Three."

Healey couldn't quit with a loser. He went on:

Which person in the following group does not belong and for what reason?
(a) C. Wright Mills
(b) Margaret Mead
(c) Talcott Parsons
(d) Max Weber
(e) Émile Durkheim

First casually, then with mounting alarm, he studied the names. The problem lay with Émile Durkheim. He *knew* who Durkheim was, but could come up with nothing more substantial than French. Although the others were familiar, how could he make an intelligent

choice without better information on Durkheim? No way.
Gambling, he circled Margaret Mead as the only woman.
The answer was "(b) Mead." *Ha! But* ... "An anthropologist. The rest are sociologists."

Mousetrapped! He should have known better than to
fall into the snare of selecting Mead because she was a
woman. Durkheim, like Weber, was a father of modern
sociology. Of course! Healey, Healey. Would you know
to come in out of the rain, idiot? Why did you forget?

Because he'd broken his brain on the luggage rack,
cracked his cranium, mangled his mind, ruptured his
reason ... was it so? Doggedly, he set about remembering
the fifty state capitals. ... Albany. Annapolis. Atlanta.
Augusta. Austin. Baton Rouge. Bismarck ... Bismarck
... Bismarck. ... Boise. Boston ... Boston. Shit. Carson City. Charleston. Cheyenne. Columbia. Columbus.
Concord. So far so good. Denver. Des Moines. Dover.
F ... F ... Frankfort. Harrisburg. Hartford. Helena.
(Ukulele) Honolulu. Indianapolis. Jackson. Jefferson
City. Juneau. Whew! Lansing. (President) Lincoln. Little
(music) Rock. Madison. Montgomery. His mind strained
like an overloaded hoist. Montpelier. (Movie) Nashville.
(Musical) Oklahoma! City. (Sporting event) Olympia.
(Bird) Phoenix. (New York hotel) Pierre. Providence.
Raleigh. Richmond. (Tomato juice) Sacramento. St.
Paul. (Witches) Salem. Salt Lake. (Railroad) Santa Fe.
(Rifle) Springfield. (Tall) Tallahassee. ... *Round and
round*.

His cerebral computer blew a fuse. What came next?
He went hurriedly to the bookcase in his outer
office—ignoring Coral, who turned and stared—seized
an atlas and scanned a map of the United States. Topeka!
Topeka had stopped him. For what reason? He'd even
been there on a conference. It was of no comfort that he'd
gone as far as Tallahassee. He had memorized the capitals
in high school and known them ever since, as though they
were graven in stone. Something was wrong, something
possibly serious.

Still watching himself that evening, he challenged Ruth

to backgammon. Losing a game he suggested another. "You like punishment, don't you?" Ruth said gaily. In her overconfidence Ruth made late errors, failing to cover points or capture his blots, but he was too far behind to win. He was ahead in the third game when Ruth, by accident, upset the board with her knee, and didn't want to continue. She was eyeing him strangely. She knows something's wrong with me. Somehow she knows, he thought.

Wednesdays, when Healey taught at the university, he traveled by taxi. On the way, glancing up from his lecture notes, he saw, just as the light was changing, *the face*. The triangular face from the highway. Peculiar upper lip. Dull eyes. He jerked his head to the rear window as the cab sped forward, but the man had turned away. Was it the same one? No, he had been mistaken: that fellow had been too short. Again he had duped himself. Rattled, he left his notes in the cab.

Noteless and harried, Healey faced his class in a poor state of mind. The medical students, polite, earnest, respectful, required a high level of sophistication, and he had little to offer that day. He launched into a lecture he knew by rote. ". . . thus, while estimates of the number of genes in a single normal human cell have varied from fifty thousand to a half million, the figure most geneticists feel comfortable with is a hundred thousand. Every gene would seem to represent both the promise of health and the peril of illness, in the ambiguous manner nature deals with living things. Each gene performs a function; failure to perform that function properly leads to the biochemical imbalances we call inborn errors of metabolism, of which, in humans, we can theorize that there are a hundred thousand—one per gene—most of which remain undiscovered, like stars in distant galaxies.

"As you know, defective genes probably figure in gout, hemophilia, sickle-cell anemia, muscular dystrophy and many varieties of mental retardation. A genetic culprit appears to lurk in diabetes, arthritis, epilepsy, schizophrenia, possibly some kinds of heart disease and cancer. Fully twenty-five per cent of all diseases may be caused by genetic malfunctioning.

"When we speak of inherited diseases we do not as yet recognize, we may refer to rare conditions, of which new ones are being spotted all the time, even though they may represent merely a new variety of diseases already known. Or we may be speaking of conditions which we do not understand to be genetic at all at present—for instance, criminal tendencies. . . .

"One day it may be possible—in fact, that day may not be far off—to identify these conditions through the study of the DNA of the fetus or the newborn child, to predict precisely what diseases an individual has a propensity toward, due to his or her genetic characteristics, and to suggest a lifetime regimen to avoid that disease. For instance, those with an inborn trait for obesity might have special diets even in childhood. . . . Yes?" Healey nodded toward an upraised hand.

"How do you account for these genetic failures to start with?"

That was the sort of ballpark question Healey found naive. "We can't," he said. "You can postulate that nature was running an experiment to try to improve a gene pool and failed—to me it's an out-and-out miracle that there are so few errors, considering the number of genes involved. Nor do we recognize where nature's experiments succeed. Or maybe the defective genes were a mistake that got passed on—nature can err too. Or it may be that what provided a genetically useful function at one period no longer does. Why do certain blacks have sickle-cell anemia? Because the sickle-cell trait provided protection against virulent malaria—the organisms don't like the hemoglobin. The individual who has sickle-cell anemia pays a price, which may be acceptable to the system if it minimizes malaria and enables the person to survive, as it did originally in parts of Africa. Another likely defensive genetic disease is obesity, which could have had survival value when food was scarce for a long period like winter. If food is scarce, marry a fat girl, my mother used to say." Pleased with his answer, Healey gestured toward another student. "Yes?"

"Doesn't the early screening mechanism you mention raise social issues? I mean, isn't it a kind of medical fascism to insist that people follow certain prescribed regimens even though they don't want to? Do they have a choice? Or their parents, if they're small?"

The question, for some reason, nettled Healey—maybe it was the querulous voice. "Sure they have a choice," he said. "No one has got to do anything they don't want do. 'Live at your own risk' might be the motto. As for parents, I can't imagine them not wanting to follow the best advice for their children." But he could: Cathy's mother. Suppose they didn't? What then? Healey became confused. "In any case, doctors per se..." What did he mean by "per se"? "...can't be expected to set social policy."

"Isn't that sort of a cop-out, sir? I mean..."

"I don't see why," said Healey steadily. "After all, there's a limit to individual responsibility. We've all got our own work to do. We have to delegate judgments, assume there are experts who can evaluate certain questions better than ourselves, have some confidence in the decisions made by the political apparatus, trust the authorities..." Did you say that, Healey? he asked himself. The way you feel about politicians? "...the general public..." The face of the troglodyte from the highway menaced his mind, making him falter.

The last section of Healey's lecture took up the building blocks of the DNA molecule, of which there were four. The language of heredity was written in a four-letter alphabet—symbolically, U, A, G, C, in various sequences. AUG, for instance, meant an order to start the production of a particular protein or amino acid regulating a part of a bodily function, while GUA was among the instructions to shut down. Suddenly, inside his head, a new voice chanted, *GUAGUA, GUA-GUA*. It sounded like *GOOA-GOOA*. Baby talk! Healey was regressing. *GUAGUA. Stop!* he pleaded. *STOP! GUA-GUAGUA*, the voice cried.

Fearful of actually uttering such nonsense out loud, Healey abandoned the lecture a few minutes early, looking carefully to see whether his behavior had seemed odd. But the class rose and departed as always—except that a couple of students might have been regarding him quizzically. He couldn't be sure.

Healey canceled his afternoon seminar, pleading an emergency at the hospital.

GUAGUA.

Healey had no further doubt that he ailed—how seriously, was the question. Because he had no objective means of gauging his condition, or even of knowing what distressed him, he began, furtively, to watch others to see whether they watched him. Undue attention, he thought, might show him how badly off he was.

That Linda Summer seemed to observe him continually pitched Healey into gloom. Did his aberration show? Did his lips move as nonsense coursed through his mind? Did he appear as distracted as he felt? If so, the scrutiny of a beautiful woman didn't help.

Wallon peered at him frequently too. What did Ad perceive? That Healey was uncertain, even clumsy at the bench? Good Lord, how ironic, Healey thought angrily, because if anybody deserved to be criticized it was Ad Wallon, who would have failed a course in freshman lab the way he upset and spilled things, costing them time. Healey smelled alcohol on Wallon's breath after the lunch breaks. Ad must have a bottle stashed in his office. What right had Wallon to stare sardonically?

Robin Frazer appeared downcast, which Healey interpreted as a sign of disappointment with the Responsible Investigator, since Robin also seemed to be appraising him. Walter Benson, Healey discovered, on turning quickly, had been examining him through the glass pane of the EM room, as if to keep a safe distance. Why didn't the little coward confront Healey face to face and say what he really thought?

On Thursday the team assembled at dawn, still hoping to meet Herman Herrmann's deadline in two arduous days. The excitement had vanished, replaced by mechanical numbness as they struggled on, repeating the steps they had taken the previous week, and temperament flared. When Benson spoke of staining microorganisms black or white, Frazer managed to find a racist analogy, reacting angrily. Queer that Robin had never displayed such sensitivity before. Queer that Benson, normally reserved, had begun to shower expletives, thought Healey, aloof at his workbench, head ringing with *She has pimples on her butt, Round and round, Beans, beans, M'm! M'm! GOOD IDEA*. Maybe they *all* suffered from stress and fatigue. *GUAGUA*.

On Friday they started early too, though they had toiled into the night. Even with the difficulties the group encountered, Healey still had hopes of finishing that day, but at lunch he gave up.

Wallon was delivering a medley of Polish jokes. "Why did the Polish seven forty-seven crash? It ran out of coal. Why doesn't Poland have ice cubes? The woman who owned the formula died. What are the only three important poles? North, South and Paderewski."

Benson stood up, small features twitching. "Cut it out! I hate Polish jokes! To me they're a personal affront!"

"Why, for God's sake?" Wallon demanded.

"I'm of Polish descent, if you want to know."

"You?"

"My family name was Besenski. My father changed it to Benson when he came here. That's why I can't stand these dumb jokes."

"Jokes about dumbness," Wallon said ruthlessly. "What's the smallest division in the Polish Army? Intelligence!"

"Fuck you. I'm going home," Benson cried, and strode swiftly from the room.

"Nice work, Ad. Well, I guess that's it for today," Healey said heavily. Without the EM photos, they couldn't continue, which, Healey decided, was just as well. He didn't like the feel of things in the lab.

Healey had intended to release Cathy Gobrin that day, but the mother, for reasons of her own, was unable to fetch the child until after the weekend. Cathy's "Hi, doctor" seemed subdued, and just as she had failed to remember Guinevere, so Lancelot had also faded, to which Healey attached no importance. The little girl brightened when Healey promised that she could go home the following week.

Healey told Olga, "If there's the slightest change this weekend I want to know." They had his country number.

On the way to his office Healey stopped at Mel Orenstein's. The busy psychiatrist sat like a queen in the midst of a hive of cubicles used for psychological testing. "To what do I owe this singular honor?" he said.

"Nothing much," said Healey. They chatted for a moment, and then Healey asked, "Did you see Cathy Gobrin today?"

"Sure. Why?"

"Nothing."

Orenstein's flat face examined him. "So why do you ask?"

Healey said slowly, "She seems a little sluggish."

"What do you expect? She thought she'd go home today. She's disappointed. Wouldn't you be?"

"I guess so," said Healey.

"Nobody likes to be in a hospital, not even a six-year-old," Orenstein offered.

"I guess not," Healey said. *GUAGUA.* "Did you give her another IQ test?"

"No. Why should I?"

"Just wondered."

Orenstein eyed him suspiciously. "Jim, is there something on your mind?"

"Not on. In," Healey said at last. He told Orenstein he'd had a ringing in his head for almost two weeks. He mentioned the fall against the luggage rack, but neglected the crazy things the voices shouted.

"Oh?" Orenstein rose. "Where did you hit your head?" Healey indicated. Orenstein pressed. "Hurt?"

"No." Orenstein applied more pressure. "No." Orenstein's deft fingers explored other areas of his scalp. "No. No. No," responded Healey.

Orenstein sat down. "Headaches?"

"No."

"Sleepy?"

"No."

"The abominable no-man," Orenstein joked. "I'm confident you don't have a fracture or a conscussion. There's nothing wrong with you that I can see, Jim. Maybe a little fluid collected under the skull, or a minor problem in the inner ear. It'll go away, I'm sure. Of course, if you want, I'll take X rays."

"I'm okay," said Healey.

At his desk Healey dialed Herrmann. He was told that the director was out of town and remembered having heard the helicopter that morning. He left word that the experiment was not, as yet, concluded. He glanced at the day's edition of *People in White* but decided he had to control what appeared to be an emerging mania for self-tests, especially since Orenstein had reassured him. He returned to the lab to get a leg up on Monday's work.

Inside, he found Linda Summer alone. "Oh, I was just finishing," she said offhandedly. This time there were no long gazes—in fact, Summer kept her back to him. Good sign, he thought: he must be acting normally again. Odd how when you go to a doctor the symptoms often clear up of themselves. Even the voices were gone, or almost: *GUA* sounded faintly.

Linda said goodbye and left. Healey finished a short time later and entered the changing room, padding noiselessly on the cloth covers that encapsulated his shoes. Hearing a rustle, he looked up as he was about to remove his tunic. The shower curtain opened and Linda Summer stood there, creamy-skinned, nude, hand on her inner thigh. She removed it instantly and remained momentarily immobile.

Lord, what a sight! Straight shoulders, pointed breasts, tiny waist, flat belly, shining flanks, red swatch...

> ...such a form as Grecian goldsmiths make
> Of hammered gold and gold enameling

Did she smile or frown? It was impossible to say as the shower curtain closed. Healey retreated to the animal room, pondering. He'd left Linda plenty of time to dress, hadn't he? Conviction wavered. Maybe he hadn't. Maybe in this confounded confusion of his, he'd rushed her, forced her (knowingly, perhaps, in some limbic layer of lust) to reveal herself to him. Yes, it must have been his fault. *GUAGUA.*

The monkey shook the bars but made no move for the wooden blocks. What's with you, Lucky? Healey asked with his eyes, reciting to himself,

> *Time will say nothing but I told you so,*
> *Time only knows the price we have to pay;*
> *If I could tell you I would let you know.*

"Yes, I guess you would," said Healey to the monkey.

WEEK THREE

DAY FIFTEEN

On Monday, rested after an uneventful country weekend, James Healey arrived at the fifth floor to find the head nurse staring at him fixedly, mouth open, as if afraid to speak. "Olga, what's the trouble?" he demanded.

The general took too long to answer. She said finally, "Something's wrong with Cathy. She's had a setback of some kind."

A nerve twitched in Healey's cheek as he scrutinized Cathy Gobrin's chart. He said, vainly trying to keep anger out of his voice, "Why didn't somebody tell me? I left strict orders to be notified if there was a change."

"I left the instructions. The weekend people goofed—it isn't like them. I only learned myself a few minutes ago."

"We've lost two days," Healey muttered disconsolately.

He moved across the hall, Olga in his tracks. Before

them, a motorized cart stopped abruptly, antenna waving. Cathy, in pajamas, sat up in bed, bent over, arms wrapped around her knees, her gaze vacant. "She wouldn't put on her clothes," whispered Olga.

"Cathy?" The little girl didn't appear to notice them. "Cathy," Healey said again.

She looked at him shyly. "Hi, dotor."

She didn't ask for a kiss, as if too timid. He administered one anyway. "How are you today?"

When Cathy said nothing, he frowned at the head nurse, who frowned back. "Cathy's definitely more withdrawn."

He repeated the question, and Cathy said finally, "Foine."

"Foine? Fine, Cathy."

"Foine."

"What was the name of the book you were reading, Cathy?"

"Bwok?"

"Book. About a king."

"Bwok. King. Don't remember."

"Try."

"Bwok." Cathy sniffled, closing her eyes.

"I can't believe ordinary food could have this effect. Is there a bug running around the wards?"

"I would have reported it at once. Anyway, Cathy has no fever, no symptomatology at all—except this."

"I don't understand. It sounds from the chart as though she's regressed steadily all weekend. What could be causing it? Cathy?" he implored, as if hoping she would open her eyes and chirp "Hi, doctor!" But Cathy only whimpered and thrashed her legs. "Cathy, what are you thinking about?"

"No-thing," she mumbled.

"At least she doesn't seem to be in pain. Nurse, she's to return to the special diet at once. I want a complete physical exam. Get the phenylalanine report to me first."

100

Olga nodded. "What about her mother? She expects Cathy to be released soon."

"Tell her anything except the truth. Cathy's going to get well."

Olga looked dubious. Cathy said, blinking, "Home go soon?"

"Soon, dear. Goodbye."

"Goodbye, dotor."

GUAGUAGUAGUA.

Healey departed hurriedly. Near the elevator he saw peripherally that something approached. He whirled to find a motorized cart aimed straight at him. He threw himself against the wall. With a tiny screech of brakes the cart stopped only a few feet from him, antenna waving. He'd been moving too fast for the vehicle's little computer to anticipate, he decided. That must have been it.

From his office Healey phoned Orenstein. "Mel? Jim. Yes, yes, I'm fine. Cathy Gobrin isn't. Don't ask me what's causing it, but all of a sudden..." Disappointment overwhelmed him. "...her condition is surprisingly like what it was when she came to the hospital two months ago."

"What?" The psychiatrist sounded shocked. "Did we push her too hard? Patients develop resistance."

"Maybe, though I doubt it. She seemed to enjoy making progress. I believe it's something physical. Maybe she's sick."

Orenstein agreed ritualistically. "If your body's out of kilter, so's your mind. Does she have a fever?"

"No. That's part of the mystery. It could be that her phenylalanine's up. I'm having it checked. I'd like her IQ tested again. Can you?"

"I'll get on it," Orenstein said.

In the lab Healey informed the others of Cathy's condition: the news seemed to shock and discourage them. Work proceeded slowly, and almost nothing had been accomplished when they broke at noon. Healey

101

returned to his office. "Anything come in?" he asked
Coral.

"Lab report on the Gobrin girl." She handed him a
sealed brown envelope.

"Any calls?"

"No," Coral said vaguely, peering at the potted plants
against which the envelope had rested. "Gracious, I forgot
to water today."

As Healey reached his desk the phone rang. "Jim? Mel.
Didn't you get my message?"

"No."

"I told Coral to have you call. Doesn't matter. Cathy's
lost a bunch of IQ points," the psychiatrist said rapidly.

"How many?"

"Hard to say with exactitude. I'd put her at IQ ninety
or less."

"Lord! That's a drop of over twenty points!" Healey's
voice wavered. "Can it be explained by day-to-day
variations?"

"Well, you can get some impressive shifts in the same
person all right, but in this case I think it's cumulative.
She must have been losing ground steadily since I tested
her last, which was a week ago. We just didn't notice. Do
you have her medical report?"

"Just a minute." Healey ripped open the envelope. "It's
not PKU. Her phenylalanine's perfectly normal."

"So what in hell could it be?"

"I don't have the other results. I'm putting my money
on a virus."

"Hell, if it's not organic, that would be good!"

"Good if we can identify the virus."

"Even if we can't, at least we can hope for a full
recovery. Her body might take care of it."

"I hope so," Healey said without enthusiasm.

Is this my fault? he thought bleakly as he hung up. Am I
in some way responsible? The questions were drowned
out by the racket that commenced in his head. *Round and*

*round, Beans, beans, M'm! M'm! GOOD IDEA, She has
pimples on her butt, GUAGUA, Please Do Not Bend,
Fold, Spindle or Mutilate* ... oh God, a new one. *Stop!
Think!*

Abruptly Healey rose, went to the bookcase in his
outer office and returned with a medical encyclopedia.
Was it spelled with a "C" or a "K"? You ought to know
that, he reprimanded himself. He tried "K" first, which
was wrong, as he'd somehow known it would be.
Creutzfeld-Jakob disease, a form of presenile dementia,
caused by a slow virus that could take months or years to
develop. Resulted in brain destruction and death. Early
symptoms: loss of memory, inability to coordinate,
anxiety, depression. Cases were occasionally reported.
How it was normally transmitted was unknown, but it
had evidently been passed by corneal transplants and by
silver electrodes inserted in the brain for diagnostic
study. ... See also "Kuru" and "Scrapie."

Kuru, probably the same virus, had once been a
leading cause of death among a tribe in New Guinea.
Apparently the virus was transmitted when the natives
smeared themselves with the blood of those they were
about to eat. The symptoms were like those of
Creutzfeld-Jakob. Cannibalism had been discouraged,
the disease virtually eradicated. Scrapie, an animal
disease, caused similar symptoms in sheep. The nasty
viruses resisted sterilization by boiling, ultraviolet light or
formaldehyde. They were extremely hard to identify
because they had no easily characterizable protein of their
own. Importantly, they caused no fever, inflammation or
other known immunologic reaction. They mocked
existing medical knowledge.

But there had been no diagnostic surgery, no
electrodes, no deaths, no sudden wave of illness at the
hospital—nothing in short, to indicate a virus, rare or
otherwise. Could it be that Cathy's delicate biochemical
balance made her uniquely susceptible to a virus whose

sole effect was to augment a problem she already had? He hoped the results of her physical exam, due tomorrow, would give him a clue.

Healey took a legal pad and wrote at the top, in small neat letters, "Virus X."

Standing behind the glass door Phillip gave no sign of recognition until Healey pulled the knob. "Pardon me, doctor."

"That's all right. Nice afternoon, isn't it? Getting warmer."

"Mmmmmm. Well, spring's coming."

"Mmmmmm," Healey repeated, not meaning to. He noted that Phillip, always immaculate, wore dirty gloves and his bow tie hung askew. He said in a friendly fashion, "Maybe you ought to spruce up, Phillip. You know those ladies on the building committee."

"Mmmmmm."

Mmmmmm, thought Healey. Was he becoming a mental sponge? Preoccupied, he watched Phillip press the elevator button for him, realizing he had touched the wrong one only when the car stopped on the floor below his. Healey blamed himself for being inattentive.

Key in hand, he hesitated before his front door. Lord he felt tired. It wasn't just the depression Cathy's relapse had caused or his growing worry that the scientific team, himself included, had been performing poorly. It was also the cerebral energy he had to expend to try to silence the voices in his brain. If they continued more than a few days longer he'd check into a hospital for a total workup. *M'm! M'm! GOOD IDEA.* But for now he was intent on an evening of peace. Some classical music on the stereo, Handel or Mendelssohn.

As he entered, a soft object struck and adhered. Snatching at his neck he found wet tissue. *Splat!* Another struck his cheek. "What..." Girlish laughter crossed the living room. "Jen!"

"Got you, Daddy!" From behind the couch Jennie

emerged holding a straw.

"She's been waiting for I don't know how long," said Ruth, smiling up from the newspaper.

"Very funny."

"Where's your sense of humor?" Ruth asked, as if surprised.

"I lost it at the clinic," Healey snapped. "Jennie's too old to shoot spitballs." Tears sluiced down Jennie's cheeks. "Stop crying," he said, thinking suddenly of Cathy.

Ruth cried, "Don't be so hard on her! She's only a little girl!"

"Not that little." Jennie ran wordlessly from the room. "What's with her anyway? She's acting like a baby."

"I told you. You're too harsh with her."

"I?" he said, astounded. "Harsh?"

"Don't shout. You'll frighten her."

"Why should I frighten her? Anyway, I'm *not* shouting."

"You are," Ruth said with an even dogmatic assurance that infuriated him. "You expect too much from her. That's why she's experiencing emotional difficulties."

It must have been that he wanted to escape from what sounded to him like prattle, but Linda Summer, naked, soared into his mind, luminous as a hologram. He pushed her out. "What difficulties?" he asked, bewildered.

"How else to explain the rotten grades she just got? Did I tell you she flunked a math test?"

"You must have forgotten," he said coldly.

"I learned yesterday. The school psychologist blames emotional upset. I talked with him today. He thinks we should spend more time with her."

"But we spend plenty of time with her. The psychologist is crazy. Did you have her eyes checked as I suggested?"

"Jennie's eyes are okay," Ruth said flatly.

Healey gave up. On the way out of the living room he found Jennie lurking behind the door. He grabbed her, pulled her down the hall, kissed her and asked, "How's my little girl?"

"Fine."

"Are you mad at me?"

"No, Daddy," she said a little timidly, making him think of Cathy again.

"Sweetheart, is your vision okay? Can you read the numbers on the blackboard, or when you take a test?"

"I have trouble," Jennie confessed.

"I thought so. You'll look pretty in glasses," he said cheerfully.

A spitball hit him on the neck as he walked to the bedroom, but he pretended not to notice. He thought of one of his mother's jokes, could hear Henrietta telling it, voice dry: a female civic leader who was inspecting conditions at a mental institution encountered a man making figures out of brick in the yard. She expressed admiration for them. The man explained that he was a professional sculptor. Then what was he doing there? the woman inquired. He'd been put away by his family because he was rich and they wanted his money, the sculptor claimed. Yes, yes, he knew that all the inmates told the same story. He didn't expect her to believe him. But the woman *did* believe him because he sounded so reasonable. She would look into his case and, if he wasn't lying, try to help, she said. Gravely, the man thanked her. As she turned to go, she was struck on the back of a head by a piece of brick. The man pointed a finger and cried, "Don't forget!"

He hadn't thought of that terrible joke in years. Why now? He visualized the mad sculptor shouting "Don't forget!" The sculptor had the face of the man on the highway.

Flo had assembled a gruesome dinner—greasy pork chops, watery mashed potatoes, limp salad ruled by garlic. "Is she trying to poison us?" Ruth grumbled.

"Careful. She'll hear," Healey said.

"I *want* her to hear."

"Why antagonize her? She's usually pretty good."

"What's the matter with you?" Healey tried to remember whether he'd ever seen the sharp line bisecting Ruth's forehead. "Don't I have the right to complain? Doesn't Flo get paid? Isn't she a servant?"

"Mmmmmm," he said, before he could stop himself. "Still, everybody has bad days. I wish you'd lay off."

"Don't tell me to lay off!" Ruth poured herself another glass of wine, and called, "Flo, come here."

Face stolid, Flo appeared in the kitchen doorway. "Yes, Ruth?"

Ruth said, with exaggerated politeness, "This dinner stinks, dear. It really does. It's fit for pigs."

Flo's large mouth opened and closed. "Send it to the cops, then!" she yelled and vanished. Moments later the back door slammed.

"You're the soul of tact," Healey said. "I hope Flo hasn't left for good."

"You take things too seriously. She'll get over it. Those people aren't long on memory."

"Those people?" he repeated, frozen.

"I wish she wouldn't call me Ruth."

"What's the promblem?" Jennie asked.

*"Prob*lem," said Healey.

"Proble*n*," Jennie replied.

"Problem, Jennie. You haven't mispronounced that word for years!"

"You're being hard on her again," Ruth said.

"What are you talking about?"

"You heard me."

"Can I watch TV?" Jennie asked.

"Yes dear. Remember the set's not working very well."

Jennie padded off to the living room. "Television?" he said in surprise.

"So? Got something against TV?"

"Just that Jennie never watches it."

"It's good for her. She studies too much. I'd like her to be more normal."

"Normal?" he said slowly, probing her meaning.

"Jennie's perfectly normal."

His eyes went to Paul for confirmation, but his son, heretofore silent, chose to read an accusation. "You mean I'm not?"

"Touchy, aren't you?"

"Who, me?"

"Who else?" Healey demanded, exasperated. He softened his tone and added, "What do you have on this evening, son? Plan to watch TV too?"

"What do I care about goddam television? Buddy's coming over. Guess we'll do some gaming."

"You guess. What's the war tonight?"

"'Nam," Paul declared. "I'm fighting the American side. I want to prove we could have won with the right tactics."

"Oh? What tactics would have won for us in Vietnam in your humble opinion?"

"That information's classified," Paul said.

"Well, that war was so stupid for us to get into that it's hard to imagine anyone wanting to refight it," Healey said. "But most wars are stupid, I suppose."

"This evening America will win," Paul insisted. The doorbell rang. "Here's Buddy now."

"Nobody's to mention Jennie's grades," Ruth said.

"Why, for God's sake?" Healey said.

"Why? Why do you ask why? I don't want the Glissers to know, that's why."

"Know *what?*"

"That Jennie's grades are down," said Ruth.

"Ruth! What's got into you? We don't care what the neighbors think. Besides, Jennie's—"

Seventeen-year-old Buddy Glisser was short and plump, with elegant speech meant to sound grown-up. Though he was Paul's best friend, Healey had never much liked him. "Hi, everybody," Buddy said grandly. "Am I interrupting? I see you haven't finished dinner."

"It's finished us," Ruth said with a groan. "Care for a little? There's plenty left."

"Oh, no thank you," Buddy said quickly, surveying the unappetizing provender. "I've just eaten and I'm absolutely stuffed."

"How about some ice cream, then? We haven't had dessert."

"Ice cream? Well, that's different..."

Paul rose. "No, we'd better get started—long night ahead. We'll snitch dessert later. And don't worry about us. We'd like to finish the war, even if it takes all night."

"It better not," said Healey.

"It's Easter vacation—almost," Paul cried.

"It still better not." Paul suddenly seemed very young.

Seeing his daughter enraptured by the TV screen and his wife, also interested in the program, hovering around the living room made Healey feel on the outside, as though he didn't belong to his family or they to him. He didn't recall having experienced the odd and lonely sensation before.

Healey went to his den to start a report on the experiment which, sooner or later, he would have to submit. When had they begun it? Three weeks ago! And it had been two weeks since he had scrubbed the first go-round because of the extra piece of DNA. How strange things had been subsequently! Healey was convinced his head was a shambles because of the blow against the luggage rack—that or (fearful as he was of even acknowledging the possibility to himself) an inherited senile trait had emerged—and yet not everything had to do with him. Like...Lucky's failure to make shapes with the blocks. Well, he shouldn't make much of that: the animal had simply tired of the game. Like...Linda's exhibition. The episode was never far from his consciousness. Reliving it, he had convinced himself that his first instinct had to be heeded: there'd been plenty of time for her to dress. Maybe she'd been daydreaming or...and/or...no...not like her....*Smile away. I can smell your feet a smile away.* Where had *that* come from? One of Paul's records....*Stop!...Please Do*

Not Bend, Fold, Spindle or Meditate.... Lord! The voices were punning now.

What a difficult job to think. His ideas tumbled over one another in a torrent. Cathy... Jennie flunked a test in math, her best subject. Her eyes? "I have trouble," she'd said. Trouble with... What was in that extra snip of DNA?... Benson's overreaction to Polish jokes... Frazer's sudden sensitivity about race.... Maybe it was only that Healey had gotten to know them better... *She has pimples on her*... Could there have been a lab accident? Impossible! A spill would have been reported. *Round and round*...

Healey examined his fingernails. He'd forgotten to cut them recently which wasn't like him. He regularly clipped his nails so as not to scratch the children during physical exams. *What* was like him anymore? Who was he? A nice guy, down deep, a little stiff, maybe, but sensible, reasonable. What was his problem? Was something wrong with his head? Think! But he didn't know what to think about. Something... except... *GUAGUA*....

If only he could objectify the situation, find correlatives that accounted for the various anomalies, isolate information that could be studied, measured, analyzed, verified, as with a scientific experiment, but he could find nothing but apparently random and unrelated facts—his inner confusion, Cathy's relapse, possible oddities in the behavior of various people and an African green monkey. They refused to add up to a single cause. Healey was back to where he had started: he'd knocked his head on a luggage rack—or impending premature dementia.

Over an hour had passed. Wearied by circular reasoning, Healey went to the kitchen for a soft drink. He watched in surprise as Ruth put a box of napkins in the refrigerator. "Think they'll spoil?" he asked.

"I'm getting absentminded in my old age," Ruth murmured.

In bed, he tried again to put himself to sleep by remembering the state capitals. This time he got hopelessly stuck at Santa Fe.

DAY SIXTEEN

Tuesday began badly. As Healey wheeled his bike to the rack outside the hospital an ambulance that rushed from the emergency unit came close to striking him. He had a glimpse of the driver: triangular face, peculiar upper lip, reminding him again of the man on the highway. But such a coincidence would have been too bizarre.

But he was not imagining Olga's downcast countenance. "No improvement. Cathy's worse, if anything. In my view..." The nurse listened as a canister plopped from the vacuum tube. She tried to open it. "The thing is stuck."

"Can I help, general?" he asked.

"I'll thank you to do your job and let me to mine," Olga said sternly. She twisted the canister hard and removed a message. "Gorbin's report won't be ready until noon.

They're all backed up in the lab for some reason." Olga straightened her cap.

The general was a bit too brusque: no doubt Cathy's condition had upset her more than she wished to admit. "Let's hope we learn something," Healey said.

The tall head nurse followed him as he crossed the hall. "Doctor, Cathy shouldn't be here in her present state. Why, she's hardly able to use the toilet anymore. We may have to put her in diapers. She's trouble for the staff, and she's upsetting the other kids. You know how impressionable they are—some of them have begun to act funny too. Unless there's an immediate improvement, Cathy should be placed in an institution, which is where she belongs, I'm afraid."

"I'll make that decision," he said curtly. He turned to the girl. "Good morning, Cathy." No response. He tried again. "Good morning, dear."

Cathy huddled in her nightgown at the head of her bed. At last she managed a tiny wave of the hand, as though she wished to be rescued. "Hi, dotor." He tried to kiss her, but the girl shrank back.

Downstairs, Healey paid a call on Lucky. The monkey returned his stare but made no effort to rattle the bars; it hardly seemed to recognize an apple.

"What's with Lucky?" he asked Wallon in the lab.

Although a diener, as they called the attendant, took care of the animals, the virologist was ultimately responsible for monitoring their condition. "It's okay," said Wallon. "Why?"

"It's not responsive."

"None of the monkeys are. They've been in small cages too long. We ought to think about moving them. It's been over two weeks and nothing's shown up, not that it will."

"How are the mice?"

"The mice?" Wallon repeated. "Mice are fine."

Wallon's breath reeked. So he was drinking in the morning now! Was he dejected? Over what? Women? His work? Wallon was definitely less effective than before, which Healey attributed to alcohol, in a vicious circle. He decided to give Ad an ultimatum: quit drinking or leave the team.

Robin Frazer also appeared dispirited. He explained at last that the night before, he'd been defeated in the squash tournament by an inferior player. Frazer couldn't get over it. Healey thought Robin a little silly to take an athletic event so seriously, but, then, he had always lacked interest in sports. He asked Frazer why he thought he'd lost.

Robin said, in the black brogue that seemed to have crept into his speech, "Just couldn't loosen up, man. Muscular tension will kill you every time."

"Mmmmmm. Why were you so tense?"

Robin said evasively, "Away from the old lady too long, maybe."

When Healey considered it, he realized that Walter Benson stayed closeted in the EM room for interminable periods, as though insulating himself from the others, and maybe he had a right to be impatient. Errors, bad timing, poor coordination, faulty communication—the experiment, plainly put, was a mess. So much had to be done over. The mistakes seemed almost infectious—Walter had begun to make them too.

Not that Healey could crow. He too was subject to errors, and Linda Summer didn't help. The competent female scientist comported herself like a high-school girl, flaunting her concupiscent wares—lips parted, arched shoulders, emphasizing her breasts—whenever he looked at her. Her ocular embrace, hard to avoid, distracted him even more than he was already.

Leaving the lab in despair, Healey bought lunch in the cafeteria to eat in his office. "Good afternoon, Dr. Healey," the cashier said. "Nice day, eh?"

"Mmmmmm. You'll go broke like that." He returned an extra five-dollar bill she'd given him in his change.

"Money isn't everything," the cashier sang. "Have a good dayayay." Or so it sounded to him.

It was after twelve, but Cathy's physical report had not

arrived. Healey dispatched Coral with instructions to extract it from the pathology lab by force if necessary. He sat in his inner office, sandwich untouched, glowering at the yellow pad on which he'd written "Virus X." He sighed and picked up the newsletter. On the same page as the self-quiz he saw:

Dr. Mr.'s and Ms.'s:
   I note in your recent article on recombinant DNA experiments a reference to the double helix, as discovered by Drs. Crick and Watson.
   Why "helix" necessarily? Why not "shelix"? Or perhaps "herlix" would do, in which case the analogue would be "double himlix."
   I believe the nomenclature "double helix" to be a blatant example of male chauvinism. Obviously, the supposed impartiality of science is a myth.
   anon. (because of fear of reprisals)

Next thing, women would want him to change his name to Herley! He laughed, along with the writer. Whoever she or he was intended satire, surely.
   He addressed himself seriously to the daily questions.

Tillie Green hates Children, but she loves _____.

Children? *Mmmmmm.* Children. What? No. No. No. Stumped! Stop! *Round and round....* At last his bothered brain contrived to furnish "kiddies."

Three rich intelligent men make a bet to see which is the most intelligent. They hire a think tank to devise a test, which is developed after much study. The forehead of each man is touched with a wand. A spot of a soot may or may not be left there. The men are told to begin tapping on the table if they see a soot spot on the forehead of either of the other two. As soon as any of them can determine whether he has or has not soot on his own forehead he is to stop tapping. If he is right he wins.

The men do not know it, but soot has been placed on foreheads of all three, whom we shall call "A," "B," and "C."

The first man, "A," ceases to tap. How has he reached the conclusion that he has soot on his forehead?

Healey plunged in, whistling inwardly. How could "A" possibly have realized that soot spotted his forehead by deductive reasoning only, without using a mirror or his hand? What did "A" know? Only that both "B" and "C" were intelligent and tapped. *She has pimples on her butt* . . . Healey fought back the voice that vied with his cognition, placing himself inside the mind of "A."

"B" and "C" have soot. Both tap. What if "A" did *not* have soot? Put "A" into the mind of "B." "B," seeing "A" and "C" tap and noting the absence of soot on "A's" forehead, has to conclude . . . In reach of his goal, Healey stumbled into a thicket of symbols—"A's," "B's" and "C's" combining and recombining until they were transmogrified into *GUAGUA*. "B," seeing "A" sootless and "C" tapping . . . *Help!*

Healey's mind worked itself into a lather. Calm down, he ordered it. "A" looks at "B" and "C" and sees soot. Suppose "A" lacks soot? "B" ("A" is thinking) would see this. "B" would also see that "C" taps. Therefore, "C" must be tapping for "B," because "A" has no soot. "B," being intelligent, would realize that he has soot. But "B" continues to tap. Ergo, "A" has soot. "A" quits tapping, proving himself smartest.

Whew! Healey could hardly believe such an essentially obvious solution had taken such colossal cerebration, almost wearing him out. It showed the poor state of his brain.

Healey's thoughts were interrupted by Coral Blanchard's arrival in the outer office. Impatiently he stood, wincing as he saw her bang into a corner of her desk. Limping as she came through the door, long face brave, like a wounded courier's, she gave him an envelope. "Hurt yourself?" he asked unnecessarily.

"I'm in great pain."

"Never marry a girl who bruises easily, my mother used to say," he tried to joke.

Coral chose to be offended. "Just because I've never married, you needn't rub it in, Dr. Healey!"

"I didn't mean to offend. Let me know if it continues to bother you," he said in his best physicianly manner.

He read Cathy's report eagerly. Never before had he wanted a patient to be sick, but if Cathy suffered from an identifiable illness Healey could look for a cure. As he feared, Cathy seemed in perfect health. Except that she had a reclusive personality and a mental age of five: IQ 85.

What could account for it? Healey had no answers, only shrill voices that chattered, chanted, screamed, ranted—a skein of sound in his head. Could they be trying to say something? If so, what? *Round and round*—a communicable disease went round and round. *If I could tell you I would let you know.* A virus would let you know by the symptoms. *GUAGUA—DNA language. Beans, beans, She has pimples on her, Smell your feet, Please Do Not Bend*—pure nonsense, but the yard-long DNA molecule did contain much nonsense, or so scientists read the unused parts of it. *M'm! M'm! GOOD IDEA.* He might be on the right track, *mmmmmm.* D-N-A . . .

Healey didn't really believe the voices sent him a message. Rather his mind, using them as clues, shaped them into a conclusion that he was understandably loath to reach: an experiment that he had conceived and been responsible for had gone awry, with possibly serious consequences. The virus engineered in the lab had an unknown piece of human DNA. It could have unwanted effects. Cathy might be displaying them. So might others. So might he. *GUAGUA.*

Rumors had to be avoided if, as seemed overwhelmingly likely, he erred, but even more importantly if he happened to be right.

He cornered his colleagues individually. Wallon first, because the virologist would be flying to Boston that day to visit one of his children who was having trouble in school. Lying brashly, Healey pretended that an absurd new government regulation required an immediate report of any mishap, no matter how trivial, during a DNA experiment.

"I upset a glass of water in the cafeteria."

"Come on, Ad." Healey shook his head. "Are you certain?"

"Would I lie?"

"You might have overlooked something," Healey insisted. "Don't tell me you haven't been drinking a good deal."

Immediately Wallon became angry, face creased. "Me? Drinking?"

"Come on, Ad."

Wallon's face crumbled like a muffin. "Maybe I have been drinking more than I ought. I've been unhappy."

"Want to tell me why?"

Wallon was elusive. "Maybe I'm in a rut, doing the same things over and over. I need something new in my life. Like a woman."

"A woman?" Healey asked with curiosity. "That shouldn't be hard to find. There are so many of them ."

"You say that because you've got Ruth! You're lucky. To most women I know, I prefer whores. At least they go home."

"You've taken to whores, Ad?" Healey said.

Wallon snapped, "Will you give me Ruth instead?" He smiled disarmingly. "I'm kidding, of course."

"Mmmmmm."

Healey took Linda aside. "No," she said, in response to his questions. "No," replied Robin Frazer in their short private conference. Finally he went to the EM room to find the little microscopist staring into an eyepiece, turning dials, haranguing the machine with curses. "Come on, you motherfucker, work, work..."

"Walter." Walter was swearing more and more.

"Walter...," he repeated.

"Eh? Sorry. Yes?"

Healey sat down, and Benson swiveled his chair to face him. He offered the explanation of the new government rule. "Walter, two weeks ago Monday, when we shut down the experiment, partly because you didn't like the looks of things—"

"Wait a minute! Wait a min-ute!" Walter said excitedly. "Wallon's been ragging me ever since, as if I shouldn't have blown the whistle and we'd be finished by now and wouldn't be stuck in this goddam lab all this time. I was only doing my fucking job. My responsibility—"

Healey was able to interrupt at last. "That isn't the issue. When you first came to the lab that day, do you remember who was already here?"

"Who was here? Oh sure. It was Wallon, the bastard."

"Anything out of the way? Any lapse from established procedure that you observed?"

"I don't remember any," the microscopist said.

"No matter how small."

"No matter how small?"

"Come on, Walter, think."

"Think," Benson repeated nervously. His forehead beveled. "Nothing comes."

"Well, okay then," Healey said. He sat still a moment, pondering. Maybe he was wrong about the whole thing. Maybe he was being too logical, looking for an overall explanation when all he really saw was random, unrelated events. Maybe he hadn't considered Cathy's condition carefully enough, overlooked some exotic pathology, Eastern equine encephalitis, for instance, a virus that attacked the central nervous system, caused brain damage and was ultimately fatal to the elderly and to young children. No, no. E.E.E. would have been picked up by the lab tests. In any case it was too early for mosquitoes, which carried the disease.

Benson, who appeared to have forgotten him, squinted into the eyepiece, cursed and took a lens tissue from a

118

box. Healey started out of the room, when Walter said, in a small voice, waving his arm. "I do recall something. A tissue in a basket. It was there when I came in at eight-thirty. Wallon should have autoclaved it. I did, for him."

Back in his office Healey tried frantically to find Wallon, but Ad had already left. He didn't have a secretary, and nobody knew where to find him in Boston.

Healey came home to find a blue-coveralled TV repairman working in the living room. He took Ruth aside and asked, "Why?"

"I want to get the set back in order. It'll give Jennie something to do over the Easter vacation."

"She's never needed it before."

"She does now. You know, kids change."

"So much?" he asked guardedly. "Did you have her eyes tested?"

"Why, yes. Her eyes are perfectly okay. Didn't I tell you?"

"No."

"I must have forgotten."

"Mmmmmm." He listened for, and missed, the familiar rattling of pots from the kitchen. "Where's Flo?"

"Didn't show up."

"I told you."

"Nonsense. She's sick, that's all."

"Did she call in?"

"No," Ruth admitted.

Ruth's overdone steak dinner was scarcely an improvement over Flo's performance the night before. Conversation among the three of them—Paul ate at Buddy's again—was desultory. Healey kept examining his daughter's bottomless blue eyes and round face brimming with innocence. That was the expression Jennie used to acquire when she'd done something wrong: he hadn't seen it in a long time. "What have you been up to?" he asked finally.

"Nothing, Daddy."

He chose not to believe her. After dinner, with Ruth absorbed in the crossword puzzle and Jennie crouched motionless before the TV screen, Healey peered into her closet and looked under her bed, finding nothing amiss. About to abandon the search, he inspected the bathroom she shared with Paul. One glance was sufficient. Jennie had smeared the mirror and walls with paint—watercolors, luckily.

He dragged Jennie into the bathroom. "Clean it up, hear? I want every trace of paint removed. Jennie, you haven't pulled a stunt like that since you were little. What's got into you?"

"I don't know," Jennie said through tears.

Ruth seemed to want to ignore the incident. "You solve it. It's your problem," she said without looking up from the paper.

"*My* problem? Why?"

"She's acting out hostility toward you because you don't pay enough attention to her. It's that simple."

"Is it?"

He kept wishing Ruth would put away the crossword puzzle and noticed that she rarely employed her stubby pencil. At last she threw the paper down. "No use. I can't do it. They must have changed styles. I forget things, can't concentrate. . . . I feel so aimless, like I've lost my way. It must be menopause." Ruth sighed from the bottom of her being.

He said, "Ruth, we've been over that. How can you talk about menopause? You're too young."

"There are cases."

"You're not one of them."

"Call it a life crisis, then. I'm bored with my job, and I used to like it so much! I'm bored with everything. Even crossword puzzles bore me. I've been thinking—maybe I should quit work. Paint full time. I've always wanted to be a real artist, you know. I'm good. I could have shows on Madison Avenue."

Healey liked his wife's miniatures well enough, but a

serious artist she wasn't. Always before, she had been realistic about her abilities; to hear her boast embarrassed him and made him want to reassure her. He went to the chaise and stroked the hollow at the base of her head, beneath the thick dark hair.

"Don't condescend to me!" Ruth wrenched herself into control. "Come on. Let's play backgammon. It'll make me feel better."

"Sure."

But on this occasion, Ruth covered the board with errors and lost three games in a row. "You must have cheated," she said ungraciously.

Healey regarded the glum face in the bathroom mirror. I'm okay, you're okay, he told himself, but he wasn't. Not okay at all, with voices clamoring in his head and the world around him gyrating crazily. Almost worse was the increasing space between himself and his wife—as though they lived on different asteroids. Again it had been weeks since they'd made love, and he went to bed eagerly.

Losing didn't arouse Ruth as winning had. Her sexless sprawl proved unassailable. He squirmed on his side of the mattress, brain active. "Something I meant to ask you," he said offhandedly in the darkness. "I'd like a redo of Jennie's IQ test. Could you arrange it in the next few days? They know you so well at the school."

Ruth sat up straight like a corpse in a horror film. "Why, for God's sake?"

Healey was prepared for the question. "Research I'm conducting on a girl about the same age on IQ variation. A comparison would...ah...be useful."

To him the lie sounded palpable, but Ruth lay back and said sleepily, "All right."

DAY SEVENTEEN

Wallon wasn't due back until Wednesday afternoon. Healey taught his morning class, cut short his seminar after lunch and returned to the hospital to wait.

Having left messages for Wallon wherever he could think of, Healey stopped at the lab. Activity was desultory, as if the experiment were winding down without anybody having given express orders, though it was nowhere near completion. Just as well, thought Healey. He visited Lucky on the way out. The monkey wouldn't take an apple.

Upstairs, he called Herrmann. "I'm afraid we won't make it this week, either."

"When, then?" Herman Herrmann complained.

"I don't know. Soon, I hope."

"I don't understand you, Jim. We'd better have a conference, okay?"

"Mmmmmm," Healey said.

"I'll be out of town tomorrow. Friday morning at ten, okay?"

Healey carefully recorded the date in his calendar so as not to forget it. He was forgetting everything these days. He'd had to leave his bicycle at the rack all night because he couldn't remember the combination to the lock. Restless, he went to see Cathy Gobrin. The little girl had been moved to a private room on the grounds that she needed special care. Coiled into a ball at the head of her bed, Cathy managed a subdued "Hi, dotor."

"Her mother will have to be told soon," Olga warned.

He muttered, "I know," but he still resisted, waiting for... what, a miracle?

Where was Wallon? Suppose it should turn out that in some fashion, not yet established, Ad had been exposed to a new virus, what then? A disease's nature, means of spread, carriers, symptomatology, prognosis had to be established, the proper authorities alerted. Of what? Of a new disease that caused... It was very confusing. Cathy Gobrin demonstrated reduced intelligence, but she might be a special case, uniquely susceptible. What other signs might there be? On the legal pad Healey wrote

Virus "X"
Symptomatology:
   Sluggishness
   Mental aberrations (voices?)
   Irritability

At the Center for Disease Control in Atlanta, which monitored serious infectious illness like Legionnaire's disease, such symptoms would hardly raise eyebrows.

Healey kept raising his head, expecting Coral to enter. Her bag was on the desk, but it seemed she had been gone a long time, and it was past 5 P.M. He paced the office, putting his finger in the potted plants. Bone dry—Coral had forgotten to water again. "Forget," "forget": the word seemed to intrude on him continually. He looked at the pad, tempted to add "Forgetfulness" to the list of possible symptoms, changed his mind and went to the men's room instead, keeping an eye out for Coral Blanchard.

On the way back he heard a tapping noise he couldn't identify. *Tap-tap-tap.* Following his ears, Healey came to a side corridor down which was the cold room where Coral stored plants and flowers. His pace quickened.

The gaunt woman stood behind the glass door, shoulders hunched under her sweater, chin trembling, eyes frightened. "Coral! What in the world?" he cried as he freed her.

"Brrrrrrrr."

"Are you all right?"

"Brrrr. I . . . brrrrr . . . think so."

"You would have frozen! Why did you stay in there?"

"I . . . brrrr . . . couldn't get the door open."

He tried the inside handle, which stuck slightly. "You couldn't figure it out?"

"I . . . must have panicked. Doctor, I'll catch pneumonia for sure!"

The dispensary would fill the prescription for an antihistamine on which she insisted. Healey wrote "Forgetfulness," then "Lapses in performance?" He was contemplating the list when the telephone startled him.

"It's me," said Wallon.

"Where are you, Ad?"

"At my office."

"Office? How long have you been there?"

"Most of the afternoon, I guess."

"You got my message?" Wallon's silence represented affirmation. "Why didn't you call? I've been waiting for hours. Don't tell me you forgot!"

"No, I just didn't want to," Wallon said. "Let's meet in the cafeteria? I could use some coffee."

The change the cashier gave him was four dollars short. Healey said, "Coffee prices as bad as that?"

"What? You must be mistaken, Dr.... Dr...."

"Healey." The woman had always known his name before. When he showed her the bills, she snatched a one-dollar from his hand and gave him a five without apology.

Wallon waited at a side table Healey had selected for privacy. He looked disheveled and needed a shave. He wore heavy-framed eyeglasses that made him seem older. "Couldn't find my contacts," he explained when Healey asked.

"How was Boston?"

"Bad. One of my kids seems to have developed a per-personality problem. They wanted to kick him out of school, but I won him a reprieve. I hope to hell he shapes up."

"Why didn't you want to see me?"

"Didn't want another lecture."

"This won't be one. We've been friends for a long time. I respect you, Ad," Healey said tentatively.

"Cut the crap," Wallon said, leaning forward.

"You really haven't been yourself recently and you know it."

"The subject *is* Four Roses, isn't it?" Wallon said, wincing.

Healey ignored him. "I remember how you acted at my house when you got furious over nothing and got all twisted up in your thoughts."

"Maybe I did have a bag on," Wallon said.

"The corny Polish jokes you baited poor Benson with. You're not cruel.... Your work..."

Wallon betrayed anxiety with a jerk of his head. "All right, all right. Perhaps the booze is slowing me down. I'll lay off. There! I've said it for you."

"Maybe you've got the sequence wrong. If you're having a hard time in your work, you might want to avoid the realization."

"Lay off!" Wallon screamed in a tiny voice. "How many neurons do I have? How many synapses? Trillions! So I lose a few..."

Healey raised a hand as if to ward off Wallon's glare. "Hear me out. Tell me, very carefully, exactly what happened in the lab two weeks ago Monday."

"You're still interested in accidents! Why?"

"I'll explain later. Start at the beginning. I want to hear everything."

Wallon lit a cigarette. "I arrived at the lab a little after eight," he recited. "Finished my coffee outside. Went in. Changed. Almost forgot to remove my contact lenses. I wonder where in hell I put them..."

"Why did you come in so early?"

"A hangover, if you must know. Case of the guilts."

"Go on."

"Jesus, you sound like a DNA...I mean DA. I was working with the SV forty virus. I took the dishes to the Zeiss..." Wallon abruptly closed his eyes as though he'd fallen asleep.

"Ad?" Healey called.

The eyes popped open. "Where was I?"

"You took the petri dishes to the microscope. From the glove box." When Wallon said nothing, Healey asked sharply, "You did use the glove box, as regulations require?"

"I..."

"Yes?"

"I'm sure I used the glove box right along."

"So you went to the glove box a good many times? And always you put plastic slips over the dishes? Or did you skip that step somewhere along the way and put the dish beneath the scope with no cover on it, as all of us prefer?" Healey reached out and seized Wallon's arm. It had the resistance of cooked spaghetti. "Tell me!"

"I can't remember," Wallon said, burying his nose in his coffee cup.

"That won't do!" Healey looked to see whether eavesdroppers had been attracted. He persisted, "Come on, it's less than three weeks."

"Seems like a year."

"To you, maybe. Try to remember."

"I'm trying, goddammit! It's...fuzzy. Maybe I...I might have looked at the first dish without a cover slip, yes. I might have..."

"Dipped the objective into the culture?"

"It's possible. Entirely possible."

"But did you?"

"Oh God. It's like my head's full of shit. I can't recall clearly. *I did, yes.*"

"Lower your voice," Healey hissed. He felt cold all over. "Then what?"

"I'm drawing a blank. I seem to see something, but I have no words. Understand?"

"Act it out. Try pantomime."

With evident effort Wallon complied. His agitated fingers had already sloshed coffee into the saucer. He raised the cup, wiped the bottom with the edge of a napkin and then, eyes sightless as a seer's, brought the paper to his forehead. The napkin's tip left a brown spot on the edge of his nose. Though an ashtray stood near, he drowned his cigarette in the cup. "I was feeling sick. I'm feeling sick now too."

"I don't doubt it. The napkin's meant to be lens tissue?" Wallon weakly gestured assent, and Healey stared at the brown spot. "The tissue passed or touched your nose. Good Lord, it had virus on it!"

"I attached no importance. I'd even forgotten. The SV forty is harmless," Wallon mumbled.

"By itself! But that stuff had human DNA in it, including an unidentified section," Healey said quickly. "The virus we designed couldn't have caused symptomatology. If this one does, it means the extra DNA is active."

"What symptoms are you talking about?" Wallon asked quietly.

"I don't know. Erratic behavior...forgetfulness ...mental aberrations. The point is, suppose the new virus adversely affected your performance. Not understanding, wouldn't you be nervous? Wouldn't you reach for a drink if only because of the jitters?"

"If this is some fancy ploy to make me give up booze, I have to hand it to you. You are goddam ingenious, Healey," Wallon shouted.

Healey laughed uproariously. "Yes, I concocted the whole thing to make you stop drinking."

Wallon seemed to shrink in his chair. "You believe I've contracted this thing?" Healey nodded. "Could it be fatal?"

"A legitimate question," answered Healey, with a hint of cruelty, "but, no, I don't think so. If it killed I think we'd already have evidence. Others undoubtedly have it too."

Wallon said slowly, "Who?"

"Cathy might well be one."

"Cathy Gobrin?" Absorbing this information, Wallon started to pant. "Good God! You're talking about IQ loss!"

"That isn't established," said Healey with a shrug. "The girl might be a special case. With me, the main effect so far is a lot of—what shall I call it?—cerebral static."

"You have noises in your head?"

Healey nodded.

"Christ. Are we infectious?"

"Not anymore, I expect. A week to ten days is standard with viruses. I don't see why this one should be different. And SV forty is neurotropic. Once it takes up residence in the brain it shouldn't be infectious. Don't you agree?"

"I suppose so." Wallon stared at him and suddenly wailed, "Do you blame me?"

Healey did, as a matter of fact, but remonstrations would get them nowhere. He said only, "I wish you'd stuck to procedures."

Wallon babbled, "Those goddam government regulations are responsible! Without them we'd have finished the week before, and none of this would have happened!"

Amazed by the *post hoc, ergo propter hoc* reasoning, Healey said mildly, "That's stupid, Ad."

"Don't call me stupid!" Wallon shouted, fury furrowing his round face. Heads around them turned. "And let me tell you something else! It's all bullshit, you hear! There isn't any new virus! The thing's impossible! You're dreaming, Healey—either that or you want to punish me!"

DAY EIGHTEEN

One reason why Healey did not at once inform his other colleagues of the situation was that he wanted to subject them to a test, the results of which might be more accurate if they knew nothing.

Wallon, of course, might have told them, but probably reinforced by a night of drinking, Ad had become unshakably convinced that the new virus didn't exist or wasn't dangerous even in the unlikely event that it did. One could still believe that, Healey had to admit, but what a rationalization! Wallon didn't want his accident revealed. "How *American* you are," he taunted Healey. "A hypo-hypochondriac like all of you. Virus my ass! Cathy reverted because of the PKU. She was damaged goods, that's all. So where's the proof of your goddam new virus? Show me. I'm from Missouri."

"Is that part of Belgium?" asked Healey with a frown.

But one individual had to be informed. Healey lured Mel Orenstein to his office to discuss Cathy Gobrin's fate. The psychiatrist announced that the little girl, in his view, was incurable and ought to be institutionalized.

"No. Not until I'm utterly sure her condition is irreversible. There *must* be a way to help her. We haven't found it yet," he said staunchly, but wondering whether he believed this himself. He added, "How does a person feel about getting less smart?"

"You mean Cathy? She hasn't the vaguest comprehension..."

"I was thinking of my own mother," Healey said untruthfully. "She's becoming senile, and she's partly aware."

"The change is gradual, and people grow accustomed to it. That's one of the problems. Their families don't realize what's happened—not at once, anyway—so you have all sorts of messy situations, without anyone recognizing the real culprit. You know, husbands and wives fighting over something one of their parents has said or done, not understanding... Where was I?"

"How the affected person feels."

"Yes. As I said, the person becomes accustomed... nature has a way of softening things." Instead of his customary staccato speech, Orenstein was talking slowly, with frequent pauses. "On the other hand, I have to admit that people are remarkably sensitive about IQ. A study of the hippies in Haight-Ashbury showed that although they rejected almost every norm of American life, they were wild to know their IQ scores. Another study says people rate intelligence tops in terms of personal worth—above sex appeal, looks, athletic ability, even riches."

Healey looked at Orenstein intently and said, "Suppose *you* suffered IQ loss, Mel. Could you handle it?"

"What a question! Everybody's IQ declines with age, which is why the tests are renormed for different groups.

But what you lose in speed you can make up for in depth—that is, if you stay alert, as I do."

"Suppose you didn't?"

"Didn't what?" Orenstein asked suspiciously.

"Stay alert."

"Adjust, I suppose. I'm a mature individual, Jim. One develops resiliency, strength, is not easily shaken..."

Healey inspected Orenstein's flat face. "It might be harder than you think."

"*What* might be harder? You're talking in riddles."

Healey laid out the situation—Wallon's carelessness, his infectivity, Healey's own disequilibrium. Orenstein looked appalled as he understood it. "It seems possible to me, from what I've seen, that functioning intelligence might be affected."

"What!" Orenstein shouted. "I can't believe it! I won't hear another word. IQ loss? Give me cancer first."

"How else can you account for Cathy Gobrin?"

"I *can't* account for Cathy Gobrin! Maybe she fell out of bed and cracked her skull for all I know. But I have no such symptomatology—I swear it!"

"You were exposed by Cathy. You had to have been. But maybe you're lucky. Maybe some people don't catch it or have symptoms. I hope you're one. Mmmmmm," crept out before he could cut it off. "Mel, is there such a thing as a self-administered IQ test?"

"Well, yes."

"Do you know your IQ?"

"Roughly."

"Mmmmmm. Would you be willing to test yourself, if only as a control?"

"Would I?" Fidgeting in his chair. Orenstein seemed astonished. "I guess so. I can't think of any reason why not—I kind of wish I could. All right, I'll do it, if only to put this nonsense of yours to rest. But I'm pretty busy today. How about next week?"

"Come on, Mel. Let's get it over with."

The psychiatrist departed, expression serene. An hour

133

later he returned to Healey's office, carefully closing the door, though Coral was at lunch. Orenstein suddenly threw himself down on the leather couch and cried shakily, "I wasn't completely honest before. I *have* noticed changes in myself. My work's been sloppy. I've been irritable for no reason, and the goddamnedest idea is loose in my head." He licked his lips with a long pink tongue. "I even heard myself say it out loud. No one heard, thank God. I'd be ruined in this WASP's nest." He faltered but went on. "It's like an obsession, but there's a voice in my mind telling me over and over that Jews are smarter than other people," Orenstein admitted.

"Do you believe that, Mel?"

Orenstein said, after a strained silence, "I guess I must. No wonder. A Jew is taught, almost by osmosis, that he'd better be smart or else, that Jewish intelligence was our principal survival tool all these centuries. Even Jewish religion implicitly makes the commandment 'Thou shalt have no other gods before me.' It took tremendous social intelligence to move from the labyrinth of polytheism to the paradigm of monotheism, and the Jews did it long before anyone else.... Where was I?" asked Orenstein anxiously.

"A voice says you're smarter because you're a Jew."

"That's why it's so goddam humiliating... to learn... I can't tell you how much... tests for people my age aren't accurate to start with, much less self-tests... I've lost IQ points... a lot... I couldn't even understand questions I would have breezed through before.... What will happen to me? To become old, yes, but old and *stupid*..." He cupped his bent head with both hands in the shape of a yarmulke and wailed, "The IQ disease... the stupid sickness..."

"I'm afraid you'll have plenty of company," Healey said.

After lunch, he talked to his team. He wanted them to take the routine blood test and then assist Mel Orenstein in an entirely different matter. They balked but at last agreed. The psychiatrist, waiting in a room used for psychological appraisals, explained that he wanted each to take an IQ test he himself had devised for exceptionally intelligent adults, in order to gauge its accuracy. Did they know their IQ scores? All did, and Orenstein instructed them to record the numbers on a form. Then, with surprisingly little protest, the scientists were taken to individual cubicles, given two sharpened pencils and mimeographed sheets Orenstein had hastily prepared, and told to begin. "Time is part of the measurement," Orenstein said. "Now don't be nervous—anxiety can affect the results."

Healey had to confess apprehension as Orenstein placed the questionnaire before them. Tests, he remembered fleetingly, had made him nervous at school. It had never been a question of flunking but of satisfying parental aspirations to have him succeed. What had been the criterion of success? Doing well in tests, it seemed. And he had excelled at them, anxiety or not. He had the kind of mentality that *understood* tests, could almost place itself inside the mind of the mind of the person who had prepared the questions. It was as much a matter of cunning and agility as comprehension. Did he still have these gifts?

Orenstein said, "Begin," and closed the cubicle door.

The first cluster of questions aimed at measuring verbal ability.

Circle the numbered word that means the same or most nearly the same as the one in capital letters.

1. RELEVANT
   (a) germane
   (b) meaningful
   (c) important
   (d) appropriate
   (e) supportive

Hesitating between "appropriate" and "germane," Healey circled the latter.

4. TAUTOLOGY
   (a) hyperbole
   (b) paraphrasis
   (c) pleonasm
   (d) ellipsis
   (e) parapraxia

He felt certain he knew the right word but failed to identify it. If only Ruth were there to help... not that Ruth seemed to have quite the verbal ability she used to.... Ruth... *Don't let your mind wander! Eliminate the wrong ones!* His mental pencil crossed off "paraphrasis" and then "hyperbole." He groped his way into the verbal thicket of "parapraxia" and stumbled out again, no wiser. He didn't recognize the word. "Pleonasm"—good God, it meant... Quick! He circled "parapraxia," hoping for the best.

Healey pushed on, identifying, eliminating, guessing.

Circle the numbered word that means the opposite or most nearly the opposite to the one in capital letters.
18. IMPRUDENT
   (a) wise
   (b) stingy
   (c) ungenerous
   (d) cautious
   (e) regulated

Which? *Come on, brain, think! She has pimples on her butt*... Stop! "Regulated"? Wait. It would be the word most like "prudent." He circled "cautious."

26. PARAGON
   (a) fault
   (b) nadir
   (c) worthless
   (d) negation
   (e) imperfection

Healey gnashed his teeth. In his head, gears stuck, wheels refused to turn. He who once compared his mind to a fine watch had only a Mickey Mouse left. Which word? He marked "nadir" with the glum sensation of being wrong.

Grogginess assailed Healey when he reached the section that appeared to measure quantitative ability.

Choose the best answer to each of the following questions.

37. 40% of 40=25% of
  (a) 16
  (b) 32
  (c) 64
  (d) 128

That was easy: 64. But though mathematics had been among his best subjects, he was soon in trouble again.

43. If one-sixth of a number plus 3 times the number equals 76, what is the number?
  (a) 18
  (b) 22
  (c) 24
  (d) 26

A precious minute elapsed before Healey checked "24."

57. If two similar triangles have bases in the ratio of 2:3, what is the ratio of their areas?
  (a) 1:1.67
  (b) 2:3
  (c) 4:6
  (d) 4:9

He couldn't see it, simply couldn't. Blindly, he chose the third answer.

73. In the following question decide which one of the numbered figures can be made from the pattern on the left.

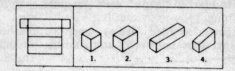

Healey circled "2." That was a snap, he believed.

Finally, there were science questions, some easy, some not:

89. In a certain population, 1 out of 10 of the men has a hereditary visual defect that is transmitted through a single allele on the X chromosome. What proportion of the women in this population is likely to have the defect?
   (a) 1/100
   (b) 1/50
   (c) 1/20
   (d) 1/10

102. The equation $_{19}^{40}K \rightarrow _{20}^{40}Ca \not{\succ} _{-1}^{0}e + v$ represents an example of the process called
   (a) alpha decay
   (b) beta decay
   (c) position emission
   (d) orbital electron capture

First of the group to finish, Healey nodded to Orenstein over the partition, turned in his questionnaire and went to his office to wait.* The results of the blood tests arrived. There were six of them, the last being a retest

---

*Later Orenstein showed Healey a copy of the test with the correct answers marked. For the questions covered they were: 1, a; 4, c; 18, d; 26, c; 37, c; 43, c; 57, d; 73, 3; 89, a; 102, b.

Orenstein had designed this test for use by graduate students because ordinary IQ tests were too simple. He had normed the results and felt them to be accurate, even with a small sample.

of Cathy Gobrin's blood. The five scientists all showed antibodies for Simian Virus 40, but all would naturally have them, having received the early Salk polio shots. The little girl had no SV 40 antibodies, nor did any of the six have antibodies that were unusual or new.

Healey pondered this information. Viruses had to leave footprints in the form of antibodies with which the immunological system fought them. Evidently the human DNA in the SV 40 had changed it into a different virus. Why wasn't it registering? More than one virus? Were they testing for the right antigens? Some viruses masked their presence. Virus X—if it existed; there was still no absolute proof—might do the same. There was, however, another way, a special test called cell-mediated immunity, which utilized white blood cells. The CMI procedure required several days in the lab and couldn't be rushed. Although it could never be used for mass screening, it might identify the enemy. Healey ordered the test for blood samples from all six. He would get the results on Monday.

It was dark outside when Orenstein wearily arrived. "I've scored the tests," he explained, "and correlated them with the original IQs. I'll assume the old figures are roughly accurate, though people do tend to lie upwards a little. Oh, by the way, what is—was—your IQ? You didn't record it."

"I forgot to. It's one sixty-five I think," Healey said.

Orenstein licked his lips and wrote the number. "All right, Summer, from 149 to 120, down twenty-nine points. Frazer, 152 to 126, off twenty-six points. Benson, another sharp decline, twenty-seven points, from 146 to 119. Here's Wallon, and it's awful. From 168 to 128!"

Healey's shock emerged as exasperation. "You make it sound like a bad day on the stock market," he complained. "Could Wallon have been drinking before the test?"

"I'm supposed to test the alcohol in his system too? I'm not a traffic cop," Orenstein retorted.

"I wish it were alcohol! On the other hand, Wallon

probably got the biggest dose of the virus. Also he was taking medication—cortisone—which could have affected his resistance. Forty points..."

Healey realized that he didn't want Orenstein to read the next number—his. He stopped, and the psychiatrist said, "You've lost IQ too." Healey wriggled as Orenstein paused, then said, with a certain satisfaction, "Twenty-five points, to one forty."

"Maybe I had a bad day," Healey said, regretting it.

"The whole group of you?" He went on, as though to soften the impact. "The numbers are all approximate, of course, but it's kind of terrifying all the same."

"Kind of! Where does it bottom out? And what happens if an average-IQ individual loses thirty or forty points? He or she would be almost an idiot."

"I have a hunch, from a preliminary reading of Cathy Gobrin's scores, that it might not work like that," Orenstein said. "Could it be that the mentally bigger you are, the harder you fall? The higher the IQ, the greater the penalty? People with more to lose would lose it. An individual with an average IQ might decline less, percentilewise."

"Do people object to taking IQ tests?"

"On the contrary. They kind of like it—or used to." Orenstein grimaced.

"Well, our people—and Cathy too—ought to be tested repeatedly until we have the clinical picture. It's not just intelligence we're dealing with, you understand. There are emotional complications. Are the anger flashes I've seen caused by the disease or the IQ problem itself? I mean, might the human psyche be enraged at the sudden loss of mental capability?"

Orenstein muttered. "Who knows what the psyche knows? We don't even understand intelligence in the first place. No definitive definition exists."

"Isn't 'definitive definition' a tautology, Mel?" Healey asked wryly. He recalled question four in the IQ test and, too late, had the answer. "Pleonasm."

"Pleonasm? What does that mean?"

"Pleonasm. A redundancy. You made up the questions, didn't you?"

"I forgot," Orenstein said, humble. "Well, the question before the house is me. I'm supposed to administer and score the IQ tests. How long will I have the ability to perform my duties if you're right?" Orenstein, it seemed, was still not quite convinced.

"The same applies to me." *GUAGUA*.

Orenstein began talking about IQ tests. They weren't necessarily reliable, he repeated, as if in self-defense. Binet and Simon, the fathers of intelligence testing—no, grandfathers: the IQ test would be seventy-five years old in 1980, though the Frenchmen hadn't used the term IQ. A German had devised it, dividing mental age by chronological age and multiplying by 100. Where was he? Orenstein asked. Oh yes. Binet and Simon saw intelligence as an attribute of behavior. (Before them, the concept of intelligence wasn't known; the nineteenth century failed to distinguish intelligence from soul, human nature, sensation, wish, consciousness, perception, etc., etc.) Binet would have resisted the notion of intelligence as a fixed and immutable number, imbued with magic by a technological society whose real ambition was to catalog and computerize human beings in order to bend them to the needs of the machine. For Binet, a truly great thinker, intelligence was the ability to adapt, learn, improve.... With us, though, it had become a mass measurement. IQ was a position on an interval scale, a measure of relative intelligence. A person with an IQ of 150 wasn't twice as smart as one with 75. They merely occupied different slots in terms of averages. About 2 percent of the population were retarded—that is, IQ 70 and below. Something under 7 percent were borderline— IQ 80 and below. The dull normals—IQ 80 to 90—were about 16 per cent. Fifty percent of the people were average—IQ 90 to 110. It was exactly the same on the ascending side: bright normal—IQ 110 to 120—16 percent; superior—IQ 120 to 130—something under 7 percent; and very superior—IQ 130 and up—about 2 percent.

"Well and good," interrupted Healey, who was familiar with this material, "but what would happen if IQ were to drop on a mass scale?"

"I imagine," Orenstein said, "that IQ would be renormed."

"Renormed?"

"Do you understand what average IQ is, Jim?"

"A hundred, isn't it?"

"By definition. But it isn't arrived at by averaging everybody who takes the tests. Originally the tests were normed, with the whole population represented by a statistical sample, and the average score of one hundred was arrived at. Over the years, average IQ rose. In the early seventies, for instance, the average six-year-old scored upwards of one hundred seven."

"Why?" Healey interrupted.

"Diet and, believe it or not, television. It gives the kids wider exposure. But average scores headed down with increasing age, until ten-year-olds were nearly back at the old average."

"Why?" Healey asked again.

"Schools, partly. They teach kind of how they always taught, and people respond as they always have. But average IQ was still higher than it had been, so to return it to one hundred, a new statistical sample was tested with harder questions. What would happen if mean IQ became ninety, say? You'd likely renorm the test with easier questions or make and standardize a new one to make the average one hundred again."

"Everything would be back to normal," Healey said bitterly.

"IQ-wise it would," said Orenstein. "Otherwise not. Definitely not."

"But is IQ everything when it comes to mental ability?" Healey asked, almost as though trying to keep fear from his voice.

Orenstein replied immediately. "I've known people—we all have—who may not test in the higher percentiles but who have good minds regardless. There are hundreds of tests measuring various skills and aptitudes, and such individuals might do much better on some of those, but the basic question is why straight IQ fails to tell the whole story in such cases. That's one of the problems in this business—a high-school kid finds his IQ isn't so hot and feels devastated. The kid shouldn't. Some people just don't do well at tests, and IQ doesn't measure creativity, perseverence, intuitiveness and dozens of other qualities displayed by the gifted and successful. IQ is a narrow-gauge measurement, and few pretend it's anything else."

"Yes, but will the sorts of abilities not associated with straight IQ be affected by the stupid sickness too?"

"I don't see why not," Orenstein grumbled. "The virus can't distinguish one kind of smarts from another. To it they're all the same."

DAY NINETEEN

There was more information for Healey to assimilate on Friday before his meeting with the director. Orenstein had plotted Cathy's IQ curve on the basis of frequent tests, the latest only just completed. "As I suspected, the drop looks roughly exponential—large at first, then smaller and smaller. If that's true, Cathy ought to bottom in the high sixties or low seventies."

"Poor little kid," said Healey.

"She's kind of a special case, don't forget. The virus probably knocked out all the gains she'd made in one fell swoop. Think of her starting with an IQ base of ninety or so."

"What about the rest of us?"

"Not enough data to predict," said Orenstein.

Ruth called, sounding wan. "I have some rotten news. I

had Jennie retested as you wanted. I talked to the school just now. Jennie is nowhere near as bright as she was."

"How many points did she lose?"

"Twenty-five, I think. Or twenty-six. I forget. It's insane. Why, she's practically *average*," Ruth said with distaste.

"That leaves her with one twenty-eight or one twenty-nine. Not exactly average. Anyway, people vary a lot in their IQ scores. It's normal."

"I must say you sound casual about it."

"Mmmmmm." But he wasn't, not at all. His own daughter! His mind began to confuse Cathy and Jennie until he saw them as one, tottering on the verge of idiocy. Healey tried to calm himself. The critical fact was that the first proof of the disease's spread beyond the hospital had presented itself. He remembered clearly how Jennie had emerged in her bathrobe during dinner that Wednesday and Wallon had seized and kissed her. Healey's dread deepened.

A funny thing happened on the way to the director's office, he was thinking a few minutes later as he left his own. I forgot his name. It was preposterous, impossible. He knew _____'s name almost as well as his own, and yet it had vanished. Disappeared from his mind like the twelve state capitals he failed to remember when biking to the hospital that morning. He had potholes in his brain, it seemed. _____? He felt even sillier because he knew that _____'s surname and last name sounded the same and should have been that much easier to recall. He started down the alphabet. Aron Aaron? No. Ben Benn? Charles Charles? Dominick Dominick? Edgar Edgar? Frank Frank? George George? Henry Henry? *Mmmmmm.* Isador Isador? Joseph Joseph? No, no, no, no. Healey was driving himself crazy and couldn't stop.

_____ didn't have his name on his office door, either, just a plate with DIRECTOR on it, which was typical of _____'s arrogance. Expecting people to know his name, he could see no point in parading it. Healey entered, smiling grimly at _____'s secretary. "Good morning, Dr. Healey!" she exclaimed. "My, you're punctual. Dr. Herrmann will see you right away."

Herrmann! He'd thought of the name the very moment she uttered it. Herman Herrmann. Unforgettable, and yet... He entered Herrmann's office, closing the door behind him. Herrmann stood gauntly by the window, his beaked nose in outline, holding a pile of correspondence, which he leafed through rapidly. "Hi, James Healey," he said. "Be right with you."

"Take your time, Herman Herrmann."

Healey sat down, pushing his chair farther from the director's carved oak desk, and tried to decide how to break the news. Herman Herrmann was not only highly intelligent, but rather immodest about it, having let slip more than once that his IQ stood at 200. His prodigious reading speed—he could read an ordinary book of nonfiction in an hour, he boasted; fiction in less—enabled him to keep up with developments all over science, as revealed by the stack of journals on his desk, which seemed even taller today than usual, and to be more than a dilettante in other fields as well. Herman Herrmann liked to call himself a futurist.

The director turned from the window without taking his eyes from the correspondence and finished reading just as he sat down and said, "I find it's more efficient to get one thing done before starting another, even if I have to rush like hell. I stylize myself as more of a shark than an octopus, though my wife says I'm too thin to be a shark. So I'm a neo-shark."

Healey sometimes had the impression that Herrmann's references to his own habits of mind and work were meant to be remembered and repeated by others, perhaps to a journalist collecting material for an article on him or, even better, to his eventual biographer. Healey replied, "If you want a job done, find a busy man, eh?"

Herrmann showed appreciative teeth. "Coffee?" Healey said no. "Well, we still have that problem. The

147

bunch I told you about—the Coalition for a New Public Health—has scheduled its demonstration for next week or the week after."

"Oh, no," Healey muttered.

Herrmann glanced at him sharply. "What's the matter?"

"Nothing."

"No? All right. Naturally we're opposed to a demonstration, but I've come up with a thought Tish Wyler likes. We give them the use of our auditorium and let them scream all they want. It'll keep them off the street. Let them have press coverage too. After all, protest is mostly narcissism. To see themselves in the media mirror is really what they want."

"Did they accept?"

"Certainly," Herrmann said at once. "And they've agreed to give us a chance to present our side. The very fact that we're willing to engage in a dialogue shows we have nothing to hide. Civilized, don't you think?"

"Oh yes," said Healey.

"We'll want our most able and articulate spokesman, of course, which means you, and possibly Ad Wallon. Are you willing? Probably they'll heckle some, but ignore it. I'll be at the rostrum in any case."

"I can't speak for Wallon."

"I'll talk with him myself."

"I'm not sure he'll be able to help you."

"My God you're cryptic today! Is something wrong?" When Healey said nothing Herrmann stroked the flying bridge of his nose and said, as though from a distance, "How's the work coming? Will you finish next week at least?"

Healey said harshly, "Herman, I don't think we can, no."

"Perhaps you could explain why?"

When Healey had finished, Herrmann's face was the color of cardboard. "I don't believe it. Tell me again. Only the salient points."

"Wallon," said Healey, shrugging helplessly, "was exposed to the virus we made. Probably it came in through the respiratory tract. It probably lodged in the lungs for a while—say a week, during which time Wallon was infectious—and then went to the brain. I don't know what the virus is—there's been no chance yet to try to isolate the protein, and no antibody has shown up—but call it the PAH virus, since the organism was designed to produce phenylalanine hydroxylase, or PAH, which catalyzes the conversion of phenylalanine into tyrosine. With the extra snip of DNA it contained, it might— probably does—cause an over-production of tyrosine, then neurotransmitters, the next step in the chain. Protein metabolism would be interfered with, and the neurotransmitters might affect neural firing across the synapses. I'm conjecturing, of course, but you might anticipate a loss in short-term memory and an effect on intelligence."

"How much for how long?"

"Those are the questions. The body might have more trouble accepting the DNA than we expected, in which case the effects might be temporary. Or the body might neutralize the PAH virus in some way. Or..." Healey had difficulty taking his own logic to its conclusion. "...the change could be permanent because the new DNA becomes part of the brain cells, as we originally intended. You could have progressive intellectual decline to almost anywhere." He spread his fingers.

"And it's infectious," Herrmann repeated.

"The new DNA changed the SV forty into a communicable disease, apparently, transmitted by coughing, kissing, even breathing."

"Is that why you're sitting across the room? Afraid you'll give it to me?"

"Maybe so, unconsciously. But I'm sure I'm not infectious any longer. I know when I got it."

"And the virus is spreading?" questioned Herman Herrmann. A buzzer sounded, and he ordered into the phone, "No calls, please. I don't want to be disturbed, no matter what." His bulbous eyes never left Healey's.

"Mmmmmm. I think so."

"You're talking about a possible epidemic," Herrmann said finally.

Healey had resisted that term. "I suppose I am." He recalled Orenstein's words. "An IQ disease. The stupid sickness."

Herman Herrmann's Adam's apple plunged and rose. "Facts are friendly—it's better to accept the truth. In the last few days all kinds of little problems have arisen here—maintenance, billing, nursing, patients. I thought it was one of those times when everything goes wrong at once, but if you're right, the stupid sickness may be spreading through the hospital."

"And beyond," said Healey, thinking of possible carriers, like Jennie.

Herrmann's gaunt face seemed to harden. "But how do you know? Maybe the IQ declines are a fluke. *You* don't seem any different." He watched Healey keenly.

"But I am different, and I know it. I can tell without an IQ test. I've lost capability. My memory's not what it was. It's hard to describe, but strange thoughts dance in my head—nonsense, mostly. That's part of it too, I think."

Herrmann said briskly, "Well, I don't have it, that's for sure. My brain is fully functional. I'm sure I won't contract it, which is fortunate. Assuming the virus exists—I'm still darned skeptical—we'll need some very clear heads around here. Could a special immunity be conferred by an extremely high IQ? Mine is..."

He trailed off foolishly, as if aware he had already imparted the number to Healey, who said, "Well, *you* seemed yourself, the way you tore through that correspondence." It was his turn to watch intently.

"Right. My functions are functional. I mean..." Suddenly Herman Herrmann pounded his high forehead with a fist, muttering almost unintelligibly, "I didn't read a word of it."

"What did you say?"

Herrmann looked away and shouted, "Of the correspondence! I went through the motions to convince myself . . . and you! I can't read the journals, either!" He jabbed a stiff, skinny finger at his desk. "Look at that pile! I haven't touched it in days. My brain, my beautiful brain, what's happened to it? I can't concentrate! My head's full of garbage! Listen, when I was a kid I knew a lot of limericks. I thought I'd forgotten them, but now they're occupying my mind like an invading army."

"Yes, old stuff comes to the surface. I've noticed the same." *Round and round, Beans, beans, She has pimples on her . . .*

Herman Herrmann was reciting: "The last time I dined with the king/ He did an unusual thing./ He stood on a stool/ And pulled out his tool/ And said, 'If I play will you sing?' Hear that? If you asked me for the second law of thermodynamics, I'd recite a limerick. Oh God." Herrmann lowered his bald head to the desktop. When he raised it his face looked older—though surely Healey imagined that. "I have the stupid sickness, all right. Another victim." Herrmann strummed the polished wood. "But where did I get it and when?"

"When did you make your last inspection of the wards?" Healey asked finally.

"About two weeks ago. I've been remiss."

"Did you kiss Cathy Gobrin?"

"How could I *not* kiss Cathy Gobrin?"

"She gave you the disease with a Judas kiss."

Herman Herrmann shuddered. "How do you know it's not lethal?"

"The deterioration would have been greater, even without fatalities, which there haven't been. That doesn't mean the thing's not serious, though."

"What a mess. Who is aware?"

"Only Mel Orenstein. He won't talk. And Wallon. But he won't talk, either. He may not be able to after a while, even if he wanted. Wallon's getting dumb, I think."

A masklike calm covered Herrmann's countenance.

"You say you don't know how far mean IQ will drop? The policy implications are unbelievable. Who's to run the country if mass intelligence declines? What about defense? In an IQ pandemic, will soldiers know how to operate weapons? Missiles, fighters? We might lose the capacity for warfare."

It occurred to Healey that Herrmann had a strong streak of megalomania and perceived an opportunity to exercise it. "That might be one good result," he said, marshaling a half smile.

"That's stupid. Now I'm sure you've got the disease," Hermann said abruptly. "You believe the Russians wouldn't take advantage? No, we have to keep the lid on. There are other reasons too. Firstly, it's still vaguely possible the virus doesn't exist. Secondly, the effects could be temporary, right?"

"Right," said Healey uncomfortably.

"Thirdly, the effects could be permanent. In all three scenarios you'd want to maintain secrecy until you knew what the facts were."

"I can't dispute that logic," Healey said reluctantly. "Herman?"

"I'm thinking about the problem, or trying to. ...There was a young man from Assizes/Whose balls were of different sizes.... I can't get rid of them! Where was I? Yes, serious business. It might be that people will have to be treated as though they're smart even if they're not. In a deterministic world, people will need illusions. Life will have to be greatly simplified. Strong leadership will be required—perhaps a group of us, whose intelligence remains higher, will have to rule.... Don't do anything yet. Wait until you hear from me. No one must know, including your family. Business as usual until the situation is clearer." Herrmann stood. "I will fly to Washington immediately."

As Healey left, Herrmann was chanting, "One ball was small,/Almost no ball at all,/But the other was large and won prizes."

152

A new man stood door that evening, and Healey asked where Phillip was. "Out sick," came the reply. Phillip hadn't been sick as long as Healey could recall.

He entered the living room to the din from the TV set, before which sat Ruth and Jennie, transfixed. His daughter blew him a kiss, and Ruth called cheerfully, "Hello, Jim. I didn't hear you come in."

"How could you over that racket? What are you watching, a quiz show? Lord, what nonsense. How do you stand it?"

Not seeming to hear him, Ruth called as he turned to go, "Dinner will be ready soon."

Healey sat quietly at dinner, trying to sift the events of the past few days. How ironic that his very success had created a biohazard. The experiment had worked, apparently—all too well. The critics of genetic transplants had been proved right—and by himself of all people. What a pill to have to swallow! He suddenly wondered whether good—which he still hoped recombinant DNA research represented—always brought the potential for evil with it. Was there a cosmic trade-off, so that benign and malign consequences always occurred together? Like life and death? Healey didn't profess to know, but on balance he still trusted that good ends would finally prevail.

Little by little the talk in the room filtered through—a concatenation of complaints, all ridiculous to him, though undoubtedly his somber mood contributed.

Ruth had been right about Flo, who had returned. From the doorway she loudly insisted that the Healeys made a slave of her. She ignored the short hours she worked.

Paul insisted that Buddy had cheated in the Vietnam war game, the final battles of which would be fought that evening.

"How can you cheat in a simulation, or whatever you call it?" Healey asked.

"Unauthorized tactics."

"Like what?"

"Sorry. Classified."

"Mmmmmm. What time will you wind up this evening?"

"That's classified too. It's a weekend."

Jennie whined about her teacher, whom she'd always liked.

"Why?"

"Mean. Picks on me. Won't let me go to the toi-toi."

"Toi-toi?"

"She's a real bitch," Ruth agreed. "If you ask me, there's a lot of deadwood at that school. I'm not at all sure we should send Jennie back. It was insane how they rushed her on that IQ test, wasn't it, Jen? Why, my little girl is the brightest child in her class, and everybody knows it. That teacher's out to get her, if you ask me. Why else would she do so badly on her math exam? She's even been talking about putting Jennie back a grade! Well, it's her fault, and the proof is that the whole class has been acting up the last few days, Jen says. I've half a mind to get that old biddy fired! As for..."

As for: her son's sloppiness (Paul just grinned); Flo's cooking (Flo had left); the low condition of *The New York Times* crossword puzzle (too stupid to fool with); Healey's insane mother, who cost them a fortune (insane now?); the dullness of her work (was Ruth in danger of being fired? Healey suddenly wondered); her boring life. Why hadn't Wallon been invited recently? she asked. "He's such fun. When he called he told me about a marvelous movie that's on TV tonight."

"Wallon called? When?"

Ruth seemed flustered. "Yesterday. Or was it today? Yes, this afternoon. Ad was home, working on his lecture notes for Aspen. He doesn't like to be alone. It makes him lonely."

"Why did he call? Did he want me?"

"You he sees all the time. He wanted to be friendly, I

suppose. The movie's a Western called *Sheriff Without a Star*. Like to watch with us?"

"Next thing we'll be having TV dinners. No thanks."

Before the movie, Ruth came to him and said, "Isn't there something funny about you wanting Jennie tested and the score she got? What do you know that I don't? Don't keep secrets from me, Jim. It isn't fair," she said, dark eyes imploring. "Is something wrong with her? Tell me!"

Healey wanted to tell his wife the truth—at least she'd have time to adjust to a new reality. But he couldn't, and, besides, he doubted that Ruth would believe him. "Nothing that I know of," he said.

Cloistered in his den, he shuffled restlessly. The article he'd started to read—when was it? So long ago—still lay on his desk, and he picked it up thoughtfully. "... rooted in a biochemical fortuity. By means of enzyme fractionation procedures, RNA polymerase was isolated ... multisubunit transcriptase ... polymerase ... multienzyme DNA replicase..." Lord! Understandable before, the text had turned into gibberish.

Spell "acrylic," he told himself. One "l" or two? Two, he decided.

Recite the names of the state capitals, he ordered, stalling at Madison.

GUAGUA.

Oh boy, he clucked at himself. He reached for "Healey's Book" and wrote, under "What Is Intelligence?":

It becomes plainer what intelligence is when you begin to lose it, as I have begun to do, it seems. Intelligence is the ability to see clearly, even lucidly. I must try to remain clearheaded, no matter what the cost. It's as though I'm on a small boat floundering in stormy seas. What do I do? I must start to jettison all my superfluous mental possessions, no matter how precious....

DAYS TWENTY
TO TWENTY-ONE

On Saturday morning Healey began an epidemiological profile of the new disease.

PAH Virus
1. *Origin:* Kellogg-Bryant Institute high-containment laboratory, recombinant DNA experiment. Virus released accidentally on Monday, March 3.
2. *Means of spread:* Oral.

Wallon spoke with his mouth close to the listener. Also, in their living room, he had coughed once or twice. Those exposed included Healey, Ruth, Jennie and Flo, whom Ad had embraced in the kitchen. Flo sang in a church choir. And Linda Summer. Healey tried not to think about her. Who else? Frazer? Benson? Lord, Wallon had spoken with Phillip downstairs. The doorman had a big family. *Mmmmmm.*

Mmmmmm. Why couldn't he stop thinking and saying *mmmmmm?* What had he noticed recently about Ruth? Healey couldn't pin it down.

The laboratory accident had occurred shortly before 8:30 A.M. on Monday, before Benson came in. Wallon said he'd felt punk all day Wednesday. Forty-eight hours, then, was the incubation period, though it might vary from individual to individual. Let's see . . . Healey had been a little under the weather that weekend, and so had Ruth and Jennie. He'd been to see his mother on Sunday and kissed her. He must have been infectious himself. Another potential victim. He might know tomorrow, when he went to visit. What about Wallon? He'd been to see Cathy on Wednesday, he'd said. The following Monday she'd begun to act strangely, though nobody had picked it up. She'd had the onset symptom, malaise. Yes, it fit. Wallon . . . went to Boston on an airplane. Suppose he'd coughed on the plane? What about Wallon's kid, the one who'd been acting up? Like Jennie, Jennie's class . . . Already there were too many potential victims to keep track of, to say nothing of the hospital staff.

3. *Incubation period:* 48 hours+
4. *Onset symptoms:*
    Malaise
    Not feeling well for several days
    Headache (Jennie)
    Irritability
    Coughing (?)
5. *Further symptomatology:*
    Forgetfulness
    Mental aberrations
    Performance lapses

The voices, certainly; Healey had no further doubt. His *I can smell your feet a smile away* and Orenstein's Jews-are-smarter voice and Herman Herrmann's limericks. Healey had to assume that all or most people afflicted with the PAH virus had, at least at the outset, strange stuff in their heads, not that they'd readily confess what.

Healey went to the kitchen, where he found Ruth emptying a tin saltshaker onto the clean kitchen table. "What are you up to?" he asked.

"That fool woman put the wrong tops on the salt and pepper."

He poured himself coffee. "Tell me again."

"Didn't you hear me the first time? I'm putting salt and pepper in the right shakers, of course."

Healey looked at the two little piles on the table and almost dropped his cup. No wonder she couldn't beat him at backgammon anymore. "Ruth, didn't it occur to you just to change the tops?"

"Why no!" she shrieked gaily. "Isn't that insane of me?"

The phone rang, and Healey grabbed it. "Jim, Herman."

Healey was tense. "Yes."

"Tell me quickly how old your little girl is and what school she attends."

"St. Mark's. She's ten."

"I'll be back to you."

"What in the world was that about?" Ruth demanded.

"They're writing a little article on us for the newsletter," he lied quickly. He had no idea why Herrmann had called. Back in his den, he added "Stupid acts" to the growing list of symptoms. But there was more to be learned. What had Ruth said? "Insane." *Mmmmmm.* "Insane." *Mmmmmm.* "Insane..." In the past, Ruth had never used "insane" that he could recall, but these days she said it continually. Like his *mmmmmm.* Paul's word seemed to be "classified." Apparently phrases wandered into one's mind like stray cats and lodged there. It was kind of terrifying, as Orenstein said. "Kind of," yes, Mel had taken to saying "kind of" repeatedly. He was appending the suffix "wise" continually, a circumlocution Healey had always detested. Healey put "Habitual new vocabulary" on the list.

In the kitchen Healey had almost dropped his coffee

cup. The team of scientists had been constantly upsetting or bumping into things. So had Coral Blanchard, but with her it came naturally. How about Coral's inability to open the cold-room door? Yes. And Robin Frazer's defeat at the hands of an inferior player? Healey added "Clumsiness—poor coordination" to his symptoms. Was good coordination, even athletic ability, a function of intelligence? He began to think so.

Healey realized an odor hovered in the room—sweet and faint. He was trying to imagine where it came from when a timid knock sounded. "Jen?" he asked instinctively.

She entered, still in pajamas though it was after noon. "Daddy," she said, sounding frightened, "Paul won't come out of his room. He's making funny noises. Mommy wants you to look."

"Paul?" he called outside his son's door. "Paul?" Hearing only a high-pitched sound, he went in. The night shades left the room in darkness, and he raised them. Torn paper, ripped boards, broken pencils littered the floor. Paul lay on the bed, fully dressed, face turned to the wall. His long body shook as he whimpered.

"Son?" Healey sat on the edge of the bed and placed his hand on Paul's quivering shoulder. "What's the matter? Are you sick?"

"No."

"Please, boy. Look at me."

Paul finally obliged, but the face he turned wore dark glasses, which, gently but firmly, Healey removed. Tears dripped onto Paul's bony cheeks. "Leave me alone," he gasped.

"Paul! What in the world? What's upset you so?"

"Nothing."

"You can tell me."

"It's..." Paul wept openly.

"Come on."

"It's Buddy. I never want to see him again."

Healey feared he was about to hear of a homosexual

episode. He said cautiously, "Why?"

"Because..." Paul's voice was curiously high-pitched. "Because he cheats." The words emerged in a gush. "If he'd only let me play one more round I would have won. I could have stalemated him, anyway. But he left at four, and I lost. I never want to see him again. I never want to play a war game again, either. Never. As long as I live. Which won't be long, I hope."

Healey might have made a joke of it had he been able to summon humor. He said uneasily, "It's only a game."

"A game," Paul whined. "To you it's a game."

"And you?"

"It's..."

"Well?"

"It's imp... impor... I can't think. Leave me alone." He faced the wall again.

"Okay, son." Healey patted him. "You'll get over it." To himself he added, "I hope."

Jennie's spitballs and paint on the bathroom walls, Paul's over-reaction—Healey added an item to the list: "Reversion to childish behavior." After much thought, centering on Orenstein's notion of Jewish intelligence, Healey introduced another: "Emergence of unresolved juvenile fantasies."

Healey stopped briefly for lunch, then returned to his compilation. The list would grow longer, he felt sure, as he continued to observe, but what he knew already pointed to noticeable behavior changes coupled with the loss of intelligence. Was that the ultimate symptom? He was considering the question when he smelled the odor again, and searching the room, he arrived at the attaché case he'd brought from the hospital. From it he extracted a perfumed handkerchief, monogrammed L.S.

L.S. Linda Summer! She, the shy one, must have crept into his office and thrust the handkerchief into his case sometime yesterday—he hadn't opened it since. What a brazen invitation! Unbelievable! The memory of her nude form danced from the wings of his mind to center stage.

His left hand crept toward his crotch. *Please Do Not Bend, Fold, Spindle or Masturbate!*

He wrote hurriedly: "Loss of inhibitions."

At dinner the kids seemed subdued, but Ruth bantered merrily, consuming a half bottle of wine. Later in the bedroom, without prelude, she told him about her two sexual affairs before she'd met and married him at twenty-two. Healey had heard those stories before and wondered why Ruth chose to repeat them.

"I was thinking that perhaps I should have had more experience before I settled down. Just think of it—only two men aside from you!"

He examined her intently. "Ruth, why did you marry me in the first place?"

"Why, because... because I loved you."

"Okay, but is that the only reason? What did you think of me?"

"You were steady, reliable, not the kind of person to chase around. I... you made me feel secure."

"So you went for security, but you had to give up something to get it. Adventure, I guess. Well, there's no point regretting the past."

"So you regret the past!" she said hotly, seeming to misinterpret him. "You're bored, I suppose! Why don't you screw around! But I get to do the same. Sauce for the goose..."

"Ruth! You've never talked that way!" Again he wanted to explain that she wasn't herself, that she had to be careful not to commit acts for which a virus was responsible, but he couldn't.

"I do now, though. Jesus, don't you get tired of marriage, Jim? Be frank."

"No," he said. Not until recently, anyway, when Ruth had started to change, when Linda Summer...

Ruth taunted him. "What are you, a schnook? Most men like some variety. They're bored doing the same thing week after week for years on end. I bet most women feel the same, only they're too goddam frightened to admit it. I'm not anymore."

He hoped she was teasing. "What do you want me to do?"

"Shake me up! Try new things! Violate me in violet time in the vilest way that you can!" Ruth chanted.

"That's schoolgirl stuff. How?"

"How do I know? I've been a housewife eighteen years. Use your imagination. Do something insane! Tie me up!"

"That doesn't especially appeal to me," he said, wrinkling his nose.

"Whip me!"

"I don't have a whip—I'm a medical doctor, not an animal trainer."

"You own a belt!" Ruth yanked at a zipper and stepped out of her dressing gown.

How short and thin she is, almost scrawny, he thought, as she stood nudely proud before him, breasts emphasized. His mind raced in neutral:

> *Once out of nature I shall never take*
> *My bodily form from any natural thing,*
> *But such a form as Grecian goldsmiths make*
> *Of hammered gold and gold enameling*
> *To keep a drowsy Emperor awake;*
> *Or set upon a golden bough to sing*
> *To lords and ladies of Byzantium*
> *Of what is past, or passing, or to come.*

"Find me attractive?"

"Sure but . . ." *She has pimples on her butt I love her.*

"Well?"

"The kids."

"Screw the kids. Anyway they're in their rooms."

"Okay, okay."

Healey returned from his closet with an old-fashioned wide leather belt he hadn't worn for years because it wouldn't fit through the loops of his trousers. There always seemed a use for things if you kept them long enough. Ruth lay on the bed, head down, arms extended, posterior slightly raised. He shook the belt nervously, and she screamed, through a mouthful of blanket, "Take off your clothes!"

"Okay," he muttered.

"Let me have it!"

"Ruth..."

"Give it to me. I want it. Now!"

He brought the leather gently to Ruth's rump, hoping her neo-masochism was satisfied. "Okay?"

"Harder!"

"No!"

"Harder, please! I want to experience pain and punishment," she gasped.

Healey became angry with his wife for the indignity she imposed on both of them. He raised his arm, really wanting to punish her for... what? For being an unwitting victim of the stupid sickness. Frightened by the sensation aroused in him, he dropped the belt. He thought with regret about a new addition to the symptoms list. "Ruth..."

"Oh, all right. Let's do it the usual way," she said reluctantly.

But Linda Summer's image beckoned, and he finally succumbed to his fantasy.

Hearing a noise, Healey woke early and followed it to the kitchen. "Flo! What are you doing here?"

"Doing?" Flo seemed mystified. "I don't understand."

"Did Ruth ask you to come in for some reason?"

"Me? No. Why?"

"It's Sunday—your day off."

"*Sunday?*"

"All day."

With an almost palpable act of will, the dark face cleared and Flo said smoothly, "I can't imagine what I was thinking about. Of course it's Sunday. I have church later on. I came in to straighten up because I can't tomorrow. I have clinic. I'm sure I told you or Ruth."

"You could have had Monday off anyway, Flo. You know that," he said. Flo visited a clinic periodically because of anemia, but Healey was sure that she meant to cover up a memory lapse. Hadn't others lied? Yes...Wallon, on not being concerned about his condition. Herrmann, pretending his vaunted IQ was intact. Ruth, feigning to be bored by the crossword puzzles. What about himself? Yes, he'd been spouting mendacities as well. But Healey didn't need more evidence: clearly, nobody cared to admit to mistakes and failures in performance. Fearful of forgetfulness, he hastened to add to his list "Defensiveness—prevarication." And then, thinking of the belt, "Propensity toward violence."

When he returned Ruth lay with her head in a pillow sandwich. They had always held each other in bed on weekend mornings, but not recently, and Healey, sensing their connubial fragility, climbed into bed intending to cuddle her. Ruth said, "Ouch."

"That was Flo. Damnedest thing...," he started to say.

"Move away. You're hurting me. I'm sore from the belt."

"Ruth! I hardly touched you!"

"Wife beater!" came her muffled yell.

When he entered the living room around noon, Healey discovered Buddy and Paul chatting amiably as if nothing had happened. Buddy wore a black jacket with metal studs over his chunky frame. Paul still had on the dark glasses—to conceal the redness of his eyes, Healey supposed. Both boys held cans of beer.

"What are you guys up to?" Healey asked.

"Classified," Paul shot back.

"Oh, that again. War gaming?"

"We're tired of war games," Paul said.

Short attention spans? "I'm not surprised. What will take its place? Studying, maybe?" He watched Paul swig his beer.

"School is basically a waste of time, I think to myself," Buddy put in.

Think to myself! How often Healey had heard that expression; only now, with his perceptions keyed to signs of the stupid sickness the redundancy registered. "Who else would you think to, Buddy?" he said tartly, annoyed because he saw Buddy—also a potential honor student, if he applied himself—as a bad influence on his impressionable son.

"Your old man's a card," said Buddy. He took a swallow and set down the empty can. "Paul, let's get out of here. We'll miss the parade."

"What parade?"

"We don't know what parade," said Paul. "It's on Fifth Avenue, like all parades. A parade's a parade."

"I have to agree with you there. What will you do afterwards?"

"Maybe shoot some pool."

"Pool? Since when have you shot pool?"

"Classified. Come on, Buddy."

Again Healey went to his mother's on foot. Probably because of the parade, cars jammed intersection after intersection. He thought again about cooperation versus selfishness. A new factor had to be considered now, the IQ disease. The day might come when drivers ignored the stoplights altogether, as if they weren't there. The prospect jolted him.

A newly minted sedan reached a red light and passed it. A young woman holding a little dog on a leash crossed with the green light. The driver swerved to avoid her. The woman started to run. The driver hurriedly changed directions again. The woman jumped. Barely missing her, the sedan raced off, passed another red light, vanished.

The dog lay still on the asphalt.

How easily that might have been you, lady, Healey thought. Or me.

"Oh, dear," said Henrietta Healey over tea, "now what was I about to say?"

"I can help you there, Mother. You haven't said anything yet," Healey replied.

"Haven't I? I thought I'd been talking a blue streak!"

"You've hardly uttered a word since I got here."

She peered at him. "Is that true?" He nodded solemnly, stirring his tea with a spoon initialed PH. For Park Hudson, not for a virus. He wished he could forget about the PAH bug for a moment. She went on, "Strange, but I thought I heard myself talk and you answer. There has been no conversation?"

"Very little. I wondered what you were thinking about."

"So I imagined myself speaking. A bad sign, isn't it?"

"Happens to all of us," he said reassuringly. Voices. The stupid sickness. So Henrietta had it too. He wished he could tell her, not that she'd understand. He wondered how arteriosclerosis would affect the disease. "Nothing to worry about."

"So you say." She bit into a cookie. "I've worried a lot recently. I haven't been myself."

"Mother..."

"Don't argue with me, James."

"All right," he said mildly.

"The book I was just telling you about..."

"Refresh my memory, please." He watched the brown liquid swirl in his cup. *Round and round...*

Henrietta examined him suspiciously. "No, I wasn't telling you. What's to become of me?" She faltered, then went on in a stronger voice, "The book is about death. Or dying, really. They aren't the same. Are you frightened of death, James?"

167

"'Fear dying, yes. Death, no.' Nice line, isn't it? It's from Lorca, the Spanish poet," he said in lieu of anything else.

"You always did like poetry, didn't you? Unusual for a physician. I didn't read much. I'm sorry I didn't. Now that I am, it's too late.... *What* was I talking about?"

"Poetry, I guess," he said, to get his mother off the subject of death.

"The old forgettery. Shocking. The point was, wasn't it—what *was* the point?... Oh yes. The book said that dying needn't be a painful or frightening experience. It can be calm and peaceful, with the right attitude." She looked at him again with clear gray eyes that could have belonged to a person much younger. "Haven't I been a good mother to you, James?"

"Of course," he said dutifully. "But to be honest, you're going in a lot of directions at once right now."

"That's because I haven't made my point. I *was* a good mother. I gave you good advice. Do you recall the things I used to tell you?"

"Yes, I remember your aphorisms, or some of them. 'Heart of gold and teeth to match.' 'Beauty is skin deep, but ugliness goes to the bone.' That was mean of you. 'Don't marry a girl who can't carry a tune.' 'Don't marry a girl who bruises easily.'... There were so many 'don't marrys' I'm surprised I did it at all!" He laughed.

"We had good times, didn't we?" Her wrinkled smile was brief. "I want you to listen carefully. You owe me one, as they say. I want to die peacefully and in full possession of my faculties. I don't want to become more senile than I've become already." He raised his hand, and again her temper flashed. *"Don't argue with me!* I'm still wise enough to know who I am, but how much longer? James, I'm going downhill. Here." She touched her head. "I've noticed all sorts of signs. The day may come when I don't know what day it is or who my grandchildren are, when I blather like a crotchety idiot." Henrietta frowned with deep distaste. "I don't want that to happen. James, you're

168

a doctor. The moment you see I'm losing my mind I demand that you give me a pill and end it peacefully for me. That is what I want. Are we agreed?"

"Mother," he said dejectedly, neither agreeing or disagreeing. Lines—whose?—floated up from a cerebral chasm.

> *Margaret, are you grieving*
> *Over Goldengrove unleaving?...*
> *Now no matter, child, the name:*
> *Sorrow's springs are all the same....*
> *It is the blight man was born for,*
> *It is Margaret you mourn for.*

That's right, he thought. It wasn't just his mother he grieved for; he also grieved for James Ewing Healey, Jr., whose decline could be measured by his inability to remember more than twenty-nine state capitals.

Ruth used a spare room with north light for a studio, and Healey found her there, besmocked, canvas on easel, working intently. "Are you interruptable?" he said.

"Sure. How was it?"

"What? Oh, Mother. Okay. She thinks she's slipping."

"For a change she's right. Did you give her something?"

"Of course I didn't! What are you talking about?" he said, thinking that somehow Ruth meant a pill.

"Money, naturally," she said, brush flying.

"Well, a little," he admitted. "I wanted to cheer her up."

Ruth's back stiffened. "I think it's disgusting of you to give it and her to take it. We have mouths to feed."

"They're being fed. Let's not start that. Did I have any calls?"

"The phone rang, but I was working. By the time I got there, the party had hung up," she said.

"I'm expecting a call," he said, sorry he had.

"About what?"

"Nothing important."

Ruth knew nothing of the call from Herrmann he waited for. He shifted from one foot to the other and went on. "I saw a dog killed by a car this afternoon. On the way home there were several near accidents."

"So what's new?"

"Only that there's an awful lot of bad driving, it seems to me. We should be careful when crossing the street, Jennie especially."

"You have a phobia about cars."

"I wish somebody would come out with a model called 'Phobia.' I'd buy it," Healey said. He squinted and advanced. "Ruth! What in hell is that?"

Ruth's peaceful little landscapes had been replaced by other subject matter. What seemed to be a courtyard contained phalluses disguised as plants. Vaginas appeared in the walls. Two women made love in the corner. A naked female perched on a wall was being eyed by a man on a stallion, both with erections.

"I thought I'd try something different."

"You have," said Healey.

The phone jangled like a warning. "Hello."

"Jim? Herman."

"Just a second, Herman. I'll take this in another room. Ruth, would you hang up this phone in a second." He waited in his sanctuary for the click; none came.

"Jim?"

Healey quickly returned to the studio. Ruth was listening at the receiver. She gave him a guilty look and hung up. "Okay," he said to Herrmann moments later.

"I called you, but nobody answered. I'm still in Washington, and the way it looks I'll be here through tomorrow at least. There's a lot to talk about."

"They took it seriously, then. I was a little afraid they wouldn't—after all, it's so bizarre."

"Oh, they took it seriously, all right. After all I'm not without influence. My reputation . . . yours . . . the IQ tests on the scientists . . . and . . . A team named Tom and Louise . . . oh Jesus. The assistant secretary of HEW—

he's organizing a task force, with my help—has a son about your daughter's age in the same school. The kid's been acting funny. They had him tested last week. He's lost IQ too. That settled the issue. We'll be at it all night."

Herrmann sounded tired. "Don't overdo it," Healey warned him. "Fatigue might augment the symptoms."

"Don't I know it! You should have heard me telling limericks to the *Secretary*. I couldn't help myself. You understand."

"Mmmmmm," said Healey.

"The report goes to the President in the morning. It will call for bringing in a team from the Center for Disease Control in Atlanta. The CDC is antisecrecy, but a goal-oriented secret—one that's kept until the facts are known—ought to be acceptable. Only a few in Atlanta will be told, in any case, on a strictly need-to-know basis. Technically, the CDC—it's quasiautonomous, you understand—is supposed to respond only to requests from local officials, but we'll find some way around that too. We certainly don't want the mayor of New York to find out until we're ready, although when you get right down to it, city hall wouldn't be much different with the stupid sickness than without it."

"I don't see how the disease can be kept under wraps if it spreads," Healey said.

"The recommendations will call for holding off on the CDC until we're sure that the effects are more than only temporary. Get started. Your bunch can be told. Find me some answers—quick," Herrmann said.

The digital clock said 11:49 when Healey woke in the darkness. He had been dreaming again, and once more he was in a car—not the station wagon but a vehicle with a cracked windshield, moldy upholstery and a dashboard that lacked instrumentation of any kind. In place of a rearview mirror hung a figurine whose eyes faced toward the back and turned red from time to time. Healey was a passenger. The driver, he saw with horror, had the triangular face of the man on the highway. "Fucking cars, fucking cars," the driver said. They were heading away from a massive hospital on top of a hill, taking hairpin curves at fantastic speeds. "Use the brakes! Use the brakes!" Healey cried, but the car lacked them. Faster and faster . . . down and down.

WEEK FOUR

FACTS ARE FRIENDLY, Herrmann had said, but these facts weren't, and that the scientists in the subbasement refused at first to accept them was not surprising.

Nor would Wallon, scowling, affirm the story. Ad wore his tunic backwards, with the buttons in front, and the absence of eyeglasses indicated that he had his contact lenses on. Two infractions. Well, it hardly mattered. Healey examined the others. Linda's red hair fell from beneath her laboratory cap—also against regulations. Frazer hadn't shaved that morning. Benson had already managed to spot his uniform with dye. And what about himself? He looked at his hands while the objections sounded. His fingernails were long and dirty.

"Prove it!" Linda Summer cried petulantly. "Maybe you're different, but I'm not. I'm the same."

"Yeah, man, ain't nothing wrong with me."

"If this is another goddam Polish joke..."

Healey read their IQ scores from a piece of paper, and instantly the mood in the low-ceilinged chamber changed from disbelief to incredulity: "It's not possible! No! No! No!" Then anger: "You've made Frankstein's monsters out of us!" "What are we gonna call it, Healey's disease?" "Take your virus and shove it." Then anguish: "What's to become of us?"

"How dumb will I get?" Wallon asked, "as-assuming your story is true? Which I don't."

"I can't answer. We'll know better after the second round of IQ tests."

The group grumbled. "All I can say, man," announced Frazer, "is that somebody better find a way outta this—or else." He stared at Healey.

"Or else what?"

"Or else I'll think of something real mean, hear?"

"Leave him alone!" Linda cried. "It wasn't Jim's fault. If it hadn't been for Wallon getting pissed all the time..."

"I didn't dream up this goddam experiment," Wallon shouted. "I'm just a hired head."

"Some head! You sure messed it up good."

"Listen, you cold bitch..."

"Keep your foul tongue to yourself. That goes for you too, Benson," she retorted.

When the lab was quiet again, Healey told them, "You see, the virus does more than erode IQ. It causes quirky behavior too, so watch your tempers. Stay in control. I'd say on balance it's best not to become emotional." Linda wouldn't return his glance. "Let's try to be patient with each other. With reduced abilities we'll have to work harder to do what we could before." Summer had her hand up like a schoolgirl. "Linda?"

"You didn't tell us your present IQ."

"Oh." He told them.

"A mental giant," snarled Benson.

By midmorning the group had the CMI report, which established beyond doubt that the five scientists and

Cathy Gobrin had contracted a virus. The pathology lab didn't pretend to know what it was.

Nor did the group in the subbasement. A virus consists of a protein coat and an inner core of DNA with which it reproduces by reordering the command system of a cell, having shed the coat outside. But while Walter Benson laboriously succeeded in obtaining its configuration—not surprisingly, PAH resembled SV 40—the new virus remained a mystery, both in what protein it employed and in what the DNA inside it did to a cell.

The scientists had several approaches, Healey believed. One was to work with the second protein that had shown up on the day the experiment had been scuttled, three weeks before, in order to establish what biochemical effect it might have in the human body, especially the brain. The organic consequences of the illness had to be studied—to that end, some of the lab animals would have to be sacrificed. Now that they had found the PAH virus, antibodies for it had to be developed if immunization was to be possible. Finally, a remedy for those who had contracted the virus had to be sought.

Healey parceled out the assignments: protein study, Frazer; molecular investigation, Benson; antibody hunt, Summer; organic analysis, Wallon, because of his surgical background; remedial measures, James Healey, Responsible Investigator.

The effort began. The viral DNA was extracted and viral protein products synthesized. They were quantified and separated by a complicated technique called isolectronicfocusing. But even when the "kinky" protein, as Frazer called it, was isolated, many questions remained. What was its function? Was this protein related to the infectivity of SV 40? Without this information it was impossible to understand, biochemically, what the PAH virus did in the human body or cast about for a method to counteract it.

The monkeys in the animal room had apparently lost even the ability to climb: the virus had to be the reason. The mice, however, appeared unchanged, indicating that the virus affected only primates. Wallon performed autopsies of the monkeys' brains, but nothing seemed physically different, nor did molecular studies of neural sections conducted by Benson reveal anything. The virus remained inscrutable. If I could tell you I would let you know, Healey seemed to hear the dead Lucky tell him.

Linda Summer deduced that the virus, though highly infectious, must be weak antigenically: it failed to send the body chemical information as to its presence. No antibodies could be found. This was sobering news, for it meant that no easy way to detect the disease in the general public existed, the CMI procedures being too difficult and cumbersome to be employed on a mass scale. An antibody might be located and an antitoxin developed, but that might require far more lavish facilities, such as those possessed by the Center for Disease Control.

Healey's analysis led him to believe that the virus (or "Healey's disease," as Frazer insisted on calling it) indeed interfered with the electrical processes of the brain. Meant originally to provide phenylalanine hydroxylase, which would convert phenylalanine to tyrosine, it was too strong a catalyst. Instead of there being too much phenylalanine, there was too little, with the probable result of protein starvation in vital brain tissue. Once the brain was seeded with the virus, over a period of about a week, intelligence suffered.

There was no evident way to kill the virus, which took up permanent residence in the brain as part of the DNA. Healey began to examine other means of controlling the disease.

On Wednesday, Healey having canceled his classes for good, pleading illness (which wasn't exactly wrong), the group was subjected to another IQ test. A little later in the morning Healey met with Orenstein in the cubicled room. The flat-faced psychiatrist asked, "When were you first kind of exposed to the PAH virus?"

"Three weeks ago today, when Wallon came to my

178

house. I'd be willing to bet that Linda got it at the same time."

Orenstein had made a crude chart on a piece of cardboard. He wrote on it, raised his head and asked, "What about Benson and Frazer?"

"I don't know exactly. Mmmmmm. Yes, they drank from Wallon's glass in the cafeteria. That was on Monday of the following week."

Orenstein wrote again and handed Healey the chart.

	WALLON IQ 168	HEALEY IQ 165	SUMMER IQ 149	FRAZER IQ 152	BENSON IQ 146
Exposure day	1	3	3	8	8
TEST I					
DAYS FROM EXPOSURE	17	15	15	10	10
IQ SCORE	128	140	120	126	119
IQ LOSS (POINTS)	40	25	29	26	27

Orenstein pointed at the figures. "It doesn't seem to matter that Frazer and Benson got it somewhat later. The first drop equalized you. Of course, I'm doing a lot of guessing."

"Let's see the results of the second test."

Orenstein showed him.

	WALLON	HEALEY	SUMMER	FRAZER	BENSON
TEST II					
DAYS FROM EXPOSURE	23	21	21	16	16
IQ SCORE	105	129	112	115	109
IQ LOSS (POINTS)	23	11	8	11	10
TOTAL IQ LOSS (POINTS)	63	36	37	37	37

Orenstein's hand covered the lower part of the cardboard. Healey exhaled heavily and said, "The decline continues."

"I'm afraid so. And the pattern is similar with the five of you, percentilewise. First you get the big drop, which is all-important for what comes next. Wallon's was the largest, for whatever reasons—the amount of virus he was exposed to, alcohol, steroids, or all three—and therefore his second drop, as measured by the test, was also the largest, being roughly half the first. Your original decline was the smallest, and you were starting with a slightly higher base than Summer, Frazer and Benson. The second test shows that you maintain your original advantage, as would follow. Also, individuals may vary tremendously in terms of resistance. My IQ was roughly the same as yours, but no longer. I'm a standard deviation below you now." Orenstein looked away and added a gravelly "Dammit."

"I wonder what accounts for this apparent resistance of mine," said Healey.

"We'll never know. People differ, that's all. But before you get cocky, remember you're losing IQ points too. Every day."

"Every day?" Healey protested.

"That's how it looks. Every day in every way we get dumber and dumber."

"You seem capable enough, Mel."

Orenstein's face reflected inner effort. "I'm concentrating hard—very hard. Also, I'm dealing with a subject I'm familiar with. Give me something new, problemwise, and you'd see the difference fast enough."

"Is that why Benson with an IQ of a hundred and nine is able to use the EM machine?"

"I assume so. Though how much longer I'm not sure. Want to see my projections for your group?"

"Do I have to?" He stared as Orenstein removed his hand from the cardboard.

Projected IQ Scores

WEEKS FROM EXPOSURE— APPROXIMATE	WALLON	HEALEY	SUMMER	FRAZER	BENSON
V	98	123	108	113	102
VI	92	120	104	110	99
VII	89	117	102	107	97

"After the seventh week, the decline is infinitesimal," Orenstein said matter-of-factly.

"Seven weeks from exposure! According to this, Wallon will arrive at an IQ of eighty-nine in three weeks."

"More or less. That'll be his new IQ for good."

"I can't believe it. What can Wallon do with an IQ of eighty-nine?"

"Well, there are studies of IQ by occupation. According to one, professional people average about 120, semiprofessional and managerial about 113, clerical and retail workers about 104, slightly skilled people 96, laborers about 94. Another, ranking in terms of median IQs, puts Ph.D.s at 140, accountants at 128, I think, with lawyers just below. There's a longer breakdown—I'll show you." Orenstein reached into his desk and came out with a photocopy. "This is a list of occupations arranged by median IQ. It's from an old study and may be out of date."

Accountant	128	Sheet-metal worker	108
Lawyer	128	Mechanic	106
Engineer	127	Auto-service worker	104
Professor	126	Bartender	102
Reporter	125	Auto mechanic	101
Pharmacist	120	Tractor driver	100
Sales manager	119	Crane-hoist operator	98
Cashier	116	Cook and baker	97
Artist	114	Truck driver	96
Inspector	112	Barber	95
Machinist	110	Farmer	93
Foreman	110	Farmhand	92
Sales clerk	109	Miner	91

'"Farmer' probably means small farmer." Orenstein said. "And there's zero or negative correlation between IQ and creativity among painters, sculptors, designers."

Healey closed his mouth to a tiny hole and said through it, "What happens to a person with an IQ of a hundred who gets the disease?"

"IQ eighty-three," Orenstein replied. "That's how I read it."

"And if almost the whole country got it?"

"The average, or mean, national IQ would be eighty-three."

"Eighty-three!"

"A person with a dull-normal IQ can function effectively, but he lacks the capacity for intelligent work."

"Meaning all the occupations listed here."

"That judgment may be too severe," Orenstein replied. "But you might have trouble finding a good mechanic."

"What else is new? And there would be more people below the dull-normal level than there are now?"

"Yes. And behavior problems. Smart people are perfectly capable of making trouble too, but you do find among the borderline population and below, especially, a greater incidence of violent and destructive behavior, untrustworthy individuals, withdrawal, hyperactive tendencies, self-abusiveness, psychological disturbances, sexually aberrant behavior."

"What a world! Who runs the show?"

Orenstein appeared exhausted. "That's not my department," he said. "I told you I couldn't handle anything new."

They spoke a few minutes longer. Orenstein had fallen asleep when Healey left. He notified Herman Herrmann, in Washington, that the stupid sickness did not seem a temporary matter, saving the details.

The whir of blades over the building told Healey that Herrmann had returned, and minutes later his phone rang. "Jim? Herman. I'm back."

"I know, Herman," he said softly. It occurred to him

that keeping a record of ordinary foolishness might be useful at some point—a kind of stupidity index, yes.

Herman Herrmann stood by a window that faced on the East River. "How are you?" Healey asked automatically.

"Me?" There was nobody else in the imposing office—another entry for Healey's new index. "I'm fine."

"Any more ... symptomatology?"

"You mean the limericks? Oh, they come to mind now and then, but they seem to be fading. Generally, I'm clear as a bell. All symptoms are go. I mean systems." The director, Healey had to admit, had never looked better, IQ disease or not. "You?"

"Yes, the voices are almost gone," Healey lied.

Herrmann scrutinized him. "What's your IQ now?"

"One twenties. I seem to be the star of the class. Orenstein wants you to take an IQ test too."

"I refuse."

"I don't blame you. The projections don't look so hot." Healey explained the situation.

Herrmann returned to his desk and sat down heavily. "The process takes about seven weeks, you say?"

"As it looks. Average IQ will plateau in the low eighties, according to Orenstein."

"Good God. What about standard deviations?"

"They'll be smaller, he believes. Instead of the bell-shaped curve, you have a kind of"—Lord! He was picking up from Orenstein now!—"pyramid, with everybody clustered pretty much together. You'll get more retarded people, but most will be within five or six points of average. Of course, that's assuming almost everybody's affected."

"A democratic virus, for shit's sake! A nation of dull normals. If it spreads, darkness will fall. 'Novus Ordo Seclorum'—a new order of the world indeed! Well, some plans have been made with such assumptions. It's still theoretically possible the disease will peter out, isn't it?"

"Yes. The virus could lose strength as it spreads. It might be that only a handful of mental basket cases will result." He winced. "At this point we have to have an epidemiological survey. We need it now. We should have had it already."

Herrmann replied, "It's been arranged. The Center for Disease Control has to be alerted. A CDC team will be here later today. In secret."

"It'd be a lot easier without secrecy," Healey stated.

"Jim, Jim, don't be naive," Herrmann complained. "Think what we have on our hands! Suppose half the population becomes stupid and the other half knows it. Why, they'd be swindled, cheated blind. You wouldn't want the dumb ones taken advantage of, would you?"

"No," admitted Healey, "but . . ." *GUAGUA. She has pimples on her but . . .* Lord, it was hard to cogitate.

"But," interrupted Herrmann with emphasis, "there's more. I've spent five days kicking around these questions with the best minds in Washington and, believe me, there's plenty involved. In an epidemic of deteriorating performance everything will alter. Procedures will have to be simplified, directions rewritten, products standardized, to avoid errors. This country's always had the capacity to make goods and machinery that last. At present we want things to break down and wear out to stimulate the economy, but that will have to change, because the intelligence to replace things may not exist. There are so many options and scenarios. Take justice. The criminal penalties will have to be unbelievably harsh to keep the imbies in line."

"Imbies?" Healey inquired.

"My word for the new group of imbeciles. After all, the race is to the swift, Ecclesiastes notwithstanding. But the swift need protection from the slow. They're liable to lunge at you when you lap them on the track. We will have to be made safe. Industrial society is effective because it has developed two superb techniques for limiting the destructiveness of the inept and using their services. Machinery and bureaucracy. Machinery is useful because it impresses people with the skills society seems to have.

It's also comparatively easy to operate, and it gives the common man something to mess with. Like sex. Sex is a form of machinery to the average man. How weird that free-floating sexuality has been presented as *contrary* to the national mores, when, in reality, sex is absolutely necessary to keep people's minds off bigger questions! *Playboy* is vital to the National Association of Manufacturers.... A team named Tom and Louise ... Where was I? Don't tell me.... Yes. Like incompetence. Myth hath it that people are fired for incompetence, when, in fact, incompetence is rewarded. Why? Better, the system says, to define incompetence as competence if stability results. Instability is the real enemy of the status quo. The terrorists know that. The terrorists are extremely stupid but have an excellent perception of weakness, like all paranoids have. ... Do an act in the nude on their knees. ... Yes, yes, terrorism will be a problem. Where was I? The bureaucracy. It will help us survive. It must implement the conditioning system. The bureaucracy will be even larger, because more people will be required to accomplish what fewer could accomplish before. It may be that some sort of collective intelligence can be developed. ... A team named Tom and Louise ... Oh dear, what was I saying?"

"Intelligence," Healey reminded him.

"Yes, computers. A master plan is being developed by a team named Tom and Louise.... Jesus! Stop it!" Herrmann shouted, as if to himself. "A team at the Department of Commerce will work on how to feed a couple of the biggest computers everything that can be programmed on how our society is run; the machines can serve as managers if such becomes necessary. Hopefully, it won't, of course, because even if things become desperate intellectually, there ought to be *some* people who retain IQs well over a hundred. *We* will have to serve as the new leadership class. By God, the servant question ought to be settled by then. There will be plenty of servants!"

185

Healey wondered whether Herman Herrmann was welcoming his forthcoming role as a philosopher-king. "But Herman," he said, "aren't you taking things to extremes? Even if the whole country gets the disease, it ought to be possible to quarantine America and let the rest of the world find a cure. It isn't as though the virus can be inherited—it's not in the germ cells, so far as we know."

"Do an act in the nude on their knees," Herrmann announced in a singsong voice. "What did you say?"

"That surely scientists from abroad can assist us if we start to go under."

"They crawl down the aisle..."

"Herman! Listen to me!"

"I am. You're a sick man, Jim. Very sick. America the quarantined! Over my dead body. The virus must become universal—America should not be at a disadvantage. Why, they'd clobber us in trade. You wouldn't see so much as a gold bar left at Knox! You think the Arabs try to exploit us now! Plans are being laid....Fucking dog-style...At the Defense Department, a high-level team...named Tom and Louise..."

"Herman," Healey pleaded.

"No, I must recite it." Herrmann pounded his head with his fists as if to punish himself. "I must! A team named Tom and Louise/Do an act in the nude on their knees./They crawl down the aisle/Fucking dog-style/While the orchestra plays Kilmer's 'Trees.' There! It's gone. Where was I? Did I tell you there's talk of a strike at the hospital?"

Youthful, clean-cut, alert, knowledgeable, the trio from Atlanta—two men and a woman—impressed Healey well, although as the interview in his office continued he increasingly doubted that they felt the same about him.

They seemed, for one thing, a little dubious about the PAH virus, and Healey, try as he did, couldn't make himself clear.

"You say it's transmitted orally?"

"I think so, yes. I mean, I don't see any other way, Paul."

"Clem, sir."

"Sorry." Clem reminded Healey of his son.

"Well, on the one hand, you claim it's seriously infectious, meaning it's a strong virus, yet you claim it's too weak antigenically to cause the production of antibodies. Can you account for that?"

"Mmmmmm, I...I...guess it's the sort of bug that doesn't need to be too powerful to infect. And in the body it's able to elude the defense system, which doesn't recognize it as an invader because of the human DNA. That's my bet, Paul—I mean Clem," said Healey, embarrassed.

"Let's try again," said the woman. "Would measles be a good model for the PAH virus?"

"Mmmmmm." He *had* to stop saying "mmmmmm." It sounded ridiculous. "Yes, it would. Same period of incubation, I believe, and of infectiousness, and..."

"And?"

"Measles would be a good model, yes." He'd had more to say on the subject but couldn't remember what.

The trio exchanged glances. *"A" looks at "B" and sees*..."Can we go over the symptomatology?" said the one called...called...Helen...yes, Helen.

"Malaise is an onset symptom, Helen," reported Healey.

"The term 'malaise' covers a lot of ground, doctor."

"To be sure...still, lassitude, headaches, feeling out of sorts are certainly characteristic of the disease in the first few days."

"But everybody feels out of sorts sometimes."

"I quite agree." Lord, Helen struck him as sexy, with high breasts and a good tight ass. Healey! Should he tell them about the voices, about Herrmann's limericks? They'd never believe him. Herman Herrmann was one of the most illustrated, no, illustrious medical men in the business. "Unfortunately, the disease is quite subtle in its manifestations."

"Surely there's more?"

"Forgetfulness is a sign, ah . . ." Rudolph the red-nosed reindeer. "Rudy."

Rudy shook his head. "It's pretty hard to screen for."

"Coughing," said Healey desperately.

"That's better. How many people whom you associate with the disease have had coughing fits?" Rudy asked, looking more cheerful.

"Fits?" said Healey. "Coughing . . . only one, I guess. Dr. Wallon, my colleague. Perhaps that was sinus trouble." He was forced to add, "My daughter coughed too."

Rudy's voice was limned with doubt. "Anything else?"

Bad dreams? Juvenile behavior? Hardly reportable symptoms. "Falling asleep at odd moments," Healey recalled. "That's been true of a few of them."

The one called Helen wrote this down with an air of determination, then said regretfully, "It's so little to go on!"

"You can't screen for IQ loss, either," Healey said. "All in all, erratic behavior seems the best signal, doesn't it?"

The trio sighed in unison. "How do you measure *that?*" Rudy protested. "So many people are erratic. We're epidemiologists, used to dealing with physical manifestations, not social ones. We don't know how to proceed. What do you suggest?"

A different kind of epidemiology would be needed, he began to realize. "Keep your eyes open." He gave them a list of possible carriers.

After the CDC investigators departed, Healey sat morosely at his desk. A decision impended that he could no longer avoid, much as he preferred delay. The situation might have been different if the hospital had been at top efficiency, but it was not; problems multiplied daily, though the medical staff blamed the maintenance force, who in the last few days had begun to talk about a strike, joined by the drivers of the ambulances the hospital maintained as part of an agreement with the city.

Orenstein believed K–B probably wasn't the best place for Cathy Gobrin anymore. On the other hand, maybe there would be a new development, something he couldn't foresee, a reason for hope. Yes, no, yes, no, yes, no... *Round and round*...

To distract himself, Healey plucked *People in White* from his in-box and saw a front-page piece on the proposed strike. An ambulance driver identified only as Buck—the reporting was becoming sloppy—was quoted as saying, "People like me don't got no chance. The hospital can afford it, and they better." *Mmmmmm*. The strike sounded serious. More to worry about! There was also an announcement of the conference on genetic splicing to be held by the Coalition for a New Public Health in two weeks' time in the Kellogg-Bryant auditorium. Herrmann must be planning to cancel it in view of developments, must have forgotten. Listed as a principal speaker was James E. Healy, Jr., spelled without an "e."

Still procrastinating, he turned to the page that held the daily questions. "Tillie Green hates sex, but she loves _____," read Healey, startled. Since when had sex been mentioned in a quiz for little kids? And with what answer? Not "kissing," as he expected, but "petting"! About to peruse the questions for adults, his eyes became tangled in the phrase "double helix." Several letters concerned the issue of male chauvinism:

> As regards this matter, I, a man, agree with the writer that science has no business imposing a double standard by using this term. Why not jettison "helix" altogether and say "spiral" instead? It serves as well.

No, it doesn't, Healey objected.

> I believe the writer of the recent letter to be a degenerate. "Himlicks" and "herlicks," to say nothing of "shelicks," is deplorable language anywhere, but especially in a bulletin

for a children's hospital. You ought to be ashamed!

anon.

Healey lost all desire to laugh; this was serious. The respondents took the controversy—could it be called that?—with such ridiculous fervor.

Nearing the fifth-floor metabolic unit, he stopped for the red light: a procession of children passed him. Was there a subdued quality about them? He must have imagined it, projected from his own mood. "Olga!" he called, not seeing her.

As if from nowhere, the head nurse arrived, cap askew. Another room lay behind the semicircular enclosure: it seemed to him that a second nurse wandered out, apparently casual, from the same doorway, buttoning her blouse. "Yes, doctor."

He said, "Where's Cathy's chart?"

"Chart? Why..." The tall nurse fingered folders, pulling one from the wrong end of the shelf. "You couldn't find it?"

"Evidently not."

The record showed that Cathy Gobrin had failed to improve; if anything, she had regressed further. Olga pursued him across the hall with clucking noises. "Doctor, I've already told you that Cathy shouldn't be allowed to stay here. She needs too much special care. The nurses are overworked as it is. Why, three of my girls are out sick today, and the others are being run off their feet. The nurses talk of joining the strike, if there is one."

Hospital politics were foreign to him. Healey's job was to heal... *GUAGUA.* He pushed into Cathy's room. The curtains were closed, as if nobody had touched them since morning. He opened them. An empty milk glass stood on the bed table. The little girl cowered on the bed, curled fetally, with twitching legs. "Hi, do...do...do...," she tried.

"Hello, dear." He approached with the idea of holding her but recoiled from the stench. "Lord, what's going on?"

The nurse said uneasily, "I gave strict orders, but her

diapers weren't changed." Healey returned to the hall, Olga behind. "Well, you can hardly blame the nurses. Nobody wants Cathy here. Why, the publicity lady ...Tish Wyler... was on the floor this morning, and she said, 'What an advertisement for the hospital!' It isn't as though we can do anything to help her. Cathy's incurable, doctor, and you know it. She belongs in an—"

"All right! All right!" Healey wanted to scream.

He acted swiftly, as though to exorcise his guilt about the little girl. A medical connection arranged an immediate transfer to Pleasant Village, a state-run institution near Poughkeepsie. Obtaining the mother's permission would prove harder, he feared, but her questions proved *pro forma*, her objections weak. Mrs. Gobrin concluded, "Will Cathy be well taken care of?"

"Very well. You can come see her whenever you like."

"Cathy will be nearer to me, won't she? I hate the long drive to New York."

She hadn't visited her daughter in more than a month, he remembered. "You'll be notified if she gets better. I still have hope."

The woman promised to execute the necessary papers.

Healey wondered how to deliver Cathy to her new home. In a rented car with a driver? But he couldn't do that, not as he felt. Healey would take Cathy himself the following day.

An hour or so out of the city, Healey saw, in a small valley, rows of neat bungalows, with a stream and a wood on the other side. A sign confirmed that this was Pleasant Village, and pleasant it looked.

"There it is, Cathy," he said. "Your new home."

The man he looked for had an office in the main building, and Healey carried Cathy inside. Dr. George Jenkins was quite old, with pendulous earlobes, a wen on his temple and liver spots flecking the backs of his hands, but his voice was firm and his eyes attentive. "There are certain formalities," he said.

"Understood. I'll take responsibility for the time being. You'll be receiving documents from her mother."

"A little unusual, but I don't suppose anyone will mind. Heaven knows we have plenty of empty beds. Perhaps I should get the girl settled, and then we can talk a moment. You might as well stay here, doctor. Oh, do you know what her IQ is?"

"In the high sixties," said Healey quietly.

"She'll live with the brighter children."

Jenkins beckoned, and Healey, administering a last little squeeze, set Cathy down. "Goodbye, dear," he said in a thick voice.

"Goo...bye...do..."

"Come along," Jenkins said, taking her hand firmly and leading her out of the room.

Jenkins was back a few minutes later with papers for Healey to sign. "You seem upset," he observed.

"I am," Healey said. "I was very fond of her. She was making tremendous progress until..." That the precise cause of Cathy's regression had not been established had been communicated to Jenkins already. He knew the rough outlines of the case, though not about the PAH virus.

"I've seen all sorts of things over the years," Jenkins responded. "Don't feel sorry for her. She's frightened now, but she'll be perfectly fine. Sometimes I think our clients are the lucky ones. Some of them, anyway. Would you like to look around?"

Healey, though he worked in inherited disease, had little first-hand experience with institutions for the retarded—"exceptional" had become the accepted term for them, which was not entirely a euphemism since it described those who deviated from the norms on both ends of the IQ scale; Healey was "exceptional" too, or had been, he reflected with melancholy. But his affirmative reply represented far more than simple curiosity. If the projections proved out, as Healey dreaded, large numbers of people would drift toward these intellectual latitudes.

"You say you have empty beds?" he asked as they stepped into the hall.

"We have the capacity to house two thousand, but I doubt if we have five hundred now. We'll be closed altogether soon. Fewer come. Better fetal diagnoses... but you know that. The state prefers to disperse the retarded to smaller places, into the community if he can be taught to 'manage himself and his affairs with ordinary prudence,' as the old saw goes."

"What do they do in the world?"

"Oh, menial jobs. Maids, waitresses, day laborers, messengers."

"And they get along?"

"Often quite well. With supervision, of course. Here's one now. He's been with us for years. He's employed as a guard." They were approaching a corridor between two buildings, where on a stool sat a short lumpy man who had a badge pinned to denim clothing. "Come over here, Peter," said Jenkins crisply. "How are you this morning?"

Peter must have been fifty years old. He said in a deep voice, "I'm swell."

"Have you been a good boy?"

"Oh, yessir. Very good. Can't I have some candy?"

"Now, now, Peter. No eating candy on the job. You know that."

"Can I ask this man for a dollar?"

"*Peter!* No begging. That's against the rules."

"A quarter?" Peter giggled.

"You are being a very bad boy. Say you're sorry."

Peter hung his head. "I'm sorry."

"That's better. Keep alert. Put your shoulders back, Peter. There's the lad." Peter gazed at Jenkins adoringly as they moved off.

"What's his IQ?"

"Seventy-five, thereabouts," Jenkins said.

"What's he capable of?"

"Oh, some practical operations, but no formal reasoning at all. Still, Peter's fairly high-grade."

"You don't condescend to them, do you?"

"No. I don't feel superior and I don't feel sorry for them. Oh, some with serious manifestations are pretty awful to look at, but, then, they are hardly conscious. Like..." He pointed toward a doorway, and Healey went to look. A collection of human shapes strewed the canvas-covered floor, some on their backs, examining the ceiling, some nodding and crooning, chins wet with dribble, some squatting stuporously, faces twisted. There were bunks and caged cribs. In one was a child with half a face. Healey turned away.

"These are extremely low-grade types, of course, down to IQ zero, or nearly. They're human artichokes," Jenkins was saying. "They don't live very long for the most part."

"Why are they allowed to live at all?" Healey wondered.

Jenkins shrugged and seemed to examine the spots on his hands. "The ones with some intelligence are subject to quirky behavior of course—fits of anger, exaggerated self-esteem, nervousness, especially when they feel inadequate when confronted with challenges beyond their reach. That's why most are better off among peers, without competition. But they are without self-pity."

"Do you ever have suicides?" Healey asked.

The old man blinked quickly. "I don't believe so, no. Not in all the years I've been here at least. Suicide's a concept, I suppose. The idea has to occur as a possibility before it can be committed, if you follow.... Yes, of course you do. I'm sorry. I've been here too long. I never expect anyone to understand me," Jenkins said courteously.

He walked Healey to his car. The grounds were fairly well kept, with simple benches and grass beginning to emerge from hard winter sod. The air had a taste of spring. "Has your whole career been spent in this kind of work, doctor?" asked Healey.

"Only the last half. I was a practicing physician, but I don't stay abreast of medicine anymore," Jenkins

194

confessed. "I haven't for the last ten years. This has been my life. I've been ever busier since I retired. I'm a volunteer, you know, though I have a pension. I go through the motions of being the director—we haven't had one since the state started to phase us out." He waved at a row of bungalows; closed windows stared emptily.

As they neared the parking lot a plain man and woman, both in denim, walked by slowly, arm in arm, mouths moving, eyes in thrall. They were neither old nor young. From their uneven gaits, rounded shoulders and blank faces Healey recognized them as retarded too. He gaped unwillingly and whispered, "Lovers?"

"I'm afraid so, yes. Tristan and Isolde are never apart, except at night. The state doesn't permit the patients to cohabit—they use the empty buildings. We don't bother to prevent them. How could we, even if we tried? The sexual urge is at least normal even if IQ isn't. You see, they have things to live for. Goodbye, Dr. Healey. Come back!"

He'd try. *GUAGUA*. Goodbye, Cathy.

On Friday afternoon the CDC people reassembled in Healey's office. The slightly incredulous tone they had used before had vanished.

Rudy said, "We've done as you suggested. We used a subterfuge—a public-health study of communicable disease patterns."

"You were careful to avoid close contact?"

"Of course!" Rudy took paper from his pocket. "Individually we have visited the following people and places. Phillip Saha, your doorman, in the South Bronx. Saha belongs to an Indian social club, and we went there too. Florence Robbins, your maid, in her rooming house and the church she attends. The schools your children go to. Your wife's office. Spouses, relatives and close friends of Herman Herrmann, Melvin Orenstein, Adelein Wallon, Linda Summer, Robin Frazer (also the Yale Club, where he played squash), Walter Benson, Coral

Blanchard, Olga Numen. There were others too, but why go on? We've checked carefully with one another and we've all reached the same conclusion. Something is wrong—terribly wrong."

"You could spot it, then. Good."

"Not so good," said Rudy. "Tracking it would be easier if it were a matter of physical symptoms. But it isn't. It's almost ineffable—you have to learn to find it in small things: lapses of memory—a couple of people couldn't remember their birthdays—some aphasia, clumsiness, a certain facial expression, call it anxious confusion."

Healey pressed both palms to the dimples in his cheeks. "Do I have that expression too?"

Rudy turned to Helen, who murmured, "Yessir. We all noticed it."

"It's something you start to sense," Rudy continued slowly, seeming to count his words, "and once you have, you sense a lot of it."

"A whole lot," commented Clem unhappily. Healey saw a bruise on his neck.

"Then there's the performance question, which is crucial. Everywhere we find these slight peculiarities, we also discover that ability has gone down. People don't like to admit it—in fact, they won't—but they're not what they were, apparently, as students, teachers, athletes, nurses or what have you. The correlation appears almost absolute. Incidentally, we had one of our people check the Boston schools the Wallon children attend. There's been trouble there too."

"Don't forget instability," said Clem, who had a slight Western drawl.

"You tell him. It's your theory."

"All right. I think instability results. Or maybe underlying tendencies are exaggerated. Many people displayed tempers. In the hall of the building where Phillip Saha lives I was physically attacked on leaving. I got out of there; I didn't want to call the police, who might have had questions. I know, I know, it's true it's a tough area, but Saha had told me, just the same, what an island of security the building was. Didn't you see anger, Helen?"

"A school principal made a pass at me. He got sore and threatened to throw me out bodily. He seemed so mild-mannered at first," Helen reported. "It wasn't the only such incident."

"A short fuse and even a violent trait may be side effects of the sickness," Clem burst in impatiently. "At least with some people."

Through the haze of his preoccupations Healey had begun to perceive individuals before him instead of faceless medical bureaucrats. Rudy, short, square, a bit red-nosed, true—Rudy the red-nosed reindeer: the stupid sickness will make Disneyites of us all. Clem, who spoke with excitement of violent tendencies, tall, angular, maybe quick-tempered himself. Helen, a little plump, but nicely proportioned. Why did she look at him so intently? She couldn't be more than twenty-five, this Helen, not of Troy, New York, unless it was Troy, New York, but just the same... Was she married? Healey! Stop! First Linda had fired the furnace of his fantasies, and now Helen fueled them too. His senses were being tricked by his disease. He didn't desire any woman except his wife, the wry Ruth. *Keep your eye on the ball, don't rock the boat, lead me not into temptation...*

"...The timing's about right. Just about this many days would be required for an appreciable number of people to be infected.... South Bronx, Harlem, Manhattan... epidemic imminent... could be of major proportions... etiology not completely understood ... symptomatology uncertain... prognosis not definite. ...Dr. Healey, do you have the PAH virus sample we asked for?"

"What?" he asked.

"Do you have the viral sample?" Rudy repeated.

The package sat on his desk. The label said BIOHAZARD, with the same symbol as the one by the other lab door.

197

Beneath was brown paper and a Styrofoam casing. Snuggled inside was a vial about two inches long containing clear liquid, enough PAH virus to infect the entire population of the United States and probably Canada. Linda Summer had cloned it.

Phillip had been absent for some days, and Healey was glad to see him when he wheeled his bicycle through the door that evening. "I heard you were sick," he said.

"No, no. I just pretended," Phillip replied in a confidential manner. "I was on retreat."

"Retreat?"

"Yessir. Everybody needs to get away sometimes, to gain per . . . a new angle on things."

"Get away?" asked Healey.

"Not physically. Mentally in my head. Mmmmmm. Do you know what I mean?"

"Mmmmmm," said Healey, whose pleasure in seeing Phillip again had already started to wane.

"I'm an explorer of the soul, you know. I went on a spirit . . . a . . . a . . . ah . . . spirit . . . a mental journey," Phillip rhapsodized, "to the farthest corners of my being, and I found myself there."

"I hope you had a good meeting," said Healey, observing that the gloves were clean, the bow tie straight. Maybe Phillip had given himself a talking to.

Phillip replied with a ponderous face, "I finally made the choice to write. Yes, to give wings to my thoughts and set them free, as a gift to the world. The world gives so many gifts that it seems only fair to give a gift in return. Do you know what I mean?"

"I guess so," said Healey, pushing his bicycle forward.

But Phillip seized the handlebar, resisted and went on, "I will compose a book. I have every intention. I shall do it. The book shall be called *The Human Manifesto*. It shall be a guide to humani . . . people."

Healey contrived to reach the service elevator, open the door, slide the bicycle past the grate and press the button.

As the car rose he could hear the doorman shouting, "Do you know what I mean? You know what I mean? Know what I mean? What I mean? I mean? Mean?"

Upstairs, he found Ruth in a cranky mood, which she blamed vaguely on the office. Healey inquired how he might cheer her up.

Flo sang spirituals in the kitchen, all too audibly. "Kill that woman for me," Ruth moaned from her chaise.

"Anything else?"

"No. I'd like to have a good time, for once, but life has no interest for me. Everything is blah. Blah-blah-blah." She looked at him sharply. "I know! Let's invite Wallon for the weekend! You know how much fun Ad is."

Healey had given the lab group the weekend off—the scientists needed rest—and planned to drive to the country in the morning. The work in his attaché case could be accomplished there as well as anywhere, if not better: the solitary surroundings might help him think. Besides, who knew when he might get to Connecticut again. Maybe not in a long time. Maybe never. But to have Wallon along in his present condition was hardly Healey's idea of fun.

"Ad's probably busy," he said to discourage her.

"No, he's free."

"Oh? How do you know?"

"I've talked with him. He's my friend too, I told you," Ruth said with defiance. Then she whimpered childishly, "Please let Wallon come."

"Ruth," he began by saying, but held off. Not being able to tell her the truth weighed on him heavily, made refusing her hard. Besides, it occurred to Healey that Wallon would free him from his wife, who had become pretty tiresome company. She and Wallon deserved each other. "All right," he said with an awkward sigh.

They arrived in hilly Connecticut before noon and stopped for groceries at a country store whose proprietor, a middle-aged man named Bunch, wanted to know about reports on New York crime that had been in the news. "No different than usual, I suppose," Bunch concluded.

"Guess not," said Healey.

Atop a round hill at the end of a gently graded drive stood the two-story house. Ruth showed Wallon, who had hardly spoken since they departed, the low-ceilinged living room with wood beams and yawning fireplace, old-style eat-in kitchen and four bedrooms, comfortable but not fancy, while Healey hovered behind, squirming at Ad's bad jokes, his wife's enthusiastic laughs and rejoinders. Before long, he announced his intention to leave them. "I'll be in the barn."

On the ground level of the small barn was the lab Healey had put in for Paul, though his son wouldn't use it anymore. (Paul, in fact, had refused to come for the weekend; he and Buddy had "plans," which worried Healey slightly, but Paul was old enough to care for himself, or should have been.) On a platform above, Healey had a rolltop desk, a chair, a light and an electric heater, which he turned on against the March chill, and set to work with books and papers he had brought. The voices were silent, he noted with gratitude. Concentration was vital.

Healey was still attempting to survey existing scientific knowledge for a solution to the PAH virus. A computer or laboratory equipment would have been of little use to him at this stage, when conceptualization was required. He had been examining ideas and discarding them. "Cure" in the conventional sense seemed to him an idle hope because the virus lived in the chromosomes. The remedy he struck on had somehow to force the virus out of its hiding place.

He began to write. "Actinomycin D would block conversion in the meaning circuit?" Meaning? Meaning that if superabundant PAH caused an excess of tyrosine and a dearth of phenylalanine, the drug might normalize the balance. Might. On further consideration he didn't find this credible, for a number of reasons, not the least being that the allergic reaction might be fatal. Try again: "Flood the body with calcium in tablets." A voice said mockingly, so loudly that it startled him, *M'm! M'm! GOOD IDEA.* The voices had chosen to return, as though they conspired with the virus to defeat him. He tried to ignore them. A hypercalcium state would cause the cell membrane of the neurons to alter electrical firing, interfering in turn with the virus's replication, he reasoned with effort. Dangers: kidney stones, thrombosis. *M'm! M'm! BAD IDEA.* What else? "Metrahidazol." This notion, he decided excitedly, had real promise. The drug made cells more sensitive to foreign substances. It was conceivable that the virus inhabited not all neural cells, but only some. These might be singled out for death from low X-ray radiation. It looked good ... *She has pimples on her but*: but the wrong cells might be killed—ones that regulated respiration and cardiovascular function. *Please Do Not Bend, Fold, Spindle or Mutilate....*

No, that didn't wash, either. His brain bungled. How badly it worked, how slow his synapses, with voices interrupting his thoughts, and with a lowered IQ to start with. How much intelligence did he have left? What about tomorrow or next week? Hurry! "Trick the virus, fool it." Some sort of viral stimulant to cause greater fecundity, then make the virus sensitive to an inhibitor like diofluorophosphate. That didn't look good, either. Try to rerecombine the SV 40 and the PAH virus. He tried to think that out, but he was becoming confused. *Round and round....*

He inspected his watch. Lunchtime was long past—he would wait for dinner. Tired, he rose and paced on the platform, looking down at Paul's lab. Healey had furnished it well—too well, considering its neglect—with outdated equipment he'd bought or scrounged from the hospital. Sinks, a stainless-steel table, burners, flasks, chemicals, a decent microscope.... What a strange progression! From milk cows and hay to scientific hardware to . . . He imagined the gadgetry covered with cobwebs because nobody understood it anymore.

Hurry! "Electrodes." Electrodes could be placed on either side of the skull. Low voltage might produce false synaptic firing, confuse the virus, cause the gene that directed viral synthesis to turn off. . . . *GUAGUA, mmm-mmm, pimples, beans, feet, mutilate, IDEA* . . . the voices engulfed him. It was no use.

For distraction he took the morning mail from his attaché case. Nothing important. Circulars. Announcements. Invitations. Junk mail. Bills . . . one from the utility. About to put it aside, Healey remembered the endless phone calls and letters required to correct the billing error. Surely another mistake hadn't happened! But why had he received another bill? It hadn't been a month. . . . He opened the envelope and his strangled sound combined fury, shock and resignation. The error had returned, like an automated albatross. It stared at him blackly. Three-hundred-odd. dollars that he didn't owe, representing kilowatts and cubic feet consumed by somebody, but not him. A computer-produced message warned that if payment wasn't received in full within ten days, the Healeys would forfeit gas and electricity. How peremptory! How stupid! Lord, he ought to be pondering how to save the world's intelligence and here he was enraged by a utility bill. But he couldn't permit himself the luxury of anger if he was to maintain his precarious mental organization as his intelligence declined. Disorder was the enemy. Nature contained contradictions. One aspect of nature favored decay. Everything wore down, from mountains to teeth. The PAH virus was part of that impulse toward degradation, which would eventually result in sameness, uniformity, the random movement of particles, total disorder, the heat-death physicists talked about. Life (how hard it was for him to theorize!), disorderly as it seemed, was an enclave of order, meaning forms. What was he trying to tell himself? Well, only that he must try to maintain formal arrangements as long as possible. Like spelling. Maybe proper spelling didn't

count for much in light of what confronted him, but just
the same it was important as discipline, even tradition.
And grammar counted too. To be avoided very careless
circumlocutions, ridiculous redundancies, sloppy sole-
cisms, tiresome tautologies and other malfeasances to
which his disease might make him prone.

From the house he could hear laughter in shrieks and
bellows. Eat, drink and be merry, because tomorrow
you'll be dull normal. Of course, with Wallon's IQ down
to his ankles, he had probably passed the point of
comprehending his state, or caring if he did. Still, to
Healey, Wallon had been foolish to try to conceal the
truth from himself, not because anything could be done
but because it seemed intelligent to know where one
stood, as a philosophical matter and a practical one too,
in case an opportunity arose to change things. In his
notebook Healey began to assemble a list of mental habits
that he mustn't slip into as the disease deepened:

Not accepting the truth
Not perceiving consequences
Being blind to danger
Being rigid
Relying too much on routine
Not understanding the impermanence of things
Processing information poorly
Failing to grasp limits
Improperly weighing alternatives

The future seemed to glitter with red and yellow lights
of prohibition and warning as he skittered down the
slippery slope of reduced IQ. But what about those
attributes he ought to hang on to if he could, insofar as
he'd ever had them? Healey began another column:

Characteristics of Creative Intelligence
Playing with notions for their own sake
Intellectual perseverance

Independence of mind
Desire for intellectual order
Originality
Imaginative use of ideas
Fluency
Flexibility
Precision of execution
Respect for forms
Divergent thinking

Healey wasn't thinking of academic intelligence. The ordinary college professor, he feared, might flounder in the IQ crisis, being the kind of person who tried to swim against an undertow and drowned. Academics, it seemed to him, were often too one-way, too boxed-in, protected by, protective of, their knowledge, and therefore might be inflexible against the disease. No—he could see this better than he had before—protection (what there might be) against the stupid sickness would require cleverness, subtlety, cunning, the ability to hold contradictory ideas in mind, to proceed on different levels at once, to...

Enough. It was dark outside, and his poor powers were exhausted. The voices hemmed him in. For once he would have a drink, maybe a couple.

But they had beaten him to it. He could hear Wallon shouting as he came in, "Why do firemen have bigger balls than policemen, Ruth? They sell more tickets!"

"Oh, Ad!"

"Did you hear the joke about..."

Healey entered almost shyly. Jennie sat on the floor, near the fire in the hearth, surrounded by little girl dolls that had come from a box in the cellar. She hadn't touched them in years. She giggled at Wallon, who, in a tight, bright T-shirt that said on the chest "Kiss Me—I'm Forty-five," under which his belly loomed like a harbinger, hulked on the couch, while Ruth perched on an antique rocker, balancing a glass on her palm.

"...the virgin who...oh, hello, Healey." Wallon stopped smiling. So did Jen and Ruth. Healey felt like a cop on a nude beach. Wallon gestured at the Scotch bottle, ice bucket and glasses on the coffee table. "Have a belt. I'll join you."

"All right. No, no, that's too much," he cautioned Wallon, who was clumsily tipping the half-empty bottle. "Go on with your jokes. Don't let me interrupt. The virgin who what?"

"Who what?" said Wallon.

"You mean, who what what?" Ruth howled, rocking vigorously.

"I don't get it. What virgin?" asked Wallon, seeming genuinely perplexed.

"The virgin who... It was your joke," said Healey without humor, as he took the drink.

"Oh! The virgin who...who...who...I forget. Here's one, though. A CIA agent was having a homosexual affair with a Russian agent from the K...KC..."

"KGB," said Healey.

"They arrested the Russian. 'Shoot if you must this old gray Red, but harm not your country's flag,' he said. No, that can't be right. 'Shoot if you must this old *gay* Red, but harm not your country's flag,' he said. Cripes! Something's missing."

Jennie's little white teeth clicked with glee. Ruth enjoyed it so much that she slopped her drink on the front of her sweater. Jennie clicked harder. Wallon went on, "'Shoot if you must this old gray...*gay*...head, but harm not your country's fag,' he said. "No. 'Shoot if you must this old gay Red, but harm not your country's fag,' he said."

"Oh, Ad!" said Ruth with a smile.

"I don't get it," Jennie said. "What does 'fag' mean?"

"'Fag' is a pun on 'flag,' dear," Ruth told her. "'Fag' means 'queer.'"

"Oh. Tell another joke, Ad," said Jennie.

"Why is a queer like a vacuum cleaner?" asked Wallon expectantly. "They both suck!"

Jennie plainly didn't understand this but said anyway, imitating her mother almost perfectly, "Oh, Ad!"

Ruth said sharply, "Jennie, stop flirting, hear? You're too young."

"Oh, Mommy." Jennie tugged at her skirt.

Wallon said to Healey offhandedly, "Hey, your wife can sure paint. She's real good."

"Which ones have you seen?"

"I don't know. Sexy ones." He pointed. Propped against the wall were a few of Ruth's lurid miniatures.

"I brought them along to show Ad," Ruth said, rocking complacently.

"Ruth!" Healey protested. "They're so explicit! I won't have Jennie exposed to them."

Ruth screamed at him, "Killjoy! Wet blanket! You're no fun!" She rocked harder until the chair went over backward, landing her on the floor. "Bottoms up!" she burbled.

Did he hate her or pity her or both? True, Ruth was an unwitting victim of the IQ illness, which in some people seemed to lower inhibitions and bring out childishness; on the other hand, this *was* his wife who burned the stew they had for dinner, laughed hysterically at Wallon's juvenile japes, played footsie with Wallon under the table (as if Healey didn't know!) and generally conducted herself like a total ass. How was he supposed to react? He wouldn't, he decided. He didn't have the resources left to try to deal with the situation. He too was a victim of the stupid sickness, which stripped him of IQ points every day, and the future of his fellow creatures might depend on him. He would have to strip himself to essentials. His lot was to be a warrior against a disease, and only that. He wouldn't feel anything! *Sick! Sick! Sick!* sounded. Oh God, a new one.

Wallon mumbled, through a mouthful of food, about his forthcoming lecture, though he couldn't recall where he was to give it. He said to Healey in a confidential tone, "I want to pub-pub-pub..."

"Publish?"

"...publish my ideas. I've simp-simp-simp, made them easier. No point living in an ivory tower. No sir, reach the people, I say. Why make things too hard? Chew big words...." (*Sick! Sick! Sick!* He means "eschew," thought Healey.) "...Who needs 'em. All words over four syl-la-bles should be removed from the dic-tion-ar-y. I don't see why newspapers should be so long, either. Keep things short and simple, I say. Com-pli-ca-tion is a way of keeping people in line.... Eh? Where was I, Ruth?"

"What?" she said.

"Your lecture, I guess," said Healey.

"Yes, my lectern. I've boiled down my ideas to the core. Science and art are the same because they make things better. Do you understand what I am saying to you? And science and art are different from politics because politics does not make things better. Is that clear?"

"Mmmmmm."

"I'm thinking of helping Ad with his lectern," Ruth put in.

"You are? Do you have time, along with your job?"

"Job?"

"Your job at the law office," he said with exasperation.

"Oh, that," she said airily. "I'm not practicing law anymore. I thought I told you."

"You forgot. When did this happen?"

"Friday. Day before yesterday."

"This is Saturday," he reminded her.

"They claim they fired me—the bastards—but in truth I had already quit. It's insane."

"The bastards," echoed Wallon. "Serves them right. They'll know what they lost."

"You can goddam bet they will, the sons-of-bitches."

"The farts," said Jennie primly.

"They're old farts, all right" her mother agreed. "Well, I'm glad I did the dirty deed. All that free time! I can practically taste it."

"Counselor-at-large," said Healey, not kindly.

"Fuck off," Ruth snapped.

"I want another trick!" Jennie yelled.

Healey went to bed before his daughter did.

He awoke at nine, surprisingly late considering how early he had gone to sleep. His brain must need plenty of rest because of the strain it was under. He gazed longingly at Ruth's upturned face. Night had obliterated new hard lines he had seen the previous evening. How sensitive she looked in sleep! Eighteen years and now this! If only he could have her as she had been. He scalloped one breast softly, thumb tracing circles on the areola, which always aroused her. *Round and round . . .*

She said with brackish breath, "Lemme sleep goddam-mit."

> *In bed we laugh, in bed we cry;*
> *And, born in bed, in bed we die.*
> *The near approach a bed must show*
> *Of human bliss to human woe.*

He rose abruptly, leaving Ruth with her head in a pillow sandwich.

Before returning to work, Healey jogged down trails through fields behind the house, partly to rid himself of unslaked libido and partly because he believed that good physical condition might be an important defense against the disease. Seeing a deer, he halted abruptly and followed silently, exultant, but not for long. Brittle branches cracked beneath his feet, and the deer bolted. How clumsy he was compared to a month ago!

Back in the barn, he reviewed his work of the day before on possible countermeasures to the PAH virus. The voices had been right to mock: none of the lines of inquiry he'd marked out looked promising. Yet there had to be a way. Problems existed to be solved.... *GUAGUA* sounded ominously. What *were* the voices? he demanded suddenly. After all, the voices were of himself. What did they represent? *Conflict*. And it seemed true upon deep reflection that some part of him was fighting some other part of him.

Genes, said one theory, came from the primal ooze. They had been independent creatures looking for a home. They'd built their domiciles by creating living things. There was plenty about this idea to argue with, but he had to clutch at straws. Genes were the stuff of DNA. So were viruses. DNAs that competed for primacy. *Conflict*. This new PAH-DNA could be struggling with *his* DNA for territory. A place to live. What did the PAH-DNA care if it produced a race of mental pygmies? Substantial scientific opinion had turned to the view that pathological microorganisms represented a rather startling contradiction in terms. They could be viewed as nature's way of ending life to make way for new life, but why did nature need agents of death? Wouldn't old age suffice? Why did nature employ surrogate killers? And why should the killers go along? It wasn't like the Mafia. *These* killers never got off. They died with their victims.

No, it seemed more likely that microorganisms "wanted"—forget about anthropomorphism for the moment—to live. Maybe they engaged in overkill; but, after all, they attacked strongly defended territory, the body, which contained genes with survival desires of their own. Yes, conflict. Suppose a battle could be staged within the human cell between the invaders and the defenders, with covert assistance to the home team? The loyalists were survival-bent too. Virus against virus. *M'm! M'm! BAD IDEA*, said a voice, meaning maybe *GOOD IDEA* if the voices were against him too.

Healey was thinking he was out of his depth—his present depth, at least—when Ruth screeched, "Healey! Phone call. Herman Herrmann again."

He went into the house and said guardedly into the phone, "Herman? Jim."

"Jim? Herman. They want somebody to come to Atlanta. Somebody to help them work out the parameters of the new illness."

"You?"

"You."

"Me? You understand the stupid sickness as well as I do."

"Be that as it may, you go."

"Look, Herman, I'm on the track of something."

"I can't go," said Herman Herrmann. "That's definite."

"Why?"

"Because . . . well . . . oh, come on, Jim. Don't be dense. I can't return to Washington, either." Healey fell silent, and Herrmann went on like a stricken man, "I can't stop the limericks. You know how I sound?"

"Mmmmm."

"It's hard to believe that my beautiful brain with an IQ of two hundred should sink to this! Jim, you have a reservation to Atlanta tomorrow. Go."

"All right, but I don't know what I can contribute."

Healey telephoned Mel Orenstein at home.

They drove back to New York that evening, with Ruth and Ad nattering in the front seat beside him. Light rain fell on stalled traffic. Just as a month before, Ruth said, "Let's play a game."

"Geography," exclaimed Jennie. "'Sussex.'"

"Suffix?" said Wallon. "Is that a place?"

"I'm bored with geography," Ruth said. "Let's play anagrams. The word is 'charade.'"

"'Red' and . . . ," Jennie said, falling silent.

Healey watched the rearview mirror. A car seemed to lurch at them. Maybe, when that old car hit us, I was injured. I'm lying in a coma now, in a hospital. That goddam imagination of mine is inventing the whole thing. There is no stupid sickness.

But *GUAGUA* sounded loud and clear.

PART TWO

APRIL

WEEK FIVE

AIRBORNE TO ATLANTA Monday, Healey, flying tourist (unlike Herman Herrmann, who always went first class, on the grounds that he needed room for his long legs), would have liked to surrender, however briefly, to the sensation of detachment from daily life that a high hurtling aircraft always offered him, but the PAH virus was never far away. He saw in the morning paper:

SCHOOLS FAIL, EXPERT SAYS

Special to The New York Times

New York City schools are in serious trouble and are likely to experience more before the crisis is over, according to a survey just completed for the Board of Education.

Violence is up and academic skills are down in large sections of the city, says the report, which also says that IQ test scores are slipping.

"What shocks me," says the author, Prof. Rebecca Hoffman of Columbia Teachers College, a prominent educator, "is the speed at which schools have begun to deteriorate. The last few weeks have seen alarming changes. If the trend continues, and there is no reason to believe it won't, the school system will have to be completely revamped to accommodate a new wave of underachievers."

Wedged against Healey's legs was his attaché case containing material which Orenstein had hastily assembled early that morning and which Healey had picked up on his way to LaGuardia. He was deep into it when he heard the stewardess say, "We are approaching the Atlanta area. Please fasten your seat belt and extinguish all smoking materials. Thank you for flying with us, and we hope to see you again. Have a good dayayay." As though in imitation a voice ranted, *Extinguish all smoking materials! Your coat's on fire!* Would he ever be rid of the voices? How crazy they were, silent for long periods until he could almost believe they had vanished, only to burst out with something unpredictable. *April Fool!* one said.

Almost an hour's drive from the airport, the Center for Disease Control, Public Health Service, Department of Health, Education and Welfare, as a sign informed, was housed in a building whose boxish symmetry proclaimed government architecture. Healey was led at once to the director, Dr. David Nagel, a lanky man a few years Healey's junior, who tersely reiterated what Herrmann had already said: because the IQ illness was without precedent (as was the pressure from important places in Washington), Nagel could justify putting information about it on a need-to-know-only basis. But he could not guarantee how long the information embargo would endure. The CDC didn't have the secrecy disease.

The virus, brought by the trio to Atlanta on Friday, was already being cultured, Nagel hoped that, with the CDC's sophisticated facilities, the mysterious protein could be identified and an antitoxin developed as protection from the disease. They might know that same week how long these steps would take. Nagel sounded reassuring. There seemed every liklihood that the stupid sickness could be contained and that sooner or later a remedy for those who already had the illness would be found. The CDC disease detectives might stumble but rarely, if ever, fell on their faces. They were good—the place reeked of competence as hospitals had once smelled of carbolic acid. . . .

There was also the epidemiological factor—to identify who had the disease and how fast it spread. The CDC maintained a Surveillance and Assessment Center (SAC) as part of the National Influenza Immunization Program (NIIP) to track the extent of "influenzalike activity in the states," Nagel explained. The system collected data from more than five hundred reporting stations—hospitals, industries, schools, laboratories, and so on—in the United States and its territories. Incoming information was instantly computerized. In this manner flu outbreaks could be monitored and medical authorities alerted. Nagel proposed to utilize this system to track the PAH virus.

"Sounds good," said Healey.

In addition, the CDC had nearly a hundred full-time field investigators spread over the country, of whom Healey had met three. The number could be increased to nearly a thousand in an emergency—trained people who were on call. Nagel proposed to throw this small army into the fight against the disease if necessary. Sections of the United States—such as New York and Boston— might be briefly cordoned off until the IQ illness was brought under control. The Deadly Virus Contingency Group (DVCG) had developed such a plan, though it had never been implemented, for use in an epidemic.

"But what *is* an epidemic?" Nagel wondered rhetorically, nodding as Helen, Rudy and Clem entered and sat at the conference table. "If a disease was bad enough— plague, say—you could have an epidemic of one or a pandemic of several. Here, since the IQ illness doesn't

seem to be a killer or even cause physical debility—
actually, it probably falls under the category of a disease
that doesn't even require reporting to public-health
officials—we need to be talking about literally millions of
people to use a term like epidemic. And we still don't have
a way to learn how many are actually afflicted."

"But perhaps we do! Measurements of performance."

"Performance appraisal isn't our bag," said Nagel
dejectedly. "We wouldn't know how to do it."

"You're all set up for it," Healey replied. "You have the
reporting system. All you need are indices."

Nagel protested, "Our field is public health."

"Isn't crime related to public health?" Healey asked
mildly. "I'm trying to suggest that the disease might bring
increases in antisocial activity."

"But why?" Nagel demanded.

"Because . . ." *GUAGUA* sounded, making Healey lose
his way. He opened his attaché case, clutched Orenstein's
notes and went on hastily, "Because as intelligence
descends you might see rises in behavior associated with
lower-IQ groups. Take criminality. There doesn't appear
to be any overall correlation between IQ and crime—
people inside and outside prison aren't discernibly
different from the standpoint of intelligence—but there is
a sort of IQ hierarchy in terms of the type of crime. Am I
making myself clear? People convicted of fraud, embez-
zlement—white-collar crimes—and even bank robbery
have the highest IQ among criminals, while the lowest IQ
is found among those convicted of rape."

"Where the rape rate jumps we'll find the IQ illness?"

"Maybe."

"But isn't it just that stupid people get caught and
smarter ones don't?"

"Well . . . it's a complicated question. I'd like to read
from the notes a psychiatrist named Orenstein prepared
for me. Bear in mind that he stayed up all night doing it,
and . . . ah . . . well, he's a little incoherent sometimes. He's
got the illness too." Healey cleared his throat and read out
loud, skipping the obscure, sometimes illiterate

passages—how Mel must have sweated to put the report together!*

"'The theoretical thrust has been to deny the connection between IQ and delinquency. The basic position of sociologists, for instance, is that no IQ differences between delinquents and nondelinquents exists. Class and race are thought to be far more important. But I believe IQ is at least as determinative, maybe more so, than anything else in terms of delinquency.

"'...a large number of studies have shown that, regardless of class or race, lower-IQ individuals commit more crimes than higher-IQ individuals. The ratio may be as high as two to one between under-ninety IQs and IQs over a hundred ten.... The data do not appear to substantiate the widely held belief that the dumber ones are caught more frequently and are therefore the ones most substantially measured. The data suggest that the effect of IQ on official delinquency is stronger than that of the parents' education or race.... Even though textbooks routinely deny the relationship, it seems to be there.... The most conservative estimate is that the official delinquents—about ten per cent of the U.S. population—are lower by eight IQ points than the nondelinquent population, which is a lot. It is said that IQ tests discriminate against low-income and minority-group children with questions like "What color are rubies?"—objects with which they've had little experience—but the differences between delinquents and nondelinquents *within* race and class can't be explained by evidence that the tests are biased in favor of the white middle class....

"'The test scores between delinquents and nondelinquents are stable. Delinquents score lower, especially juvenile delinquents. Such notions as IQ tests don't

*Before his death, Melvin Orenstein told Healey that he had relied heavily on Travis Hirschi and Michael J. Hindelang, "Intelligence and Delinquency: A Revisionist Review," *American Sociological Review*, Vol. 42 (August), 1977, pp. 571-87.

measure innate intelligence, that intelligence can't be part of any respectable theory on criminality, that IQ tests measure only the socioeconomic status of the respondents, and so on, seem fallacious. The truth is, or seems to be—using statistics from whites alone—that IQ competes successfully with class and race as a determinant of crime.... In terms of crime, people aren't equal. Low-IQ people commit more of them. This is a problem that an egalitarian society does not like to confront.'" Healey put down the paper.

"Go on, Dr. Healey," Nagel said, seeming less skeptical.

"Well, what are the typical crimes committed by juveniles, for instance? Physical assault, vandalism, car thefts, stealing in general, and a variety of minor offenses—drunken driving, truancy, malicious mischief, shoplifting. It ought to be easy to assemble a complete list. There should be other indicators, beyond simple teenage delinquency. Absenteeism, maybe. Major crimes like unpremeditated murder. Poor school performance. Visits to physicians—people will sense something's wrong with them. Tranquilizer sales—the stupid sickness makes the victim nervous, I can tell you that." *GUAGUA*. His hands trembled—not discernibly, he hoped.

"Well, I just wish we had better data on the relationship between crime and IQ before we go out on a limb on this," Nagel said.

Rudy replied, "The HEW computer may have statistics on the relationship of crime and IQ."

"Find out," Nagel told him.

Formerly an auditorium, the large room was crowded with computer consoles and tables covered with work sheets. In front stood a map the size of the state. Electricians were installing lights that marked every American city with a population over fifty thousand.

By late afternoon a tie-up between the HEW computer and the PDP 11/40 used by the SAC system had been made, and the printout began with only Healey, Helen, Clem and Rudy present.

ACCESSION NUMBER: ...   09900.00.001917

TITLE: STATISTICAL SUMMARY OF
                              THE FEMALE OFFENDER
                              PUBLICATION DATE: 71
                              PAGES: 48

AUTHOR(S):   ANON

CORPORATE AUTHOR: TEXAS DEPARTMENT OF COR-
                              RECTIONS
                              BOX 99
                              HUNTSVILLE TX 77340

SPONSORING AGENCY: TEXAS CRIMINAL JUSTICE
                              COUNCIL
                              BOX 1828
                              AUSTIN TX 78767

SALES AGENCY: NCJRS DOCUMENT LOAN PRO-
                              GRAM

ANNOTATION:
STATISTICAL DATA ON THE FEMALE OFFENDER IN THE
TEXAS DEPARTMENT OF CORRECTIONS IS SUMMARIZED.

ABSTRACT:
THE TYPICAL FEMALE OFFENDER IS NEGRO, 26 YEARS OLD,
MARRIED, RESIDES IN AN URBAN AREA, IS A BAPTIST, IS A
FIRST OFFENDER . . . IS IN GOOD PHYSICAL CONDITION,
HAS EDUCATIONAL ACHIEVEMENT OF 6 YEARS AND 5
MONTHS, AN IQ OF 83, WAS SENTENCED ON A DRUG
OFFENSE, DID NOT HAVE A CO-DEFENDANT, IS SERVING A
MINIMUM OF 2 AND A MAXIMUM OF 5 YEARS, HAS NOT
SERVED A PROBATED SENTENCE AS AN ADULT OR
JUVENILE, HAS NOT VIOLATED PAROLE, HAS NOT BEEN IN
TDC PRIOR TO PRESENT CONFINEMENT, HAS NOT
ATTEMPTED ESCAPE WHILE CONFINED, HAS A GOOD
DISCIPLINE RECORD WHILE IN THE DEPARTMENT OF
CORRECTIONS.
32 TABLES

"Let's concentrate on teenage crime," said Healey.

ABSTRACT:

THE MAJORITY OF DELINQUENTS ARE BELOW AVERAGE IN INTELLECTUAL ABILITY BUT CULTURAL FACTORS, MOTIVATION, AND ADVERSE TESTING SITUATIONS AFFECT THE IQ SCORE. NECESSARY EDUCATIONAL PROVISIONS AND PROPER TEACHING METHODS CAN BE EFFECTIVE IN SOCIALIZING THE GIFTED DELINQUENT....

ABSTRACT:

DATA WAS COLLECTED IN WASHINGTON, D.C., AN AREA SHOWING A SIGNIFICANTLY HIGH DELINQUENCY RATE. AGE, IQ, AND GEOGRAPHICAL LOCATION WERE CONTROLLED, RESULTS SHOWED THE DELINQUENCY-PRONE GROUP TO BE SIGNIFICANTLY MORE IMMATURE AND REPRESSIVE... THAN THE CONTROLS.

IT WAS FOUND THAT THE PROBATION OFFICER VIEWS INTELLIGENCE AS AN IMPORTANT COMPONENT IN ANTI-SOCIAL BEHAVIOR. IN A SURVEY SAMPLE OF 48 ADJUDICATED DELINQUENTS 31 PERCENT WERE FOUND TO HAVE IQ'S OF BELOW 70. THE DELINQUENT GROUP SHOWED MARKED IMPAIRMENT IN MOST CRITICAL ADAPTIVE ABILITIES WHEN COMPARED WITH NORMAL CONTROLS....

There was much evidence of this sort.

Rudy said, "Okay. The correlation between delinquency and lower IQ seems to exist. Even if only the stupider ones got caught and were measured for IQ it would still exist. The question is whether IQ loss caused by the disease will result in crime. Why should it?"

The voices were ringing in his head again, but Healey tried to summon an answer. "Let's suppose many people have at least some antisocial tendencies. They're kept in check by the perception that the penalities outweigh the benefits. What's worth going to jail for? Not much, for most people. But with less IQ that perception might be blurred. Besides, the stupid sickness has emotional aspects; juvenile or childish sides of the personality assert themselves." He stole a look at Helen-of-Troy, to find that she had already preempted their eye space.

"God help us if this is true," said Clem. "Let's go to work."

The four of them worked on the text that would go by teletype to major CDC centers and by telephone to full-time field investigators. In essence it said, report at once changes in behavior that can be measured statistically. A number of "indices" were cited: petty crime, sexual assaults, arrests, murders, in no particular order. Absenteeism also appeared.

It was late. Healey had a reservation at a small hotel across the street for easy access to the CDC. Clem and Rudy vanished.

"Party of two," said the hostess, leading the way. Helen had come with him to provide succor for a visiting dignitary, it seemed. Over dinner she asked him many questions about his work but none about his marital status, though he inquired politely about hers: married and divorced. Evidently she wasn't curious. And why, after all, should it have mattered, their relationship being purely professional? Healey told himself.

It was not really arranged that Helen visit his room—rather, the two simply continued to talk softly about the IQ crisis as they boarded the self-service elevator and he pressed his floor. She excused herself and went to the bathroom while he paced fretfully, telling himself she'd come upstairs to use the john. Lord! And she was looking better to him every moment, with her clean skin, ebullient eyes, full body, dark shiny hair. *I love my wife but oh you kid*, a voice laughed at his libido, and he rejoined in angry silence, *No! Shut up!* He wouldn't have the voices interfere . . . but the voice had been telling him something. His disease was causing him to fantasize irresponsibly. *Sick! Sick! Sick!*

He stood by the window, staring out, engaged in interior battle, when it occurred to him that Helen had been absent for a long time, nor could he hear noises from the bathroom. He turned to find her in bed.

Buttbuttbuttbutt! He gasped, "I'm married!"

"I know," she said cheerfully. "I read about you in *Who's Who*."

He felt almost like a virgin, after eighteen years of fidelity. How energetic was she, his young playmate, how different her fiery fury from his wife's practiced languor. He'd forgotten to call Ruth as, on trips, he nightly did. He'd phone tomorrow. Tonight... *M'm! M'm! GOOD IDEA*.

Like freshets, the reports began to trickle in at noon the following day, becoming a stream and by late afternoon a river.

The information was processed by the small computers almost instantly and the results analyzed by the four of them—no one else being permitted into the chamber. The plan called for a comparison between present and past of what Rudy called "antisocial statistics" based on figures supplied by the HEW computer. A blinking red light on the massive map meant that antisocial acts and destructive events—automobile accidents and fires had been added to the list—had recently risen in a particular city. The rate was extrapolated. If it looked to the four observers as though a critical point had been reached, the light would stop blinking, meaning that a city had "gone under," as they phrased it.

Tuesday night, when Healey and Helen returned to the hotel, New York, Boston and Washington, D.C., were flashing. All were in the midst of turmoil. Other Northeastern cities were flashing too. No city had gone under yet.

Wednesday morning, Chicago flashed, then Milwaukee and Madison. By noon, flashing lights had crossed the Mississippi.

Before Healey returned to New York a sober conference took place in Nagel's office. They agreed: too late to contain the disease. "Now it's in the lap of the laboratories," Healey said.

226

"Bad news there too," Nagel replied. "This bug's a difficult customer. My people estimate it could take as long as six months to decode the protein. That's happened before."

"Six months!" protested Healey. "The virus will be everywhere by then!"

"Let's pray a lot of people are immune," Nagel said.

Helen drove him to the airport. She cried when she kissed him goodbye at the gate. "It's like one of those old movies when the characters know they won't see each other again because they're traveling different roads. Well, it's been a wonderful interlude."

GUAGUA. Goodbye Helen.

Just outside of New York the airplane dived angrily, engines whining, wings creaking, passengers—seat belts trapped—screaming hysterically. There was no need to ask why: another aircraft roared by, missing them by feet.

No mention of the incident was made from the cockpit. "Thank you for flying with us," squealed the stewardess. "Have a good dayayay." But it was night.

The terminal seemed normal, surprising him, who had half expected chaos. He climed into a taxi and said to the driver, once they were under way, "How's New York? I've been out of town for a few days."

"'Bout the same."

"What about all this crime I've been hearing about?"

Shoulders hitched. "Don't believe what you read in the papers. Everybody wants to give this city a bad name."

Mmmmmm. Well, statistics were statistics even if you didn't happen to witness one; people might have a hard time accepting changing circumstances.

The driver went on, "Lot of accidents, though. Never seen so much bad driving in my life. Fucking teenagers." He swerved to avoid a car that suddenly braked for no apparent reason.

Entering the apartment he called, "Ruth?" No answer. He went to the bedroom, carrying his bag, and called again, so as not to startle her, "Ruth?"

"That you?" Ruth said from the bathroom, whose door was slightly ajar.

"Who else?"

"Eaten?"

"On the plane. Where are the kids?"

"Jennie's in bed."

"So early? It's only eight o'clock."

"I'm punishing her for flunking another test, though I must say she's not the only one. A lot of kids are doing bad. They're talking about using a . . . something-shaped curve at the school. They never have before," Ruth said chattily.

"Bell-shaped," he replied, sitting on the edge of the familiar bed. Healey realized that he dreaded seeing his wife, fearful his Atlanta adventure would be inscribed on his face. "Where's Paul?"

"With Buddy. They're looking at cycles. Paul wants one."

"Motorcycle? Over my dead body."

"You'll have your work cut out. He's got his own dough and he'll be seventeen soon."

"I'll talk to him. *What* are you doing in there, Ruth?"

"Sitting on the john. Oh, did I tell you on the phone? Flo upped and quit yesterday, just like that."

"You didn't tell me," he muttered.

"I must have forgot. After all these years, without a day's warning. That black bitch even wanted her vacation pay, of all the nerve! I told you that woman was no goddam good."

"She must have had a reason."

"She said something about being sick."

"Can you hire somebody else?" he asked.

"Do you know how diff-diff-diff . . . hard it is to find a dom-dom . . . maid?"

"Mmmmmm." He heard motion. "What's taking you so long?"

"Combing my hair. I want to look nice for you." That sounded more like Ruth, and guilt stirred in him like a snake. She went on, "What were you doing down south—or did I ask?"

"I told you, consultation for the government."

"I'm so scatterbrained these days." Ruth sighed loudly.

Healey's eye fell on a small box by the clock radio, but as he reached for it his wife emerged. *"Ruth!* Good Lord! What in the world?"

"Well?" Ruth said with a proud smile.

"I ... I ..."

He needed a moment to accept the transformation. He took her in from toe to head, as though trying to avoid the worst as long as possible. Pointy sequined slippers. Sheer pink dressing gown, sequined around the waist, that showed filmy black panties and a transparent black bra, which pushed her small breasts high and close together, imparting cleavage. Shiny lipstick and eye shadow, neither of which she usually wore. And, good Lord, the hair!

Ruth's hair was no longer dark. Dyed blond, it stood out from her head like the brim of a hat. The hairdo was very possibly the ugliest Healey had ever seen.

"What do you think?" she asked impatiently.

"Huh?"

"Don't you love the way I look?" she implored.

"Why, sure," he said softly.

"I'm glad you do because..." The smile on her bright lips faded. "But you don't, do you?"

"Well..."

Ruth stamped her sequined foot. Anger lay just beneath her powdered skin, like capillaries. Had she been drinking? He thought so. "I knew it! Why are you such a square? This hairdo is the latest fashion. What do you know, anyway? What right have you to criticize?"

"I didn't criticize," he insisted.

"You don't have to. It's all over your fucking face. Stop laughing at me!"

"Laughing? Who's laughing?"

"Your dimples are laughing. You probably don't like my gown, either. I get all dolled up and you find me ugly."

"Who said you were ugly, Ruth?" Healey began to lose patience.

"I'm not ugly! I'm attractive! To other men, anyway."

"Stop it."

"I won't stop it! Listen, why have I gone to such pains?" she screamed. "To turn you on, that's why. To get something going between us! Hell, there's not much now. Admit it!"

"We've been married a long time. You can't expect..."

"I do expect! I'm all woman, one hundred percent. What do I get from you? Once every two weeks, if I'm lucky and if I beg for it. Who calls that living?"

Healey retorted, "Whose fault is it? You're the one who never wants to."

"Why would I want to, considering what a lousy lover you are. You should have gotten laid more before you married me. A lot more."

"Thanks. How come you haven't complained before?"

"I didn't want to hurt your feelings, but I don't care anymore."

Healey was aware that Ruth was on the defensive and said whatever she could use as a weapon against him, but there was nothing he could do about his own reaction, it seemed. He had to reply. *Round and round...* "Seriously, Ruth, you're full of shit."

"Oh yeah? Perhaps I know more than I used to."

A nerve jabbed in his jaw. "Meaning what exactly?"

"Meaning..." Ruth collapsed on the other side of the bed, burying her face under a pillow, and sobbed methodically. Her shoulder stiffened when he touched it. Healey reminded himself of the need to avoid raw emotion in his present precarious state. He went to the living room intending to play a record to calm himself but stood still before the console, wondering whether there was any way to rescue domesticity. Healey didn't believe that he was a lousy lover—Helen hadn't seemed to think so—and maybe he could manage to overlook the indictment of his amatory abilities if he kept in mind that his wife was sick. He was, he realized, divided about their

230

marriage. Ruth became increasingly impossible; just the same she was as much a part of him as his blood. But what had she meant when she said that she knew more than she used to? Idle words, surely.

Healey wasn't ready to give up on Ruth, not yet. He'd try to convince her that she was glamorous, a belle of the bedroom. As he entered in the hall he heard a small voice. "Daddy?"

"You're awake," he said.

"Mmmmm." Jennie lay cuddled by her animals. "Daddy, I'm scared."

He kissed her. "Of?"

"The shouting. What is it? Is there a problem?"

"Your mother and I are having a little fight, that's all."

Jennie said, sniffing, "Can't we be like we was?"

"I hope so, hon. Good night, now."

Ruth lay on her back, eyelids taut. He said, "Darling...we all say things we don't mean sometimes...pop off...lose our tempers...paint ourselves into corners. Forgive and forget isn't the worst advice....I think you're lovely. I like your gown, your...ah...striking hair. Ruth, let's cool it, huh?...Ruth...sweetheart." Her eyes stayed shut. His own, casting about, found the small blue box by the radio. He opened it, examined the contents, tried to remember, raged, "Ruth! Couldn't you even bother to hide the evidence!"

"Evi..." She sat up straight.

"This!" He shook the box. "Contact lenses! Property of Dr. Adelein Wallon, I bet."

Ruth sank back and said, "I don't know what you're talking about."

His voice was sharp as an ice pick. "Do you deny they're Wallon's?"

"Perhaps he left them there."

"Perhaps? He *did* leave them here."

"Perhaps he was taking a rest."

"Perhaps he was taking a rest. Why was he taking a rest on our bed?"

"Perhaps he was tired."

"Jesus! What was he doing here in the first place?"

"He came to visit," she said, examining the ceiling.

"You are—were—a lawyer, Ruth. You know what obfuscation is."

"Ob..."

"Cut the crap. Why did he come to visit you? When I was away, I assume," Healey said hotly.

"He doesn't like being alone. Me neither," Ruth replied. "I guess he lay down to rest while I was watching TV."

"And removed his contact lenses?"

"What do I know about his habits? Perhaps his eyes were sore."

"What kind of fool do you think I am? Wallon spent the night!" he yelled at her. "You must have hustled him out early in the morning so the kids wouldn't see him!"

"The kids saw nothing."

"Oh-ho! There it is," Healey said. "Let's not play games, Ruth."

"Games?" Her gaze crept to his face, to the box and to his face again. "Okay. So I've slept with Wallon. Okay," she said defiantly.

Confusion covered Healey. He had strayed in Atlanta, after all. Sauce for the goose.... But could his casual encounter with a strange girl in a strange place be equated with his wife having lain in their marital bed with one of his good friends? He couldn't square the two events. Sadness, mordant melancholy stabbed at him. Was his marriage to end? Was nothing to be done? Should he simply sit and stare at the pouty mouth, absurd blond hair? "Ruth..." He groped for acceptable phrases. How hard this was! "...you...we...are not ourselves."

"Guess we're not. Maybe it's about time we—"

"Wait. A while ago I told you about an experiment? Well, it went wrong. We produced a bug that affects intelligence adversely."

"Ad..."

"Reduces it. Makes people stupid. Causes us to do

232

strange things we wouldn't have otherwise, like your affair with Wallon."

"What's strange about it?" she demanded.

Healey swallowed hard and said, "I know you find him amusing—God knows why—but is he worth it? What can you see in him? Wallon's an idiot."

Ruth said nervously, "He's not as smart as I thought, but he has redee-redeem... nice qualities."

"Such as?"

"Guess," she taunted.

Healey threw down the box. "Won't you listen to me? There's a disease. I have it. You have it. Wallon has it."

"I was trying to explain. Ad told me about it. He doesn't believe a word. Me neither."

"Look what's happened to Jennie's IQ," Healey said in desperation.

"The kid's got psychologic troubles, I told you."

"And you! The crossword puzzles, your job.... Can't you tell the difference?"

"You've changed, but I'm the same," said she.

"Are you *that* stupid?"

"Please don't call me stupid!"

Please Do Not Bend, Fold...Unable to restrain himself he ranted, "A month ago, would you have dressed like a whore?"

"A whore," she repeated.

"Maybe that was too strong."

"Oh no. Don't try to take it back. That cuts it. I get all decked out for you and now I'm a tramp. You really showed your true self that time! We're all washed up. I mean it."

Healey pressed both palms to his cheeks. "Ruth..."

"You heard me. I've been con-con... thinking about it for days. Tonight was a kind of test, and you failed. Don't ask me to change my mind. No way!"

After a long silence he said reluctantly, "But what will you do?"

"Move in with Wallon. He's asked me. Jennie's coming with me, and it's all settled now. I've talked with a div...div...div...lawyer and there's nothing you can do. Nothing! Paul can stay here until he decides."

Dazed, Healey asked, "Decides what?"

"Stick with school or hit the road."

The center cannot hold; mere anarchy is loosed upon the world.... What rough beast..."Ruth." Healey was, he realized, crying. "I can't accept it. Maybe our marriage wasn't perfect—I can see that more clearly now—but to break up after all these years just like *that*! It isn't reasonable. It isn't right. It isn't fair to the children. It isn't fair to us. We need time. Look, we're sick people."

"Speak for yourself."

Healey rose early from the uncomfortable couch in his den and left the apartment before the others stirred. As he wheeled his bike across the lobby, Phillip accosted him.

"Dr. Healey!"

He turned. "Yes?"

Phillip was clipping on his bow tie as he ran forward. "Dr. Healey!" he repeated with urgency.

"Yes? What do you want to say, Phillip?"

Phillip's mouth moved. "Don't remember."

The trip quickly became an acoustical and physical hazard, with autos attacking the intersections in a threnody of horns. Cars lunged at his bicycle as if it were invisible. Pedestrians turned street into sidewalk, jostling him as he rode. A red apparition roared down the street, an elephant of a fire engine with twirling lights and a jumble of sounds. From the other direction came a smaller but shriller monster whose markings identified it as an ambulance from Healey's hospital. Because of the traffic, both vehicles were forced to use the center of the street, and they approached each other on collision course. Which would give way? Healey wondered as brakes brought them to a stop, front to front, decibel pitted against decibel, flasher against flasher, almost as if the rights of life competed with those of property. The way he felt about people that morning, Healey was tempted to cheer for property.

The smaller vehicle squeezed adroitly by the fire truck, and as it passed him Healey had the briefest glimpse of the driver's profile. The man from the highway! Once more his disease tried to turn imagination into reality. No! No! Healey shrieked in silence. He had enough on his mind already.

It would be a busy day—conferences with Herrmann and Orenstein, phone call to Atlanta, visit to the subbasement lab and God only knew what else. Pushing Ruth from his thoughts he plowed through routine administrative matters that had accumulated in his absence, then turned briefly to *People in White*.

The typographical errors seemed to be increasing; so were the letters on sexism in science because of the phrase "double helix." The strike threat remained, Healey noted unhappily. The ambulance driver, whose full name was Vergil Buck, had emerged as a leader.

In the elevator, he pressed the button for the fifth floor by habit. The door opened, and he debated whether to get out. Cathy doesn't live here anymore! He watched the doors close and descended to the lab.

The sight of the four scientists at work before 8 A.M. made Healey consider the heavy traffic he had encountered: did victims of the PAH virus rise early for some reason? Maybe they forgot the time as part of their general disorientation. He dismissed this idea as far-fetched; that the disease was spreading rapidly there could be no doubt, but that enough people had already been affected so as to create a nonrush-hour traffic jam seemed inconceivable.

Kellogg-Bryant was another story. Where the stupid sickness had originated it had taken root, as revealed by the numbers of calls on the lab phone from people dialing the wrong extensions, by small but significant breakdowns in services—dimming lights, unwashed or broken equipment arriving through the autoclave from the "kitchen." At one point the lab became insufferably hot—somebody from maintenance, it seemed, had mindlessly turned up the outside thermostat. In the subbasement they might be in their own world, but, like a placenta, it required the womb of the hospital for survival.

Healey had been in touch with his colleagues by phone from Atlanta, and an area of research been decided on. Though the odds were long, the idea seemed promising: to find, using shotgun experiments, a piece of human DNA which would neutralize the PAH virus by shutting off its basic protein building blocks. Success would be indicated by the failure of the PAH plaques to turn blue when subjected to Robin Frazer's assay. If it worked, the new DNA-virus could be administered by injection. In the brain, it might effectively arrest the stupid sickness. Whether the victim's intelligence would return entirely or partially or simply remain at its present level was unknown.

Not only did this approach offer some chance of success, but it was also practical. The necessary ingredients were already on hand, and the scientists had complete familiarity with the requisite techniques, having performed them again and again for more than a month. Had new skills been asked of them they would doubtlessly have failed. As it was, they worked by rote, ignoring one another like autodidacts: Benson, cursing constantly as he turned dials in the EM room; Frazer, chanting to himself in dialect as he did his delicate assays; Summer, humming love songs and leering at Healey as she recombined DNAs; Wallon, gesticulating at no one as he grew great quantities of SV 40, far more than they would ever need, but Healey preferred not to speak to the virologist on this subject or any other.

Healey could hardly bear to look at the man who had trysted with his wife. Ursine slob! Wallon was a fool; that Ruth could tolerate him was proof enough of the poor estate of her brain. Wallon had an IQ of less than 100 now—below average (or what had been average). Ad was an intellectual insect, beyond contempt. Healey delight-ed—what was the German word?: yes, *Schadenfreude*, exactly—in his former friend's cerebral collapse, the ruination of his reason. Woe to Wallon, drifting in a Sargasso Sea of stupidity. Whereas Healey was smart, he reminded himself repeatedly. He retained an IQ in the 120s and would not dip much lower. Orenstein had said. *I think, therefore I am.* That he could still think well was a fact Healey pondered with no little satisfaction.

Thus engrossed, he almost forgot his appointment with the psychiatrist. As he rushed by her, Linda whispered, "Sorry about you and Ruth." So Wallon (who refused to meet Healey's eyes) was already spreading the word, and Linda didn't look at all sorry.

"Good news and bad news," Orenstein said in Healey's outer office. "Which do you want first?"

"Some good news is definitely in order," Healey responded.

Abruptly, the flat-faced psychiatrist went to the blackboard and after many erasures succeeded in writing:

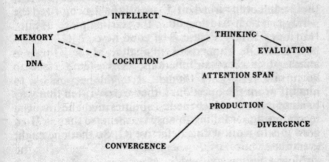

"This scheme," Orenstein said carefully, "represents an analysis of what intelligence might be thought to consist of. Convergence refers to thinking that leads to a single correct solution, such as: four plus seven equals what? Intelligence testing relies solely on convergent thinking. Divergence refers to thinking that leads to a number of correct solutions: how many uses are there for a paper clip? The testing of creativity relies heavily on divergent thinking. Production is how the mind assembles the results. I ought to add 'speed' beside it—where's the chalk? Here it is, right in my hand! How long, or even whether, an idea continues to move down the line kind of depends on the attention span. If it's long enough the idea emerges as a thought. Now, a thought is influenced by how the thinker evaluates it and by what he does with it, cognitionwise. Cognition—the machinery—is influenced by previous experience—that is, memory, the storage cells which DNA or RNA molecules apparently provide. Memory feeds into intellect as well as thinking, for the intellect has to appraise the thought as against what is already knows before it decides to accept, reject or file the idea for later scrutiny. The intellect, therefore, may be seen as a kind of final authority in the thought process, which begins with convergence and divergence. Convergence refers to thinking that leads to a single correct solution..."

Jesus! Orenstein had begun again, like a tape recorder that hadn't been turned off. Evidently he'd memorized the windy spiel but had forgotten the starting place. Healey raised one hand. "Please. The good news, Mel."

"What? Oh. I undertook an analysis of the IQ tests in terms of intellectual functions," Orenstein's staccato voice said hastily. "I thought it might be possible to identify from the questions—they were written that way to some extent—which mental abilities might be involved in answering, or failing to answer, them, so that... How hard it is to work with a defective IQ! So that one might get an indication of... where was I?"

"The abilities involved."

"The abilities involved?"

"Tell me."

"I'll try. I really will. Don't blame me if I fall on my ass. Well, I tried to correl... relate the questions to mental functioning. I think I'm right—I can't be sure—in saying that only *certain* functions have been affected by PAH."

He went to the blackboard and checked "memory," "cognition" and "attention span." "Everything else looked to be intact."

"I don't understand."

"You're not yourself either! What I'm trying to tell you is that it looks like the IQ illness mainly impairs memory and speed of thought. That's all."

"What's so hot about that?"

"You are slow, slow, slow! I'm telling to you that our brains are still physio-physio..." Orenstein assumed an expression of tremendous determination. "...phys-i-o-log-i-cal-ly sound. Everything's there. We're thinking slower, and memory has been short-circuited—accounting for the IQ drops—but if a remedy were to mat-materi... be found this very instant, we'd have our brains back sooner or later. The disease has put them in storage. Of course, it may be that we can't get them out, but if we could they'd be as before. Our brains haven't been destroyed, it appears."

"So the IQ effect isn't—doesn't have to be—permanent!" Healey said with excitement that rapidly left him. "Which still leaves the question of what to do about the virus."

"Yes."

"Give me the bad news, Mel."

Orenstein said bleakly. "I've calculated the IQ drops for you and the other scientists. I'm afraid I underes... figured too high—except for Wallon. He has a different curve. I've got some new bottom lines." He took a crumpled paper from his jacket and handed it over.

Projected IQ Scores

WEEKS FROM EXPOSURE— APPROXIMATE	WALLON	HEALEY	SUMMER	FRAZER	BENSON
VII	93	106	100	101	95

"What!"

"Expo...exponential math is tricky," said Orenstein apologetically. "A small change in one part of the equation makes for important shifts in others. As I see it, while upper-IQ types will suffer a little more than I previously thought, average intelligence won't be any lower than I first pro-jec-ted—if it makes you feel any better."

"Not much."

"That's not all," Orenstein continued. "Let's assume that the static we've experienced—voices, rantings, and so on—have a relationship to our imaginations. There's little doubt that high-IQ people have more imagination; it follows that they have more static in their heads. Static almost certainly interferes with interior communication. You've noticed that, I'm sure. It makes it harder to think and therefore effectively reduces IQ further. How much I don't know, and at the rate I'm going I never will. I'm heading downhill fast."

Healey left the meeting with Orenstein shaken. He had counted on retaining a level of intelligence which, while not commandingly high, might be sufficient for the tasks ahead. Beset by voices and equipped with a plebeian IQ, how could he devise the sophisticated answers the PAH virus would require?

"You're early, Dr....Dr....Healey. How stupid of me!" Herrmann's secretary told him.

"Not according to my watch."

"Well, you are," she insisted. "Dr. Herrmann's in the john. Won't you go in and wait?"

He wasn't early—he would have put money on it. "It is you who have changed, I have remained the same," Pericles told the Athenians, and people had been saying that to him. No one quite knew who they were anymore, himself included.

On Herrmann's carved and polished desk lay a newspaper. Healey took it and read:

SAT SCORES DECLINE SHARPLY

Special to The New York Times

PRINCETON, Apr. 3—The Educational Testing Service reported today a dramatic drop in the scores of college-bound high-school students who have recently taken the Scholastic Aptitude Test.

SAT score averages have declined each year since 1963. Until this year, verbal score averages had declined a total of more than 40 points, and a similar but less dramatic decline had occurred in mean mathematical scores, ETS officials said.

But the new drop has been much sharper than before, embracing both verbal and mathematical skills. Among the explanations cited are race, permissive schools, drugs, TV watching, the use of nonacademic criteria in awarding scholarships, and poor motivation.

Some experts have begun to ask whether some broader social phenomenon might be involved.

"Good afternoon," said Herman Herrmann. "I mean good morning. Where was I?"

"In the john, I was told," said Healey.

Herrmann's long face frowned. "I haven't been talking to you?"

"Not yet."

"Well, there's the disease for you. In the crapper I thought I was talking. I was telling you that in a country of the blind a one-eyed man is king." Herrmann's bulbous eyes regarded him solemnly. "Original, yes?"

The pile of professional journals had outgrown the desk and stood along one wall like a woodpile. "Sure, Herman," Healey said.

"The point is, a different kind of hier-hierar...class structure will be needed. The leadership will come from those, like myself and yourself, who retain intelligence levels forty points or so above average." Healey considered telling Herrmann of Orenstein's discovery—that former intellectuals were likely to be stupider than previously thought—but could find no benefit in

241

upsetting the director. "We haven't yet decided whether to make the new aris-tocracy visible. If so, absolute respect for it must be inculcated. We'd give the group some flashy title the populace will fall for, like 'ecology wizards,' something like that. But it may be better for the rulers to stay in the background. The question's under debate."

"Who's debating it?"

"Why, the best minds in the country. Gorgeous brains from Harvard, MIT, Caltech, RAND, the Hudson Institute, the Center for Advanced Studies, Stanford Research Institute, University of Chicago, inside the government—I can't tell you who, but you'd recognize the names. We're meeting as often as we can, in small groups, comparing results by telephone. We'll put together a report before very long. Where was I?"

"The new aristocracy," Healey prompted.

"Yes, the new class. This group will have to make laws and set standards for the others, who will require a changed system of values and in-in-incentives.... Said the dour Duchess of Dray...Stop!" Herrmann was becoming excited. "As things stand now, by and large, we reward intelligence. Even the accum-accum...making a lot of money is taken as a sign of being brighter than the rest. A nation of imbies will need things to strive for, but they'll be different things. Physical appearance, say. There'll be an awful lot of beauty and muscle pageants, as well as marathons of one kind or another, even sex marathons. Our group has suggested making head size the sign of intelligence, as Galton once believed. Quite brilliant, don't you think? As I said before, everything will have to be rewritten and simplified, especially rules and regulations. The bureaucracy will be enormous—that can't be helped because people will have to be told what to do practically all the time. Individualism must be discouraged, because individuals will be incapable of achievement. Everything will be done by groups and committees, which reminds me..." Herrmann's massive Adam's apple bobbed.

"Of what?" Healey asked finally.

"I forget. Anyway, efficiency will be the big problem. We can probably keep them happy with quiz shows, amusement parks, sports and sex contests, but how do we make them *work*? There will be very stiff penalties for mal-mal... maling... fucking off. Like the bureaucracy, the police force will be huge—I expect you'll have one cop or security guard for every ten people or so—but we'll need a bigger incentive than that. I favor starvation—a real carrot and stick. You work, you eat. You don't work, you don't eat. Period. No exceptions. I don't have to tell you that none of this is for public consumption... Said the dour Duchess of Dray..."

"Herman! When is the stupid sickness to be announced?"

"There are problems," said Herman Herrmann slowly. "The export situation."

"Export? Oh God, you mentioned that. You mean giving the disease to others."

"A free gift!" Herrmann exclaimed. "The whole world must get the illness. The Defense Department is culturing the virus in quantity. If America happens to develop a remedy first, we can supply it selectively according to our national interest. You might want to give the Russians five years' worth of stupidity, say, which ought to undo their economic plan completely. Yessiree, this bug has real po... po... potential.... It's been a jolly good day..."

"But how would you infect them? Surely not with missiles!"

"I can't reveal the delivery system, but think of CARE packages. How in hell does it go? At last! I have it! Said the dour Duchess of Dray,/'It's been a jolly good day:/Four cherry tarts,/Three brimming farts,/Two shits and a roll in the hay.'"

For Healey, the scheme was so deeply, egregiously, unthinkably stupid, base and self-defeating as to leave him wordless. However, the best and brightest had dreamed it up, Herrmann had said. Maybe Healey was wrong. What did he know, with an IQ shortly to be barely over 100? Meathead! He felt the first stirrings of an intellectual inferiority complex.

"... is scheduled for next week," Healey heard Herman Herrmann say. "I'll make the introductory remarks, then you come to the podium, after which the Coalition for a New Public Health will do their thing."

"Herman! You don't mean to go through with it!"

"Business as usual," Herrmann said with a premonitory chuckle. "Oh yes, I know what I was trying to remember a while ago: the strike. They've got a grievance group. I'd like you to meet with them tomorrow, as part of our committee. I must be in Washington. Most of our personnel are too dense to handle it now."

"I hate committees. The lowest common denominator rules," Healey replied. "And what do I know about labor and strikes?"

"You don't have to. Stall them. They'll soon be too stupid to strike," Herrmann said absently.

Before he went home, Healey telephoned Helen in Atlanta. "How does it look?"

"Lousy. You'd think it was Christmas. Twinkling lights all over. New York..."

"Can you talk louder? I can't hear you."

"Sorry. New York is bright. The Big Apple may go under, it seems to us. And..."

"I still can't hear you."

"That's because I didn't speak. We've got a little light in Atlanta. I wonder how it will feel."

"What will feel?"

"Being stupid," Helen said in a deeply depressed voice. "I'm with Socrates. I'd rather be dead than dumb."

He had decided to forgo the bicycle, which was just as well. It had been stolen, he discovered. The rack to which it had been chained was also gone, ripped from the cement.

He took a cab. "East Seventy-fourth Street," he said. The driver headed uptown, turned left and then left again. The wrong direction! "I said *east*." Oh God, north. Then west. Wrong again. Lord! "Pleasepleaseplease. Turn *right* here." The cab went left. "Let me out," said Healey. "I'll walk." He dreaded the apartment, whose emptiness had loomed all day. He wondered what he would do that evening. There was no point working; his concentration wouldn't hold. Call his mother, whom he had been neglecting. Write a letter about the utility bill....

But there were people upstairs and a foyer filled with bags and boxes. Ruth said through a mouth that looked as if it had been sewn shut, "We'll be gone in fifteen minutes. Our things will be picked up in the morning. Don't talk to me anymore."

"Did I speak?"

"You are now."

"Ruth, do you really want to do this?"

"Yes."

Shaking his head, he left the bedroom, where Ruth was packing cosmetics with intense self-preoccupation, and, pacing his disconsolate domain, passed Paul's room, from which he heard a little voice say, "Mustn't do that. No! Buddy," she giggled. "Paul!" Could Healey be hearing right? He waited. "No!" Jennie said again, half alarmed but half not.

"Now, now, sweetie," came Buddy's voice. "Girls have to grow up. Open your knees. We only want a peek."

"Boys...," Jennie softly beseeched.

Healey rushed into the room to find Jennie outstretched on the bed. Paul held one of her bare feet, Buddy the other. Both crouched. "You bastards," Healey cried. He lunged at Paul, who somersaulted backward onto the floor, and then at Buddy, who jumped away, pants bulging, shame and anger on his pudgy face. Jennie's legs snapped together like scissors. "Pull your skirt down, Jen," he told her in a softer voice.

"Oh, Daddy, help," said Jennie, who didn't sound terrified or even entirely glad to be rescued.

"Paul, what in hell are you doing?"

Paul looked momentarily contrite but, perhaps sensing that Jennie's complicity had undercut Healey, who, in any case, felt shaky because of his wife and daughter's impending departure, chose defiance instead. "Mind your own business."

"Yeah," said Buddy.

"You guys have been molesting a child. Do you understand what that means?"

"We was just playing around," Paul answered.

"Playing around! Jesus! This is serious! Buddy could have raped her." He stared in fury at Paul's friend and then at Paul. Maybe his son would have raped her too. Jennie began to blubber.

"Bullshit," said Paul.

"You want to wind up in jail?"

"Bullshit," said Paul. "Nobody's putting us in jail."

"You carry on like that and you'll get there."

"This guy's nuts," said Buddy.

"Scram, Buddy. Beat it," Healey ordered.

"You scram," said Paul. "This is my room. Keep outta here."

"That's it. Paul, leave." He raised his fists. "And don't come back," Healey shouted.

"Don't worry," said Paul. "I won't."

And so he was alone, lips closed, keen face empty as he padded softly in slippers through soundless rooms. How fast it had happened! He could hardly believe it. His life whirled like a centrifuge. *Round and round* . . . One day he would be old and stupid, as Orenstein said. His existence had become pointless, without hope. Healey found himself examining an open window whose billowy curtains seemed to beckon.

He opened "Healey's Book" and read what he had written on suicide. ". . . I believe suicide to be a biologically stupid act . . . if we consider intelligence precisely as the possession of self, then suicide becomes stupidity in those terms. Broadly considered, life *is* intelligence." How naive he'd been! He hadn't fully understood depression. Healey felt like a piece of excrement that deserved to be flushed. . . . Quickly voices started to chatter: *Please Do Not Bend, Fold, Spindle or Mutilate... Beans, beans.* Yes, he was hungry. Eat! *M'm! M'm! GOOD IDEA.*

The fridge appeared to contain almost nothing of substance but TV dinners. He had one in the stove when the phone rang. There was no one there, but the call reminded him of one he'd intended to make. "Mother," he said on the kitchen extension, with false cheer.

"Ah...ah...James. I'm glad you tele... called. Been missing you," Henrietta said with difficulty.

"I've missed you too, Mother. I plan to come by this weekend. How have you been?"

"Oh fine. I...no, why fib? I'm not myself anymore. The old forgettery's out of control, James. I won't remember my own name if it goes on like this! But it can't. I..."

"Yes, Mother?" She cried in the silence, he thought.

"I'm not ready for a pill yet—I *haven't* forgotten that—but I have to go to a nursing home. No point delaying..." He wondered guiltily if he should take his mother in—he had plenty of room. But she would have to be cared for, and he might he be in no condition to help anybody, including himself. Besides, where—*who?*— would he be in the coming weeks, months, year, should his life last so long?... "James?"

"I'm sorry, Mother. I was feeling a little sad."

"Don't pity me, James Healey! I don't want it!" Henrietta was right; pity helped no one. Especially self-pity. His. It is Healey you mourn for. "But there is one thing. I told you about selling off my poss-poss-poss..."

"Possessions?"

"Exactly. I'll have an auction. I want you to run it."

It was futile to protest. The auction would be held on Sunday.

Healey warmed and swallowed the packaged dinner without tasting it. He returned to his den, where he composed a tough letter about the utility bill. The phone rang again, but he heard only heavy breathing and a click.

It frightened him a little; if there had been plenty of crank callers before the IQ epidemic, what would it be like after it?

He opened "Healey's Book" to a fresh page and after contemplation wrote: "What do people fear most?" Death? That was too easy. Most people accepted death. Senility? No, it seemed too remote. Loneliness? Many suffered it—look at himself this evening—but was loneliness the ultimate fear? He didn't think so, except in a philosophic sense. Stupidity? People couldn't fear what they didn't know about, namely the IQ illness. War? Again too remote. Poverty? *Mmmmmm*, but no. The bulk of Americans didn't expect ever to be poor. Well, what, then? Why had he written the question? What did he fear most? He had it. "Other people." Jesus, it was true, wasn't it? Other people were the agents of fear. Who else deprived you, cheated you, beat you up, killed you? He thought about genes again. If those genes were pools of selfishness, competing with other genes of the same species in order to triumph, to mindlessly prove themselves fittest and best, then what hope was there except the intelligence of social order? He was suddenly convinced that Herman Herrmann's futuristic vision was in error. Men and women couldn't be coerced, as the director and his highbrow group believed. Minus intellect, selfishness would prevail—he'd already seen it on the streets. Stupidity would lead to anarchy....

A ringing sounded again, making him jump. He raised the dead receiver but heard the buzz again. The house phone.

In the foyer he picked it up. "Somebody to see you."

"Who?" Healey said.

"Didn't get the name." Click. Procedures had started to crumble in the well-run building.

Probably it was a mistake. His watch said past eleven. The night man had pressed the wrong lever. He started back to his den, when the doorbell rang. His one eye scrutinized the hallway suspiciously through the wide-angle lens inserted in the door, seeing no one.

What's this? He put on the night latch and opened the door, standing back to avoid possible gunshot. "Who is it? Is anyone there?" No answer. Nothing. In bewilderment he heard female laughter. "Okay, Jim, the game's up," a husky voice said, and Linda Summer stepped into sight.

Healey was more than a little nonplussed. The situation could not be compared with the one in Atlanta, where, surprising himself, he had made love with a sweet girl who had freely chosen to do so without the slightest pretense that the affair was anything other than a lively liaison of lonesome libidos. But this was decidedly different. He had recently (good God, that very evening!) separated from his wife of eighteen years and ought properly to have undergone a period of mourning, even if Ruth would sneer at it. He was not promiscuous. And Linda suffered from a disease which, among its effects, destroyed inhibitions, while he, though a victim too, appeared to have greater resistance than others who had the illness. In his straitlaced soul Healey believed that he should not take advantage of this beautiful, backward woman.

"Come in," he said. He added, "I didn't expect you."

"I don't guess you did," she said. She entered, carrying a small suitcase. "But here I am."

"Yes, I can see that," he said nervously, taking her coat. "To what do I owe the honor?"

"You've got to be kidding," she said.

"But . . ."

She seized and kissed him deeply. "I love you."

"But . . ."

"I've wanted this for a long time." She reached for his belt buckle.

"I have too, but . . ."

"I thought I'd shown you." She undid his belt buckle.

"Mmmmmmm. But . . ."

"You're a little slow at catching on." His trousers fell to the floor.

"But..."

She tugged at his underwear. "Maybe you don't like me?"

"Oh, I do, but..."

"Let's go to bed, doc."

"But..."

"But *what?*"

"But I want to change the sheets."

"Linda, you're magnificent," Healey exulted.

"More," she whispered, "more, more."

"You look tired, Dr. Healey," Coral Blanchard said to him the next morning.

"You don't look so hot yourself," he snapped, instantly sorry.

Coral wailed, "I'm not! I've been reluc-reluc...afraid to tell you for fear you'd laugh, but something is very seriously the matter with me, doctor. It's no pimple this time. Something's wrong with my head. Inside of it," said the gaunt, white-haired woman earnestly.

"I'm sure there's nothing—"

"But there is! I've got a brain tumor! I know it!"

"Coral, you don't. Believe me."

"What makes you so sure?" the woman said.

"I *know*. Get X-rayed if it'll make you feel better."

"All right, I will. A tumor is nothing to fool with. Don't forget your meeting this morning. Dr. Orenstein called to remind you."

"Yes, dear," he said.

Coral had looked anxious, poor thing. Would she have felt better if she knew about the PAH virus? He doubted it. Still, the truth had to come out soon. He could only pray helplessly that the export scheme was a perfervid product of the IQ illness or that it would flounder somewhere along the way. Jesus! The enormity of it confounded him. If only progress could be made in the lab or at Atlanta toward finding a rapid remedy, but PAH had so far stymied them completely. And he, preoccupied with as serious a matter as could be imagined, was forced to turn his muddled mind, his attenuated attention span, to the business of a strike!

The phone jangled. "My name is Donald Donnelly," said an elegantly flanneled voice. "Counselor-at-law. I specialize in matrimonial matters. I represent your wife." Another distraction! "Mrs. Healey is, naturally, concerned about what's happened. She wishes to be fair, but to be forced to leave your domicile after eighteen years of marriage has been an enormous shock."

"*Forced* to leave?"

"Well, perhaps 'forced' isn't quite the right word," said Donald Donnelly. "But how much can she bear? She's none too strong to start with, you know, and the abuse to which she had been subjected has caused enormous psychological strain. Call it mental cruelty."

"Mental cruelty?" He repeated the phrase to himself.

"The women you have flaunted in her face. That you criticize her constantly—for her clothing, for instance. That you withhold her connubial rights. That you neglect your daughter and have threatened your son with physical violence. Worse, that you have subjected her to whipping. . . . I have a list."

"Listen, I'm in a hurry," said Healey.

"As I said, Mrs. Healey desires to be fair. She wants the apartment, of course, as a home for herself, and your children, and the country house, to have somewhere to go in the summer. The car must be hers as well, but since she's not vindictive, she requires only two-thirds of your salary." Speechless, Healey drummed the desk top with his long fingernails. "I thought merely to communicate the situation to you. I can discuss the details with your attorneys."

"I don't have attorneys, Mr. Donnelly. Ruth knows that."

"No?"

"None. I don't have a lawyer, either," Healey said. "I'm not a litigious person."

"You'll need a lawyer," warned Donald Donnelly.

"Give me a little time."

A little time! The thought of lawyers and courtrooms after the full impact of the stupid sickness cheered Healey slightly. Those argumentative attorneys wouldn't remember the name of their profession, much less the fine points of the law; judges would spout banalities about plaintiffs and defendants none of whom would recognize which side they were on. A little time and Ruth wouldn't know which way was up! *GUAGUA.*

A confident smile still played on Healey's lips when, slightly late because of the phone call, he reached Herrmann's office, where the strike meeting was to be held. "Go right in, doctor," said the secretary. "They're waiting."

He already knew who would represent the hospital—himself, Orenstein and Tish Wyler from public relations. Tish gestured across the room at Olga Numen, wearing her uniform, cap askew; at a ruddy-faced man in coveralls, introduced as Bart, from the maintenance staff; and at a man who stood, as Herrmann often did, at the window, looking out. He wore a white uniform, had tight blond curls and seemed almost columnar from shoulders to hips.... He turned, revealing a triangular face with vacant, dark, wide-set eyes over a short nose and queer upper lip. The man from the highway!

"And Mr. Buck, from the ambulance drivers," Tish Wyler announced.

"Vergil. V-e-r-g-i-l," mouthed the man. "Vergil Buck."

Healey sat down hard. Was this, in fact, the same man? He was no longer sure. It looked like him, but then again it didn't. It had been so long. Was he imagining that this was the same person, or wasn't he?

The man called Vergil Buck examined Healey with what seemed intense curiosity—as if he too was remembering the scene on the shoulder of the highway—but without surprise, as if he had expected to meet him in that very room. Or did Healey imagine that as well? Buck might be merely sizing him up as an opponent at the bargaining table, a perfect stranger. *Round and round ...*

Tish Wyler addressed them, declaring herself the personal representative of the admirable Herman Herrmann, who could not be with them. Lifting her buttercup face as though to invoke lofty purpose, she said that while good salaries and working conditions were essential, the Institute, which existed for people, had to come first. Contributions, on which it depended, had been extremely slow of late. Antything beyond small adjustments could not be considered, Tish Wyler said, fumbling frequently for words.

Olga Numen, whose cap now lay in her lap, spoke for the nursing staff. "First," she said, "we want time off for periods."

"I'm afraid I don't understand," said Orenstein, who was taking notes. "A time off for periods?" He scratched his gray head.

"Why are you so dense?" nurse Olga said, showing temper. "For menstrual periods."

"I see," said Orenstein, blinking into the silence. "Any objection from our team?"

Healey took his gaze from the ambulance driver. "How would we know whether a woman was actually menstruating or whether the discomfort justified staying home?"

Olga pointed her cap at him. "Dr. Healey! Would a woman lie about something so personal as that? Shall I move on? The girls would like their uniforms styled in Paris by a leading cout-cout...designer."

"What a *sweet* notion," purred Tish Wyler, "to make the hospital chic. It gives one ideas. A restaurant, some attractive stores, maybe a tennis bubble on the roof, a disco."

"What about the patients?" Healey asked.

"Bedpans," said Olga, ignoring him. "We believe it possible to have automated bedpans. And we want shorter hours."

"How short?" questioned Orenstein.

"Not more than six hours a week."

"A *week*?" Tish cried.

253

"A day, I said."

"Oh, that's better."

"That requires four shifts instead of three," Healey argued.

"You are a re...react...con...conserva...a real son-of-a-bitch, Dr. Healey."

"Shall we hear from the others? Maintenance. What's on *your* mind, Bart?" said Tish Wyler.

"Bigger brooms," announced Bart, "with longer handles."

"Write that down, Mel. Bigger brooms with longer handles. What else?"

"Vacuum cleaners are too slow."

"Too slow?" cried Tish.

"They don't move. Guy down in the basement says they could be compu...com-put-er-ized to run themselves. He's a whiz, that one. He knows how to run the hospital carts. The ones with the wands."

"Charming. Computerized vacuum cleaners," Tish said innocently. "Is that all?"

"We want longer lunch breaks instead of shorter errs."

"Errs?" asked Orenstein politely.

"Errs! Of which there are twenty-four in a day! A three-err lunch. Plus more vacation. Three there too."

"Also three," Healey interpreted. "Three what?"

"Months."

Tish said, "Let's hear from the ambulance corps. Vergil Buck?"

"Louder sirens," said Buck at once.

"Louder sirens," repeated Tish Wyler.

"Faster ambulances. Lighter stretchers."

"Faster ambulances. Lighter stretchers."

"Bonuses."

"Bonuses?"

"For bringing in business," said Buck grimly from the peculiar upper lip.

"I don't think we understand, Mr. Buck."

"For bringing people to this hospital instead of other hospitals! We'll go find them. And guns. Umbulances should have guns. For protection."

Vergil Buck, Healey decided, was demented as well as dumb. He said dejectedly, "Let's table the ambulance question. Anything else?"

Buck spat. "Higher pay. People like us don't got no chance. The hospital can afford it, and you better. If not, well, you heard of a strike. And you'll get one like you never seen." That, to Healey, sounded like the highway man.

"What do you have in mind?" asked Orenstein, starting to write.

"Double," said Buck.

Orenstein looked up. "You mean double pay for overtime, something like that?"

"Double, dammit!" Buck held up two fingers. "Double what you pay us now! Plus overtime and bonuses."

"We're far apart," Tish Wyler wailed.

"Tough shit," said Vergil Buck.

"More. More. Much more."

"Angel..."

Over the weekend the team labored in the lab, still searching for a piece of human DNA that would neutralize the PAH virus. The Responsible Investigator had begun to wonder whether the research had been focused too narrowly, whether some other approach existed, perhaps obvious, but found himself unable to proceed in any direction other than the one he had already set for himself. He appeared to have lost flexibility, the ability to think divergently, his creative gifts. A vise clamped his mind.

On Sunday, Healey took time off to go to his mother's. In a taxi-cab—frequently lifting his eyes to make sure the driver took the right streets—he picked up *The New York Times* he had bought that morning and looked at it more carefully. Healey was old enough to remember the *Times* when it had been called "the gray old lady," when international news was featured, when crime was downplayed. The *Times* had been careful, reliable, profoundly responsible and dull. Today's paper was different. The columns had been reduced from six to four. Photographs, some in color, dotted the front page. The news stories were short, and most featured crime.

CITY IN THROES OF MAJOR CRIME WAVE

6 Shot on Parke Ave.

Swindle on Wall Street

Crime Jumps Elsewhere

Inside the paper Healey found two items that interested him.

IRS REPORTS TROUBLE

The Internal Revenue Service said today that unprecedented difficulties were swamping it.

Millions of people are no longer able to fill out their income tax correctly. They do not seem to understand the forms. IRS offices throughout the country are besieged with requests for help. No explanation was forthcoming.

Jesus, he'd forgotten about his income tax. Would Ruth and he file separately or together?

MASS IQ DROP PREDICTED

Permissiveness Is Blamed

Americans for Freedom, a conservative group, says that recent trends indicate a sharp decline in U.S. intelligence has begun. It claims that liberalism is responsible.

"What we are seeing," said a spokesman, "is the end result of years of spoiling our children, who have been taught that self-gratification is the aim of life. It's the liberals' fault. They've convinced everybody that hard work is unimportant because the society will take care of you no matter what you contribute. We think it's high time that traditional American values toward work and study are reasserted."

How like people to create paper villains! Well, it wasn't their fault this time; they just didn't know the facts, although they soon would. Then what? How would they react? Anger? Despair? Indifference? The answer might be critical.

When Healey arrived for his command performance at the Park Hudson a dozen people waited in the dining room. Surely, some of them at least had the IQ illness, he reflected, yet they looked their normal selves, as he had seen them in the lobby or Henrietta's apartment. The stupid sickness was invisible; the group of well-dressed older men and women resembled any such gathering. How extraordinary that a virus that wreaked such an extraordinary change within the human body should leave no outward trace.

Healey joined his mother, who sat, cane at her side, at a table crowded with her "cherished possessions." She told her guests, "You are aware that I have spent much of my life in travel"—this was pure hype on the part of Henrietta, who had been abroad perhaps twice and then briefly—"and during my wanderings I have gradually col-lect-ed many rare and wonderful *objets*, some of which are set before you. You know of my int-inten...plan to leave here, and so with sadness I must part with them, because where I go I cannot take them all with me, as I would have wished. I must also dispose of my precious furniture and valuable books, many of which are first editions with fine leather bindings. Though I would much prefer to give them away, to charity and to you, my dearest friends, I find to my em-ba-emba...shame that my financial condition compels me to sell them for hard cash. My son James will conduct the auction, as my poor old forgettery is no longer up to it. James?"

"Yes, Mother."

"You may begin, my son."

Henrietta handed him several pieces of paper on which, with many misspellings and corrections, she had compiled a list of her precious possessions along with descriptions, most of which were fictional. "The first item," he told them, clearing his throat, "is a glass egg from...ahem...Venice. Apparently it's from the nineteenth century. Do I hear five dollars?" Henrietta rapped the floor sharply with her cane. "I meant ten."

"Ten," said Judge Crum.

"Twenty," said a lady in blue silk and pearls.

"Twenty-five," the judge bid.

"Thirty," said blue silk crisply.

"Forty," came from Judge Crum.

"Fifty," said blue silk with determination.

"To hell with it! Seventy-five!" the judge shouted.

"Eighty!"

"Eighty-five!"

"Ninety!" announced the woman in blue silk.

There was silence, into which the woman smiled in triumph. Healey stole a look at his mother, who frowned darkly, shaking her head. "When I think ...," she began.

"I must have it. A hundred!" roared Judge Crum.

"Going, going, gone!"

Henrietta snickered, whispering, "I told you about greed, James."

WEEK SIX

"AD QUIT TODAY," Healey wrote in his desk calendar under Monday. He had started to record events there, fearing he could no longer depend on his once-swift memory.

Ad had touched him in a way. Healey had just emerged from the elevator in the basement and was heading toward the stairs to the subbasement lab when a door opened. The corridor behind it led to the ambulance entrance and thus the street—as if Wallon had chosen this means of access so as not to be seen in the hospital, and no wonder! Healey's ex-friend, wearing an old lumberjack's shirt and filthy khakis, arrived unshaven in a cloud of whiskey and tobacco fumes. "Jim?"

Healey turned and said, "Yes?"

Wallon placed a heavy hand on his shoulder. "I'm sorry."

"For what?" Healey said defensively.

"Well for . . . Does it matter? What is, is."

"Yes." He hesitated. "How's Ruth?"

"Fine."

"The kids?" he asked.

"Fine. Jennie's on Easter vacation." How many days since his family had evacuated? Only a few. Things were collapsing fast. "Paul and Buddy went out on the road. I heard on the radio that the roads are filled with kids."

"If you don't know where you're going any road will take you there," Healey remarked.

"Huh?" Behind his contact lenses Wallon's eyes shifted nervously. Healey tried to recall what Ad's IQ was now. Somewhere under 100. "I don't under . . . get you. I came to say I is sorry for how it turned out; that, and I is through."

"Through?"

"Sci-ence isn't for me anymore. Ruthie and me going to make a new life for ourselves."

"Good luck," Healey said briskly. Wallon was useless in any case. As he turned, Wallon clutched at him. Something like his old intelligence seemed to flicker. "I'm . . . ah . . . all confused. It's all so strange. I keep wondering if I'm myself. Am I, Jim? Tell me, please."

"You're the way you are."

"Oh." On Wallon's broad face brightness died.

At his desk upstairs, Healey glared at the calendar. Time was the enemy of their intelligence. A remedy for the stupid sickness still eluded them, while at the hospital conditions deteriorated alarmingly. A strike would bring total paralysis. Yet the work had to continue. He still hoped to stumble—if his skills held long enough—on human DNA that would countermand the PAH virus. The equipment needed was essentially simple—even the electronmicroscope was no longer vital. The experiment could be performed almost anywhere. Healey began to consider another site for the lab.

He looked up to see Coral in the outer office, lowering the watering can to plants. "Coral," he called softly, trying to keep mockery out of his voice, "that won't do any good."

"Why, doctor?"

"You don't have any water in the can."

She stared incredulously, first at him and then into the empty can. Dropping it, Coral went to her desk. Her shoulders heaved.

"Now, now, it's all right," he said gently as he stood by her desk. "You used up the water, that's all."

"There never was any water in it," Coral sobbed. "I forgot to fill it. My brain's gone, eaten away."

"Come on. Did you have the pictures taken?" She shrugged assent. "Well, what did the X rays show?"

"Nothing."

"Well?"

"That doesn't mean a thing!" cried Coral. "Tumors can be hard to spot and you know it!"

"You're all right," he insisted.

"I'm not!" Coral whimpered. "I'm not myself in dozens of ways. I'm terminally ill." She looked at him with terrified red eyes. "I'll kill myself rather than die of a brain tumor. I really will."

"Coral..." Healey was familiar with her hypochondriacal outbursts, and this wasn't one of them. She'd looked as if she meant it when she spoke of suicide, which he could understand all too well—he had been strongly tempted by the open window. It was absurd that the government still withheld the information—*that* was the stupid sickness for you! He decided to tell Coral Blanchard the truth. He would inform others if ..."Coral, you don't have a brain tumor. You have something else. You're not the only one. I have it too. It's a virus, a nasty one. It reduces intelligence," he said earnestly.

Coral regarded him with open suspicion. "What did you say?"

"I said there's a virus loose that does strange things to the brain, like serious impairment."

"Dr. Healey, how could you lie to me? Now I know I

have a brain tumor!" Coral fled into the hall.

He started to follow, but she was gone. Glancing at her desk, he saw the hospital newsletter and retrieved it. The bulletin had shrunk to two pages and seemed to him a farrago of folly. Had the staff unlearned how to spell, he wondered, reading the daily quiz? "Tilie Grene hates . . . If four belie dancers lose betwene them twenty pounds in eight hours of dancing, how many belie dancers would be needed to lose ten pounds in four hours of dancing?" Even for his injured intellect the answer was easy: four. He looked at theirs: eight. "Srs: I red in *People in White* that 'double herlicks' has been sugested as a substute for 'doubl helix.' I disprove strong. I'd just as leaf drop this term. Female lesbanism is enuff of a problem already . . ."

The newsletter noted that the anti-DNA-experiment demonstration would be held Friday. Again he wondered what would happen when the news of the PAH virus got out. A lot of people, plainly, wouldn't believe it, but some would. They might become enraged—the more he thought of this, the more likely it seemed—at the scientists who had created the problem. Again Healey pondered a haven, a place where they could work in peace. The Connecticut house? A possibility, yes, but the man who ran the store knew him, or Ruth might arrive. Was there anywhere better? Yes, he had it. Pleasant Village. One of the empty bungalows. Perfect. Healey started to make plans to evacuate the lab.

"Linda"—Healey was testing: *testing, testing*—"is it clear to you what we're trying to accomplish in the lab?"

"Certainly."

"Tell me what it is."

"Moremoremoremore." They lay in his bed.

"I'm serious. Tell me."

"It's an experi-ment."

"Yes, yes. But what is the ob-jec-tive?"

"Part of the microscope."

He sighed. "What is the purpose of the experiment?"

"To make us smart," she said in a girlish voice. "Did I pass?"

"I guess so."

"More, honey."

"Well..."

"Dr. Healey! Skicyypinngotl. Tllinnoto. Zkizkie. Don't you think?"

"Quite right, Phillip! It makes a lot of sense."

● ● ●

TAX SYSTEM ON VERG OF COLLAPS

On Tuesday, following another unsuccessful meeting in the office of Herman Herrmann, who still conferred in Washington, Vergil Buck accosted Healey outside.

"You," said the man with a triangular face roughly, "are the one holding this thing up. You are the one making the trouble."

"Maybe we'd get somewhere if you scaled down your demands."

"Scales," said Buck with a look of dull wisdom, "is for fish."

"Scales are also for weighing things," Healey returned, "like justice."

"Smart guy! Save the wisecracks for when you're being a physic. If we don't agree it's your fault. I'll get you for it."

"You said that before, I think," said Healey. "Aren't I the guy you bumped on the highway? Tell me!"

"What highway?" asked Vergil Buck, in cunning or innocence.

"I just got the final check, James! I made five thousand dollars from the auction! I'm very content."

"This is Dawnald Donnelly. We spoke last week. Have you ob...sec...gotten the ser-vi-ces of a coun...at-at...law-yer yet?"

"Give me a little time."

"I have just finished my life's work, Jim, and in the nick of time, before darkness descends over me. Using anal-anal-anal...*analyzing* the results of IQ tests I believe that I was right. Jews are kind of more in-intell-intell-i...*Jewishwise!*"

"It's Helen. We've got it!"

"You mean you've found something?" Healey said excitedly.

"Something's found us," Helen replied slowly. "The sickness has reached the CDC."

"Hello, this is Dr. James Healey speaking. I received a notice this morning that you're about to turn out my lights for nonpayment of bills. I've been trying to reach you all day, but the line's been busy. There is no balance due. I have the past bills, canceled checks and a letter from your company to prove it."

"When is your service to be term-term...cut off?"

"Friday, I think. Yes, Friday."

"You called too late. Nothing can be done."

"What do you mean, nothing can be done? I just got the letter this morning! And it's only Tuesday!"

"Too late."

"Listen," Healey screamed, "let me talk to someone in auth-auth...who's in charge!" But by the time he got this out the line was dead.

It was a few minutes before five. He kept dialing to busy signals until a recorded message told him to telephone in the **morning**. He marched down to the lab in dudgeon; from the **corner** of his eye he noticed Coral's bag perched on her desk.

"Son-of-a-bitch black bastard."

"Walter!" Healey protested.

"Just let him cuss on, 'cause it don't harm me any, and

it gimme somethin' to listen to. If I tire of it, I can shut that funky li'l honky up whenever I wants to."

The bag was in the same position on Coral's desk as it had been the night before. "Oh Christ," he moaned out loud, and raced into the corridor. Returning, he dialed quickly, pressing wrong buttons before he finally reached the morgue.

"This is Dr. Healey on the eighth floor. H-e-a-l-e-y. That's right. Dr. *James* Healey! Will you *please* pay attention! There's a dead woman in the cold room on the eighth floor. She's been there all night. Don't ask me what she was doing there! Bring her down on the double, and I want an autopsy of her brain right away. No, her brain. Jesus, what's the matter with you? Brain! B-r-a-n-e!"

He wrote in his calendar, "Coral commited suicide."

The roar of helicopter rotors on the roof told him that Herman Herrmann had returned. Stepping down the hall a few minutes later Healey felt that he was being followed. He turned, to see a motorized cart behind him. It stopped when he did, antenna waving gently.

A few minutes later he looked again. There were three carts now, side by side. And they were closer.

Healey dived into the elevator.

"We're far along. The Pres-ident's scheduled to ad-ad...talk to the nation Saturday. He'll tell them the truth, or some of it. The stupid sickness is coast to coast. Did you know the CDC has it?"

"Yes. Herman..."

"Operation Export is under control, thanks to Defense. They were able to finish delivering the packages just in time—while pilots still knew how to fly. There were complaints about over-flights, but it didn't come to shooting because they thought we were sending food gifts and they were puzz-puzz...cur...oh well. The packages were landed by submarines too. They'll be gone over, but their scientists don't know what to look for, so they'll find nothing. How are you coming on a solution?"

"I'm still trying. Nothing yet. Herman..."

"We have almost finished the plan. Soc-society is to be divided into three classes, as it is now, but instead of upper, middle and blue collar, people will be sorted into prime, choice and good, like beef. People are familiar with that system."

"Herman, the announcement can't wait. There's already been a suicide. It's becoming dangerous here, and outside the hospital too. There's a crime wave. As for the demonstration, things are just too vol-vol-volatile!"

"No! The demonstration must be held! The packages are still being delivered. Business as usual! I must return to Washington immediately after the demon-stration. I will leave by hel-heli...chop-chop...whirlybird."

"Do you have the autopsy results on Coral Blanchard? B-l-a-n-c-h-a-r-d."

It was sad, Healey reflected while he awaited an answer, how detached he was from the fact of Coral's death. It wasn't as though he didn't care; he did. But he felt selfish, for himself and others. A remedy to the stupid sickness was all that mattered. Sadness couldn't be indulged in. Anything that distracted his dwindling attention had to be avoided. He had to hone his sick intelligence.

"Who?"

"Coral Blanchard was her name. You brought her down from the eighth floor this morning."

"Well, there's no record."

"You mean you *lost* her?"

The mail on Thursday contained another cutoff notice from the utility and a card from Paul postmarked St. Louis. "Dear Dad, I'm sorry we had a flapp about Jennie. Buddy and I didn't meane any harm. We were just kiding around. I am fine. Buddy and I have cycles. We are staying in a youth hostile and plan to move on. Never had more fun. Glad I quit school. See you sometime, okay? Love, yure son."

"I was almost killed today," he wrote in his desk calendar.

Vergil Buck had been the assailant, he was convinced. That morning he'd walked to the hospital for the exercise, and nearing the entrance he sensed a presence behind him, turned and leaped in the same motion. The ambulance slid by, siren off, missing him by inches, and disappeared into its tunnel.

Suppose he had been struck? He would have counted as a statistic, but not much more. In the last few days traffic fatalities had become so commonplace that the police hardly bothered to investigate.

"There is no record of a notice to shut off your elec-elec... power."

"Are you sure? I got one."

"I'll check your records once more. What did you say your name was?"

"But you just checked my records! H-e-a-l-e-y, James E. Healey, dammit!"

"... I have a H-e-a-l-e-y at that address."

"That's me."

"There is no record of a notice to shut off your elec-elec..."

"You *still* can't find her?"

"There is no record...."

Antennae waving gently, eight delivery carts ringed him as he stood in the corridor, wondering what to do. Cry for help? He'd look like a perfect fool. They were only carts, after all.

"Move on," he said out loud, as if the carts had ears. "Go on about your business. Shove off."

The carts looked heavy. They were about four feet high, with tiers of shelves loaded with equipment like sheets and bedpans, and a motor underneath. They crept toward him, backing him into a wall, penning him in. One swerved at him. Raising his foot he shoved its bumper. The cart gave but only a little; it had brakes, he realized. Another came from the side, striking him lightly on the hip.

They were crowding him, jostling with one another for the space to attack, antennae swaying. One cart lunged; Healey stepped sideways. The cart banged into the wall, cracking plaster. Healey jumped upon it and waited until the other carts wheeled away.

He backed off from the motionless vehicle, whose antenna had ceased to wave. What had Bart, the fellow from maintenance, said about a computer whiz?

"... banking as we know it will be out of the question. Most people won't be ca-ca-capable of writing checks. But they mustn't be allowed to have large sums of money, either—it will be too simple to steal from them. It was a Greek who first suggested that money be made too heavy to carry, to discourage its use. Money will all be big coins. Computers must be responsible for fi-fi-financial transactions. There will be a single credit card—"

"Herman!"

"The so-called mass media will be vital. Advertising must do its share to whip up en-thu-si-asm. People will be slow. They must be forced to purchase com-com-commodities or the economy will founder. It is for that reason that we have decided to permit the use of automobiles, though the accident rate will be frightful."

"Herman, please."

"We see sex as a kind of safety valve. The mass media must promote it. Forni...inter...carnal...screwing will be compulsory."

"Herman, I'm trying to tell you there's a madman on the maintenance staff who knows how to program the motorized carts to attack people!"

"There once was a maiden medieval... *How* does it go?"

270

• • •

Heading for Mel Orenstein's office to discuss the IQ projections, Healey heard the cry from far down the corridor. He ran, then faster. A cart with a bloody bumper, antenna slowly waving, stood like a creature from outer space over the body of the psychiatrist, whose head was crushed. Healey kicked the cart as hard as he could and then permitted himself to scream.

"All right, everybody listen."

"Shit fuck asshole..."

"You jus' cuss on, li'l ol' man, 'cause I don' mind, y'hear? 'Cause I'm a black man, and you white folks know we is easygoin'—"

"Listen, I said! Try to pay attention. You've got some brains left so stop acting like children. I still need you. We've got to leave here. I want the equipment packed. Everything that will fit into boxes. Don't forget the cultures, including the SV 40."

"My micro-micro-micro..."

"It's okay, Walter. The Zeiss will be enough. Now, how do we get the stuff out of here? Robin, can you drive an ambulance?"

"Sho can."

"Moremoremoremore!"

Friday morning, at seven sharp, the digital clock stopped turning. Healey, awake, had been watching it idly, thinking of time. He said, "Fuck! They cut the electricity after all. Linda...no, sweetheart, there isn't time for that...get up and pack your bag, okay?"

Downstairs he said, "Goodbye, Phillip. I'm going away for a while. Take good care of the building." Phillip stared at him wordlessly.

They took a cab to the hospital. Because of the wrecked cars on the streets, progress was slow. As they were halted before a newsstand Healey hopped out and bought a paper. A banner headline said:

LOST: OUR INTELLIGENCE?

Special to The New York Times

WASHINGTON, Apr. 11—Informed sources revealed today that a top-level debate is under way at the White House on a possible mass decline in U.S. intelligence.

There is no agreement about whether the decline is actually happening, but many authorities are convinced that it is. As evidence they cite numbers of statistics, including reading scores, automobile accidents and widespread social dislocation resulting in vastly increased crime in the U.S.

Some believe that American IQ will sink to 83, which is dull normal. If this controversial fact is true, the question is how to run a complicated industrial society on such a meager IQ base, or whether it can be run at al.

Several reasons for this tragic event—if it is actually happening—have been mentioned. One is that the U.S. is a victim of a Soviet brain-scrambling operation. But others claim that the Soviets have, or will soon have, the affliction to.

Others believe that the mass stupidity is the result of a disease called "the IQ illness" or "the stupid sickness" caused by a new virus created and accidentally released during a DNA experiment in New York, though the sources were not clear as to details.

Dissenting experts deny that there is a new virus or that the IQ drop is taking place. "What you're seeing," said one, "is a spontaneous rebellion against a system which makes too many demands on people. Fighting the system is hard—it's easier to become ineffective. It's catching too—you have here a remarkable example of a psychological epidemic which sooner or later will go away." j9jjlloolk

"So the story's out," Healey muttered as they arrived at the hospital. He peered at the crowd before the auditorium. "Linda, would you go to the lab and wait? Tell the others we're leaving soon."

Healey pushed past shouting people wearing sandwich boards and carrying banners. Near the entrance he halted and stared.

Ruth, hands dirty, hair uncombed, hawked her pornographic miniatures, which lined the wall, while Jennie cried for people to take a look. Ad Wallon squatted on the sidewalk, three cups before him, one containing a marble. "Win a dollar for a dollar," he was saying. "All you gotta do is guess where the marble is. Here we go." He put the marble under one of the cups and shuffled them quickly.

Healey put a dollar on the sidewalk and said, pointing, "That one."

"I'll be goddamned. He's right!" He looked up. "Jim!"

"You never were much of a magician, Ad," he said with a flipness he didn't feel. Jesus, my wife! My kid! "Hello, Ruth, Hi, Jen."

"Hello, Daddy," Jennie cried. "Why haven't you been to see us at Unca Ad's house?"

He scooped her up and kissed her. "I've been pretty busy, Jen. Soon I will."

"No you willn't!" Ruth declared. "Not until you get an at-at...lawyer and settle this thing with me."

"Give me a little time," he said.

"Gimme time! Gimme time! That's all you say to Mr. Donahue or whatever it is. It's been months now."

"You only left home a week ago," he reminded her.

"A week? Is that all? You must be mis-mis...wrong."

"Ask Ad."

"What does he know? Ad?"

"I dunno. Who wants to win a dollar?" Ad called weakly. "I better make it this time. That was my last buck. Got a buck, Ruth?"

"Not for you to piss away."

"Jim?" Ad pleaded.

Healey handed back the dollar he had won and went into the building.

● ● ●

By 9:30 not a seat in the good-sized auditorium remained, with standing room filled also. Backstage, Tish Wyler ran up to Healey, hands fluttering. "I never expected this! There are crowds *outside* too. You saw the piece in the *Times*?" He nodded. "Dr. Herrmann has told me it's true and that the vi-vi... bug was developed in your lab."

"I'm afraid so."

"I've seen changes in people, though not in myself, thank God. I don't have it, do I?

"I'm sure you don't."

"The sched... program must be changed," Wyler said anxiously. "We'll put on our side first. There are reporters here. I can't have Dr. Herrmann exposed to hos-hos... nasty questions. I'll say he has to leave for Washing-ton, which is the case. The helicopter's already on the roof. The policy Dr. Herrmann has decided on is for us to deny any knowledge, at least until he is safely gone. He has a major role ahead. *He* is what matters now."

"If you say so."

Herman Herrmann strode to the lectern, eagle nose jutting, eyes abulge. "Ladies and gentlemen, welcome. This is a solemn occasion, but before we commence perhaps a small rhyme will lighten our spirits. 'There once was a maiden medieval/Who lived in a forest prime-val...'/How does it go? Damn! Well, no matter. We are here today to discuss a major scientific issue—the pros and cons of recombinant DNA research. My hope is that we can be dis-dispass... objective and not descend to the sort of emotionalism which has marred so many gatherings on this controversial topic. You there, quiet please! Certainly, this subject is important enough to merit careful scrutiny (although I must say a great deal of advanced thought has already gone into it), which is why we're here. Damn, how *does* that limerick go? Let us reason together. Leave us not squabble. Leave us stick to the facts and not engage in wild surprises. I mean, surmises. We must remember that the entire future of science will not be settled in this room today; DNA research is only a small corner. Can we, then, stay calm?...A bounder espied her...

"Unfortunately, I shall not be able to spend the entire morning with you, as I have pressing business—I have to have my suit cleaned! Ha-ha—in Wash-Wash...our nation's capital. But Dr. James Healey of our staff is present and accounted for. I meant to say that Jim is here to tell you about the DNA research he has recently concluded, with complete success. We believe that a major breakthrough is in the offing in the field of inherited disease, because of Jim and his col-col...co-workers. But I'd like Dr. Healey to tell you about it himself. He will answer your questions. Thank you."

As Herman Herrmann left the microphone he could be heard to say, "A bounder espied her/And plied her with cider..."

A snigger came from the audience. Banners unfurled:

> WE SHAL NOT BE CLONED
> OUR FREEDOM IS PERELED
> "I WILL CREAT THE PERFECT RACE"

"Will he answer all our questions?" a voice shouted.

"I'll try," said Healey from the lectern, wondering what to say. He couldn't claim the experiment had been an unqualified success, nor could he tell them that, because of him, they no longer knew how to spell. What a bind! *GUAGUA*.

"Our objective was...," he began.

Others banners appeared:

> HELIX IS SEXIST
> WE WANT DOUBLE PAY
> WHO MAID US DUM?

Howling people with reduced intelligence demanded their dues: Double shelix! Double wages! Down with DNA! A madhouse! He had to quiet them, leave the room intact, get on with a remedy before night fell on the world. He raised a hand and shouted into the microphone, over the hubbub, "If I could tell you..."

An older man rose, whom Healey recognized as a famous biologist. Microphones stood in the aisles, and he was handed one. He said, in a foreign accent, "I wish to reply that the Germans were in-in-interested in selective breeding. They believed in eugenics, which led to concen-concentration camps. The Nazis never said 'No!' to an experi-ment. There are ethical questions.... DNA research has the support of the state. Is science slave to the state? That is what happened under Hitler. It must not happen here. Human genes must be protected under all cir-cum-stances. Scientists must prevent ir-irre-irrespon-irresponsi-irresponsib-irresponsible... irresponsibility."

What? thought Healey. Because the Nazis cremated their victims should furnaces be outlawed? He listened glumly as others seized mikes in turn. "Who is behind DNA research? The corporations! Should we permit corporations to grab control of new life forms? Should we tinker with ev-o-lu-tion for the profit of a few? We are against the ma-nip-u-la-tion of nature... escape from the lab... give us all cancer... germ warfare... No! No! No!"

Someone called to Healey, "Do you believe in med-dling with the mys-ter-ies of life?"

"Mmmmmm."

"Do you favor 'double shelix' as a term?"

"No."

"Are you for double wages?"

"No."

And then, almost timidly, as if the dreaded question had been saved for last, "Did a DNA exp-exp-experiment go wrong?"

"Yes."

"Have our brains been affected?"

"Yes!" he shouted.

Silence imploded, total silence. This was it. Either

they'd accept the worst, wait patiently, and hope that means to save them would be devised or they'd revolt against the inevitable, in which case help would be that much harder, or impossible, to achieve. Which? Yes or no?

Silence. Silence had to mean assent.

But Herman Herrmann was on his feet, wandering toward the lectern, a smile spreading his lips. The director, the symbol of authority, leadership and intellectuality, cracked into the microphone, "I have it. 'There once was a maiden medieval/Who lived in a forest primeval./A bounder espied her/And plied her with cider,/And now she's the forest's prime evil!' Ha-ha. Well, don't you imbeciles get it?"

"No!" they screamed in frustration and folly.

"Get *him!*" growled Vergil Buck, running down the aisle.

Herrmann's eyes seemed to leap from his head. "Tish! To the helicopter! Quick!" Herrmann's long form disappeared through the exit near the stage, with his publicity person hopping behind. The screaming crowd surged after him.

Walking slowly, Healey reached backstage unobserved and went through the rear door into the hospital building, where an elevator dropped him to the subbasement. The equipment had been packed in wooden crates and stood on dollies, ready to be moved. "Hurry," Healey said, pushing one through the inner airlock. "Follow me."

He went down the corridor to the emergency unit. He would have employed force if necessary, but the drivers were still with the crowd upstairs. An ambulance stood at the dock, gleaming under the fluorescent lights. Now that he thought of it, he hadn't seen an ambulance around the hospital in several days. Probably the drivers were refusing to work. "Okay, load her up. Plenty of room. What's that box doing there? Never mind, there isn't time. Robin, you drive. Be careful, hear! Robin, stop a second." Healey leaned out the ambulance window.

Above, Herrmann's helicopter thunderously strained to clear the roof, but ropes had been tied to the pontoons. One dangled down the side of the building, with a dozen people still clinging to it. The craft leaned, righted, tipped again, struck the edge of the roof, plummeted to the street and exploded as bodies crashed to the cement, among them one wearing a pointed cap.

A man with a triangular face raced from the ambulance tunnel. Healey couldn't hear the words, but he knew what Vergil Buck mouthed as the ambulance sped off: "I'll get you!"

An isolated institution for the mentally retarded was the last place anyone would look for them, Healey thought; after the episode at the hospital he feared pursuit.

Dr. George Jenkins pulled on a pendulous earlobe, blinked and said at last, "I can't think of any reason why not. The water and elec-elec...power are still on in the bunga-bunga...cottages. You can eat in the cafeteria."

Healey asked about Cathy.

"She's fine. Want to see her?"

"I guess not."

As the ambulance reached the cottage, Healey pointed to two stooped figures in blue denim walking arm and arm. "Jenkins calls then Tristan and Isolde. That'll be us one day unless you're a good girl and do exactly as I say," he said to Linda, who shuddered. "Okay, let's unload and set it up as quickly as poss-poss...as we can. Here's what I want to try. Attention, please."

The SV 40 had been in his thoughts before, and on the drive to Pleasant Village he revived it in a new form. It wasn't much of an idea, but he didn't have another one and wasn't sure—judging by the increasing slowness of his mind—if he ever would. Recombined with the PAH virus, which they had brought with them, the SV 40 might in some way compete with the new virus. Frazer's blue assay, if the biochemist could still accomplish it, would tell the tale. Everything else, in any case, had failed.

The laboratory, hurriedly improvised in the bungalow, was a far cry from the facility in the subbasement with its air locks and glove boxes, but there was no point worrying about contagion; and if they lacked major equipment, such as a centrifuge, the requisite biological materials had already been prepared and waited in neatly labeled dishes, test tubes and vials—Healey had seen to that. It was now a matter of skillful mixing, heating and testing—for which the scientists were still sufficiently expert, he judged.

During the afternoon expressionless faces with sullen eyes had appeared at the windows, and that evening torches could be seen in the fields. A soft knock sounded, and Jenkins appeared in the doorway. He said brusquely. "The re-tard ... little people are frightened. They think you've come to do them harm. You'll have to leave."

Healey protested, "But we're all ready! We only need a couple of days."

"I'm sorry, but if you don't go, they'll burn the building down. There's nothing I can do."

They dismantled the lab and packed the ambulance that night. In the morning they were back on the road.

"Hey, wow! This is some trip! Where we going now, boss brain?" said Robin Frazer.

"Connecticut," said Healey. "I've got a house there. It's stocked with food. We'll risk it."

"Okay, boss brain, but that's where I git off. I've had it with the honky in back who does nothin' but cuss, with this chick who can't keep her cotton-pickin' hands off you, and with you too, if you don't mind ma saying so."

"Don't you honky me, you shit-face black buck!" Walter screamed through the transom.

"Okay, fellas, knock it off," Healey rejoined. After a while he sniffed and called, "Walter, what's that smell?"

"It's the nigger," said Benson.

"Now there's a li'l ol' man can't own up to his own farts," Frazer replied.

279

"Shut up, you guys." Healey inhaled deeply. "Something's wrong, Robin, stop."

Healey climbed into the rear, pushed boxes around and came at last to a stretcher on one side of the ambulance. Beneath it was the long black box which in his haste he'd noticed but not registered. He saw: a coffin. He raised the lid. Coral Blanchard lay inside. Those fools at the hospital! Where had they been taking her? To a crematorium, he supposed. They'd put the box in the ambulance and forgotten it.

Healey closed the lid and returned. "It'll be cramped, but Walter better ride with us in front. We've got a corpse on our hands. We'll bury her when we arrive."

They drove through Connecticut woods and hills. The ambulance had a radio; on it were frequent though garbled reports of the stupid sickness and the events of the day before at the hospital—James Healey was mentioned by name. Suddenly Robin said, "Look down dere."

On a curve below was a cluster of cars and men. Healey muttered, "A roadblock. They must not want company here."

"End of de line, I guess. Them folks ain't goin' to let us through, I betcha."

Healey thought carefully—carefully as he could. The others still wore white uniforms from the lab, dirty though they were, and they still had their caps. Only he wore civilian clothes. Gauze masks hung from hooks by the stretcher. If the men on the roadblocks had the stupid sickness, they might buy it. Said Healey, "Listen carefully."

Red lights revolving, siren splitting the air, the ambulance sped on. "Hit the brakes." The ambulance ground to a stop inches from a car blocking the road. "Turn off the siren."

Among the men carrying rifles Healey recognized Bunch, the proprietor of the little crossroads market. He leaned out the window and demanded, from behind his mask, "What's the reason for this?"

"You can't go through," Bunch shouted. "Turn around and leave. We don't want strangers. Especially not from New York. We're free of the stupid sickness here, and we don't aim to get it."

"You don't understand," said Healey.

"Don't under-under-understand what?"

"Look in back. Don't come too close."

Coral Blanchard reposed on the stretcher. Across from her sat Summer and Benson, whitely gowned and masked.

"What is this?" said Bunch in a shocked voice.

"That woman's dying."

"She looks dead to me," said Bunch.

"She isn't. The stupid sickness makes her seem dead. But she's dying. She's extremely infectious."

Bunch leaped backward. "The stupid sickness doesn't kill, the radio says!"

"That's what we thought too. She'll be the first fatality if we don't hurry. I'm a U.S. Army physician. I'm attempting to get her to a military hospital in the northern part of the state as fast as possible. It's the only place in the world equipped to deal with this. If we can get her there on time we may be able to save her." His mask slipped off, and he lowered his head, adding, "And others later on."

"What do you think?" Bunch said to his cohorts.

"Let 'em through. Fast. Get 'em out of here."

"You can go on. But you've got to promise not to leave the ambulance under any cir-cir-cir... conditions until you're out of the area."

"Promise," said Healey. The ambulance roared on.

The house was just as he'd left it. They buried Coral in the soft soil of what, that summer, would have been the garden. They unpacked the ambulance and hid it in the garage.

Healey refused to let the scientists rest. Again the equipment was assembled, this time in the barn, and again the work began. In the evening Frazer yawned and said, "These bones goin' to bed."

"No! We're sticking with it."

"You stick with it all you wants, but not me," said Robin. He gazed at his plaques under the glare of strong light. "'Cause, you see, boss man, this idea of yours, it don' work."

On television they watched a replay of the President's morning address.

The President confirmed that a new virus was loose. The virus lowered IQ—the President did not say by how much. No cure existed, but one was being sought and would soon be found. There was no need to be apprehensive toward other nations—the IQ illness was becoming universal. The federal government remained strong and must be trusted. The public must exercise extreme self-control, remembering that people's abilities were limited. Drive carefully. Be honest. Report to work. Do your duty. Obey your leaders. A complete set of regulations would be issued on Monday, when the President would talk to the nation once more.

Though, doubtless, the President used a TelePrompTer, though his vocabulary was monosyllabic and his sentences short, though he evidently strained to retain composure and convey the competence of his command, he could not avoid the tiny slips and lapses characteristic of the IQ illness.

To Healey, the President appeared terrified.

There must be something. What?

He left Linda in bed moaning, "More, more, more." Downstairs he found Benson cowering in a chair and Frazer, in a loincloth, heating a huge pot of water.

"Now what?"

"Ma brekfus," said Frazer. "Don' he look good?"

All three of them were useless now. There was only him, and what did he retain? He tried to remember the state capitals but had only reached Concord when his mental engine gave out. It wouldn't be long before he was incapable of serious form-form . . . concept-concept . . . re-re . . . The words wouldn't come. His brain was mired. Think! *GUAGUA*.

In the barn he disconsolately examined the strewn equipment with which they had failed to find the proper answer—and which before long he wouldn't know how to use. Week seven was almost upon him. Feet shuffling, head bowed, he climbed the stairs to the landing, opening "Healey's Book," which he'd thought to bring with him. Under the stupidity index he inscribed, "James E. Healey, Jr."

Again he read his entry on suicide—no, the urge had gone. In fact, he was shrouded by a certain peace, as if his intelligence were cushioned by soft material in which he could bury his lethargic brain. It was almost comfortable—why fight? Perhaps he had misjudged the problem all along. In the end, stupidity might be good. A stupid person didn't look different, wasn't of less personal worth, wasn't inferior in any way save one, which consisted of the ability to process information, to ask and answer more complicated questions. So what! He could see how intellectually arrogant he had been, how deeply proud of the absurd digits that represented his so-called IQ, how secretly smug about his superior smarts. Yes! What did brightness solve? Nothing. What did it cause? Trouble. If he'd been dumber he couldn't have done the DNA experiment. . . . There was something fall-fall . . . wrong about that argument, but oh well! Too many brains caused half the problems in this world. Phillip was right after all—compassion mattered more. What had Helen said? She'd rather be dead than stupid. Bet Helen didn't think that way now! He felt warmly toward her and the whole fellowship of fools. Brightness might fall from the air, but it was without substance.

He picked up a pen and printed slowly:

WAS SOCRATES RONG?

Maybe intellect is not so desirable as the Greeks said. Their philosophers claimed it was better to be an unhappy human with self-consciousness than a happy animal. I am no longer convinced. Smart people make waves! Nuclear weapons. DNA experiments. When we are all stupid we shall be equal! Stupid people are nicer people! We shall be happy, yes! Imbies of the world, unite!

Reading this over, he disagreed entirely. There had been a certain joy in writing it, in being able to stake out a position even though it wasn't his—not yet. Diseased genes tried to lure him back to the mental mud from which they'd come, but he wouldn't heed, not if he could help it. Maybe he couldn't spell anymore, but if he used his will—Oh, he thought, my will, my will! My willpower is still there, yes—he could avoid sinking into the ooze, at least for a little while. *Physician, Healey thyself!*

Outside again, he saw Linda in a bathrobe leaning against the building, fingers between her legs, while Robin chased Walter around the yard with a stick. Healey aimed himself for open country, forcing his feet, trying not to shuffle. Think! Laboriously, he reviewed everything he remembered—how much was he forgetting?— about the PAH virus. Virus occupies neural cell. Virus causes overproduction of phenylalanine hydroxylase, resulting in shortage of phenylalanine. Virus...

Perhaps that was the wrong approach. He tried to concentrate on the virus itself rather than the chemical reactions it caused. The virus was a biological package of SV 40 surrounding human DNA with the PAH piece. But the package could not be of a random size, he thought with difficulty, in small words. It had to meet certain rigorous specifications in order to find a niche in the chromosomes. If the package was wrong, it might be rejected as too hard to handle. Therefore... Healey was on to something.

Ahead he heard a rustle in a copse. A deer, he thought, approaching cautiously. Branches parted, and Healey beheld a triangular face.

He could scarcely believe it. Was he dreaming? Healey dug long fingernails into the heel of the same hand and experienced pain. No, he was there, and so, unhappily, was the other, whose grin contained no merriment. "Why are you here?" Healey was able to ask.

"You," said Vergil Buck.

"Me? Me?"

"You." He stepped from the bushes holding a small blue gun. "You come."

"Why?" called Healey.

"Come," said Buck impatiently.

"Go 'way. Get outta here!"

But Vergil Buck had traveled there for a reason and would not be easily dissuaded. As if in proof of Healey's hypothesis, the man—*was* he the one from the highway?—said, "No."

So this was how the world ended, with a bang, not a whimper, after all. Holy shit! How fucking ironic! Here was Healey, his conceptual apparatus, or what remained of it, on the brink of success, only to have hope shattered by a loud noise. No, of course not, he would hear nothing. His brain would be blasted before the sound reached him. Would there be any sensation? Healey dully doubted it. But Buck hadn't shot yet. "Come where?"

The gun pointed toward the road. Should Healey attack? Time was everything; he couldn't lose much of it. Don't be a bigger fool, he told himself. Walk! He did, slowly, Buck behind him, until he saw the battered car. Was it the same one? "Get in," said Buck opening the door on the driver's side. "Move over." Healey complied. Vergil Buck climbed behind the wheel, started the engine and, holding the steering wheel in his left hand and the gun in his right, maneuvered the vehicle onto the road.

"Where are you taking me?"

"To trial," said Buck.

"Trial?" Healey squirmed in misery on the tattered upholstery.

"For making us dumb."

Healey sighed tremulously, pressing both palms to

unshaven cheeks. The idiot evidently intended returning him to the hospital for proceedings of some kind—what a mockery of justice that would be, tried by a jury of fools! In the auditorium, maybe.... He *had* to escape and get back to the barn, no matter what he had to do to Vergil Buck, who didn't deserve to breathe. In the meantime, he must keep talking. "How did you find me?"

"Saw picture of house in office. Found address on card. Followed a map," said Buck, pride in his vacuous voice.

"Must have been a pretty simple map," Healey muttered. "How'd you get by the roadblock?"

"Weren't none."

Because of their short attention spans, Bunch and the others had probably forgotten why they were there. Concentrate. Did the nitwit beside him really believe he could make the curves driving with one hand, with one eye on Healey? Rattle him. If he crashes and you're killed, what difference? Soon be dead re-regardless. Healey laughed contemptuously. "Don't blame me for making you dumb, Buck. You was stupid already."

"Oooooh," said Vergil Buck. He waved the gun and the car swerved. "Have half a mind to..."

"That's about the size of it," needled Healey. "Half a mind."

"Ooooooh."

"Tell me, once and for all. Was you the guy hit me on the highway?"

"Don't talk," Vergil Buck said.

"Come on. You got nothing to lose. Was you?"

Buck said nothing.

"That's right. Better give the road your full at-at-attention, Buck. You got none to spare."

Vergil Buck spun off the pavement and sent the old car rattling down a dirt road. Healey knew where it led: not far down the steep grade was an abandoned granite quarry. Vergil Buck must have scouted the area first, but why? What could the cretin be thinking? "What's on your little mind, Buck?" he said, sounding much cockier than he felt.

Vergil Buck still said nothing. A horrid suspicion dawned on Healey as the car stopped. Buck jabbed the air with the gun and said, "Ge⁺ out."

Healey complied. "Now listen..."

"Over there." Healey went where directed, a quarried place with rock walls rising on three sides of him. "Take off your clothes," ordered Buck.

"What for? What for?"

"Strip," said Buck. "Shoes. All."

"But..." *She has pimples on her butt*...The gun threatened, and Healey undressed, shoes and socks as well. What did the son-of-a-bitch want? Buck stared at Healey's penis, shriveled in cold and terror. Was Healey about to be raped? Buck's tongue curled on his upper lip. Jesus! *Please Do Not Mutilate*...But the gun rose, and Healey knew for certain that the moron intended to kill him. Clothing was identification: to have the victim remove it saved trouble and mess. Healey's fingerprints could identify him, not that the police would have sufficient brains to apprehend the murderer, but Buck didn't realize that.

Shit! The injustice! goose-pimpled Healey was thinking as he stood on his bare feet. He should have refused to remove his clothing, not made Buck's bloody scheme any easier; but there had been no choice, after all. Buck would have shot him then; but like this, he was still alive in his crypt of dark rock. But why hadn't Buck pulled the trigger? Healey focused on the gun barrel, which wavered. Buck trembled, couldn't get a bead. The moment his hand held steady Healey would dive. *Keep talking.*

"I got all the luck, don't I?" Healey said hurriedly. "I was born smart. You was born dumb. That's a big difference."

The triangular face twitched angrily. "People like you been telling me I was dumb my whole life," he said in a strangled voice.

"Sur-prise, sur-prise. Would it be smart to call you smart?"

"Oooooh."

"You're no genius, just the opposite."

"I'll fix you. "But the gun wavered even more.

"Where your IQ is I tie my shoelaces," Healey said.

"Oooooooh."

"Your IQ is so low you could trip on it."

"Aaaaaah!"

"I've known dogs smarter than you," Healey droned on.

"Uuuuuh," raged Buck shrilly.

"It's not your fault, Vergil Buck. You were probably a grown man before you learned how to talk.... You couldn't help it, Vergil.... You didn't de-serve it.... It was your mother. Your mother was a pinhead, Vergil. She had a point on top.... Your father's eyes were so close together they touched.... Your sister had ears like an elephant.... Your brother wiped himself with his nose."

The pistol jerked violently, and Buck seized it with both hands. Healey jumped. A bullet splattered on rock near his head, but he was in motion, feet churning, hands outstretched. His rush carried Buck backward to a pile of stones. He fell down, Healey on top of him. Healey heard a hollow sound. Buck went limp.

Healey got up. Buck had struck his head on a stone, but already he stirred. Left there, he would only follow, intervene again. Healey took the gun from Buck's hand, placed it to his temple and fired.

He hobbled back to the barn, thinking hard, but not about being a murderer. If the package was wrong... Before, they had re-re-recombined viruses and DNAs in test tubes and always failed to find the remedy. Suppose the recombination occurred *within* the cells of the body, he thought with difficulty. Introduce a substance that would merge with the other virus and either reduce its impact or release it from the host DNA so that the body would be able to take care of it? Maybe. But what substance? Something that would ape the PAH virus. . . .

He had briefly considered it before and rejected it as too dangerous: SV 40. Flood the neural cells with Simian Virus 40.

They had plenty of SV 40 because Wallon had cultured it copiously. How should it be administered? By injection into a blood vessel which would carry the neurotropic virus directly to the brain, there to do battle with the other—virus against virus, a clash of microorganisms. It might work, but it might not. And even if the SV 40 succeeded, the antibody response could bring shock and perhaps death within minutes.

Fill syringe with SV 40, he commanded himself. Swab arm with alcohol. . . . Outside, the others shouted like children. Better not have them present even if shock set in; their help would be worse than none. Put wooden bar through slots in the barn door, locking it.

The sound must have attracted them. A knocking sounded. "More, more!"

"What boss man doin' in dere? Don' he like us no longer?"

Healey tried to remember the capitals but failed to pass Annapolis. Two!

GUAGUA. "Healey's Book" lay open at a small table with a cot alongside. He raised the needle but hesitated, afraid of death.

"Fuck-face Healey," Walter said through the door.

But he wanted his brains back above all. Healey injected himself in the vein. He watched the colorless liquid drain from the syringe. He sat down at the table.

"De mo' I tink about dis here virus the mo' Ah'm sho dat whitey dreamed it up for usin' on de niggers. 'Cause whitey want de black man to be dumb. But black man ain't dumb, no suh, he jus' po'. So whitey figure way to make de black man dumb, wid a sickness for messin' up his brain. Den he cure de honkies, but leave po' Robin as

289

he is." The door rattled, and Robin's tone turned fearful. He pleaded, "Please! Please gimme some-a dat cure. Please gimme some, please..."

"Please!"

"Please!"

Their importunate voices faded. Healey tried to remember the state capitals but couldn't—not a single one. He wrote:

> heley, you is reley stupud now. you did a terbul thing. you maid you dumer than you was. before you could still funschion, sort of, but if somebudy axed you the name of your swetehart... if I could tell you I would let you gnow. metehead. scrambled branes, fizzician, helix thyself...

Chills assaulted him. Hiccuping heavily, he dropped on the cot and watched the roof beams whirl. In his bag of pain and desperation he could dimly hear pounding on the door, but for him it was over. Goodbye, Jennie and Paul, goodbye Linda, goodbye brain. Goodbye, you big dumb-assed world. He was dying. Goodbye. *GUAGUA.* Goo-goo.

He dreamed of two armies of monkeys on a field whose surface was covered with fibers. The monkeys of one army were blue; they beat their chests with hairy fists, gesticulated horribly, hopped about, showed fangs. Their opponents were smaller, resembling Lucky, the African green. They were organized into platoons and carried clubs. On they marched....

Goo-goo. *GUAGUA.* GUA meant "stop" in DNA language. Stop the production of... what? In this case, pheny...phenyl...phenylalanine...phenylalanine hydroxylase! Yes, stop! Healey realized he was actually thinking this! Albany, Annapolis, Atlanta, Augusta ...Lord, it worked!

He checked his watch. Several hours had passed since the injection. He readied three hypodermics and opened the door. The scientists squatted outside, though it was cold and nearly dark. Healey held up a syringe and said, "Come here."

In the morning Linda said, "Where have I been? I have a terrible headache."

"Me too. The PAH virus is still being de-degraded, I imagine. We're not ourselves yet."

"Are we still stupid?" she said.

"Not as dumb as we were. The relaxation curve is the mirror image of the exponential. We'll recover half our lost intelligence at once—maybe we have already—and then over the weeks it'll return in ever smaller amounts until we're back to where we started." He added, "I hope!"

Linda moved her smooth body away from him. "Where we started? So what am I now, an adult-adult adulteress? When Ruth's herself she'll come running."

"Maybe not," he said finally. There were so many problems to settle. His mother hadn't gone to a nursing home yet and wouldn't have to. Paul would return, Healey felt certain. Jennie's future depended on what happened between him and Ruth. Helen: they'd been for each other—how would she put it?—an interlude. His brain whirled and *GUAGUA* sounded, though faintly. "I think she really wanted out, IQ illness or no."

"I don't care about her. What do *you* want?"

"I . . . I guess I'd had it with her too, though I didn't know it. You . . ."—the words sounded foreign, but he meant them—". . . develop in-er-tia in a long marriage like ours. Love gets mixed up with habit. It doesn't occur to you that anything's really wrong until you're forced to change course. I'm grateful she has Ad Wallon—they'll be fine together."

"You're not jealous? Be honest."

"Not much."

"I don't believe you."

"Really, it's true. It doesn't matter to me. I'd tell you if it did. I'll have to explain to the kids, and I'll miss them.

291

But Paul will be off to college soon, anyway—I'm sure he'll want to go after this—and Jennie can live with us on weekends."

"*Us?* You haven't even asked me!"

"I am now, though," he said seriously. "I love you."

"How much?" she said with a smile in her voice.

"More and more and more," said Healey.

They thanked him first, but inevitably complaints began. "Did we have to suffer so long?" said Walter Benson as they went down the drive in the ambulance.

"Yes, why didn't you think of it earlier?" asked Robin Frazer. "Ouch, my head."

"I did. I rejected it because it was so dangerous, and then I forgot it. No wonder. I could have died, you know."

"He'll want a medal next," said Linda.

Frazer said, "There's a lot to be thought out. A tremendous amount of SV forty must be cultured, and we'll have to start somewhere. Suppose we use the hospital for a base. Will we have to fight our way in? Most people won't take kindly to being stabbed in the arm with a needle."

"We could use nebulizers," Linda suggested. "A perfume spray bottle would do it."

"If you can get close enough," said Benson grumpily.

"*I* can get close enough," Linda said, giggling.

Healey said tentatively, "You three were willing enough to be injected, weren't you? Even when traumatized."

"I was scared of being stupid. So was this honky here," said Frazer.

"Listen, you son-of-a-bitch..."

"Knock it off!" Healey cried. "The point is, the sickness terrified you, didn't it? It certainly terrified me. If people can be persuaded a remedy exists, they might come flocking." He thought of Herman Herrmann's plans for employing the media. "We could use tele-tele-television."

"People may be too suspicious to respond," said Frazer.

"I wonder. Let's find out what's happening."

Healey switched on the radio, surprised at first because the reception seemed normal. He remembered then that people contracted the stupid sickness, not equipment. When machines broke down and repairmen no longer knew how to fix them, the failures would start—*would*, unless the public could be made to listen. Turning the dial, Healey heard shouts and screams. What was being said? Dog food...crotch itch...sexy swingles bar.... Commercials! The broadcasts seemed to consist entirely of advertisements, broken only by a few bars of music.

At last he found the sole news program. A voice said slowly: "...in Washington the President announced that we must recognize that we is less smart, because of the IQ illness, which nearly everybody has. We must try to be patient and careful, said the President, and remember that the best is the enemy of the good, said the President, who added that we could be as intelligent as before, maybe smarter, if we all work together and use our col-col-col...united intelligence, like a hive of bees. Well, the President's optimism doesn't seem justified here today. All traffic is stopped on—I can't read your goddam handwriting, Fay—a major road because they raised a bridge and can't figure how to lower it. Airline service has been sus-suspended because of the crashes. According to rumors, money is about to be pretty much illegalized, so the stock market is way up despite the mass of mistakes on Wall Street—you have to put your money somewhere— but that's about the only bright spot. Schools are closed, since teachers can't teach any better than students can learn. Teenage gangs run wild. The theatres are mostly closed too, as is the opera, ballet, and sym-sym-symphony and the public library—who reads books? Nobody reads much of anything except porn-porn-porno-graph-ic (there!) magazines, and there are lines at the porn movies too. Judging from this weekend, the fun is gone from sports. Athletes can still play but not smart. According to predictions the birthrate is about to soar. The stupid sickness is not inherited, but doctors believe it will inevitably spread to future generations."

Minutes passed for loud commercials, and then the voice returned: "A surprising number of people, however, welcome the new disease and claim it's a blessing in disguise. They say that we was too smart for our own good. Life had grown too com-pli-cat-ed because we had so much brains. Folks couldn't figure things out anymore. We didn't know where we stood. We was confused all time. We felt we was inferior because others was superior. It weren't fair. What right did one person have to a high IQ while so many was stupid? We will all be equal, or just about, in the new world. We won't have any nucular war because nobody can work the weapons. So we give up a few things! Who needed big words and fancy ideas and college degrees and that kind of shit? Did intelligence bring happiness and peace of mind? No! Life will be better now. That's what a lot of people say, and maybe they're right."

Healey said, "Robin, there's a little grocery store down the road. Stop at it, will you?"

Bunch, the proprietor, examined him warily. "Don' I know you from somewheres?"

"I've been shopping here for years. Jim Healey, remember?"

"Rings a bell. Seems like I seen you not long ago."

"Mmmmmm," said Healey. When his mask had slipped at the roadblock.

"What can I do for you?"

"Jim," Linda said in a low voice, "we ought to buy out the whole place. He has everything marked down. He's selling soup at a dime a can."

M'm! M'm! GOOD IDEA, sounded jokingly in Healey's less muddled mind. Would he have to endure the voices forever? He didn't think so. Steadily they lost strength. "Everything's pretty cheap, Fred. What happened to inflation?"

"Inflay...?"

294

"Never mind. You've got the stupid sickness, haven't you?"

"Which?"

"It's not leprosy. Fred, there's a cure."

"Cure for what?"

"You know what. You want it or don't you?"

"Whatta you talking 'bout? Git off my back. Scram outta here."

"Fred..."

"Whatta you, some kind of doctor?"

"You know I'm a doctor. Think."

"A U.S. Army doctor?" Fred said, peering at him.

"It makes no difference. Do you want to be cured?"

"Don' know what you're talking 'bout."

"Okay. Come on, Linda," he said. "Let's go."

They had nearly reached the ambulance when Bunch appeared in the doorway. He said timidly, "Doctor, help."

"One more stop," Healey insisted.

"We haven't time," Frazer said.

"I don't want a medal, but indulge me, please," Healey said. *"Please."*

Having told Healey where to find Cathy Gobrin, George Jenkins submitted to the injection meekly, then staggered to his desk, where he instantly fell asleep.

Healey put a needle into the narrow arm and waited for Cathy to wake up. It was crazy of him, he knew—a vestige of the illness—for much waited to be done at Kellog-Bryant. Yet something remained to be considered, and a ward for the retarded seemed an appropriate place. The sluggish people stayed away.

One day not far off he would be asked, "How do you feel about recombinant DNA experiments now, Dr. Healey?" What would he say? Would he agree that science had no business meddling with the mysteries of Life? On the whole, he didn't think he would, no. Maybe the error was placing too much emphasis on physical containment, as in the P-4 facility, as though human judgment was nothing to worry about. Better to be absolutely careful about people. Better to make sure the microorganisms were safe. Better...

But, he told his imaginary interviewer as he turned to the little girl, don't forget we found a permanent cure for her. We did that! We accomplished it! And hundreds of thousands of human beings can be helped! Saved! All those genetic diseases...

Cathy Gobrin opened her eyes at last. "Hi, doctor!" she said in a faint voice. "Kiss."

He kissed her.

She looked around and whispered, "What's happened?"

When he could tell her he would let her know.